PAINT THE DESERT

Book 2 – Golden State Trilogy

A Christian Contemporary Novel

Dawn V. Cahill

PAINT THE DESERT

Book 2 – Golden State Trilogy
A Christian Contemporary Novel

"Arise, cry out in the night: in the beginning of the watches
pour out thine heart like water before the face of the Lord:
lift up thy hands toward him for the life of thy…children."
Lamentations 2:19

Cover design by Dineen Miller

Edited by Steve Mathisen, Odd Sock Proofreading and
Copyediting

Formatting by Rik, Wild Seas Formatting
(http://WildSeasFormatting.com)

To my beautiful mom, my biggest fan when I was still an author wannabe.

Thank you for believing in me, Mom!

Prologue

San Rafael, California

Rich St. John revved the souped-up engine in his kelly-green '68 Camaro and relished the satisfying roar. "Yes!" He slapped a high five on the black dashboard. "Attaboy, Richmobile. You're a lean, mean, green machine, baby."

He gave a celebratory whoop. What dude his age wouldn't want a car as hot as his? Killer car, smoking hot girl, and a dream job—yeah, he had it all.

Since good fortune had smiled on him lately, he took it to mean he would ace his Spanish test this evening. He could almost hear his mother telling him not to get too smug when life was going well because life could turn on you in a heartbeat.

Mom would know. She'd for sure had her share of hard times. Most notably when his dad left her for another woman. But today life smiled on Mom, honeymooning in Hawaii with her new husband, Jon.

Remembering his mother's words, uneasiness snaked over him. What if life did turn on him? Just as quickly, he shoved the thought from his mind and sent a text to Kassidy. *Hey Babe. Richmobile running sweet. Whoot!*

He roared out of his mother's driveway and made his way through the neighborhood, double-takes and admiring glances following in his wake. He tossed a grin and a thumbs-up at each smiling face. At the boulevard, he hung a right, then a left onto the 101 which would take him to his six-thirty p.m. class at Ignacio College.

He pulled into the college parking lot with fifteen minutes to spare and straddled two spots, crossing his fingers for luck. *Good luck, dude. Buena suerte.* Too bad Lady Luck was such a fickle mistress. He shuddered and crossed the fingers of his left hand to be doubly sure. He had to ace this midterm to keep his GPA at three-point-oh. Anything below, his dad would stop paying his tuition.

Mom didn't believe in luck. Only in her God's providence. Either way, Luck or God, he sometimes wondered why some people were so blessed, such as himself, and others not so much. Like that unfortunate woman in San Anselmo who got shot last night in her own garage. By an unknown assailant, said the news. For no apparent reason.

What would make a person shoot a stranger for no apparent reason?

Reaching for the door handle, Rich made sure the Club was securely fastened onto his steering wheel and grabbed his backpack. "Voy a hacer bien en el examen." He worked his lanky frame out of the car. "Si, si, voy, voy." He wasn't sure that was correct syntax, but hey, it was only his first time taking Spanish.

First stop, the cafeteria for his weekly beef 'n' bean burrito. Heaven in a flour wrap. The line was five people deep when he reached it. His stomach growled and his mouth watered as the line crept forward. But another odor mingled with the taco bar's meat and cheese. Someone nearby either hadn't showered or hadn't brushed his or her teeth in days. Maybe both. He wrinkled his nose and glanced behind him. A pair of eyes as yellowish-green as a cat's regarded him from under a black hoodie. The guy clutched a guitar case, swinging it jerkily back and forth.

Maybe he was homeless. What was he doing here? And that face … it reminded him of something. Or someone.

Rich held his breath, turned his back on the guy and filled his plate. After paying for his food, he found a table and hurriedly wrapped the thick tortilla around the aromatic filling, then headed to room 242, munching as he went, mumbling Spanish conjugations between each mouthful.

He wolfed down the last bite just as he arrived at the nearly-full classroom. He waved at his teacher and then grabbed the test Mr. Hope handed him.

"Geoffrey Hope?" called a voice from the doorway. Richie sniffed. That odor again. He spun around, and his brain froze.

A black hoodie. A click, sharp explosion, screams.

Something jerked him backward.

Unworldly pain.

Then, nothing.

Chapter One

"Say ah, honey." Meg Paulson, laughing, popped a french fry into her new husband's mouth. The delicious Maui sun bathed her and Jon in cozy warmth like a sauna. The ocean beyond sparkled like a sea of champagne. Hawaii in September: Paradise on earth, the travel sites claimed. They weren't kidding.

Her husband's arm around her shoulders intensified the heavenly afternoon's warmth. She pulled her Hawaiian-print blouse from her pants' waistband, letting the ocean breeze cool her skin. A sudden gust jostled a strand of wavy hair into her face and sent the rest rippling off her back. "Beautiful hair," Jon had declared the first time he played with it. He'd wrapped golden tresses around his fingers and run his hands through their thickness. She'd never seen the need to change what God gave her, instead kept it natural, a few shades lighter than mousy brown. Just the way Jon liked it.

Her phone buzzed, but she ignored it. Everyone at home knew they weren't to be disturbed. She groped in her yellow capris' pocket and pushed the mute button.

Their wooden picnic-style table, stained red, sat off to the side of the outdoor café, where they could be alone. But someone approached their table anyway, a friendly smile on his face. "Aloha," he greeted them. "Mind if I join you?"

Meg caught a brief flash of annoyance across Jon's face, quickly covered up by an equally friendly grin of his own.

The man, his round face, dark eyes and complexion identifying his native Hawaiian heritage, held her gaze, hope in his eyes.

Jon shifted, the sun flashing on his black-rimmed glasses. "Sure. Have a seat. Nice to have some company. I'm Jon Paulson, and this is my wife, Meg."

"Glad to meet you." The newcomer held out a hand. "I'm Teo Yepp."

Meg felt her lips twitch. But the man didn't seem to notice. He eyed Jon. "Where are you all from?"

"San Francisco," Jon answered with a handshake. "We're on our honeymoon."

"Hoʻomaikaʻi ʻana," he replied with a knowing wink. "Congratulations!"

"What did you say your name was?"

The man handed her a business card. *Mr. Teo Yepp*, it said, *Owner. Moonlite Cruises, Inc., Lahaina, HI.*

Meg held out the card for Jon to see. He cleared his throat, then coughed. "What's this Moonlite Cruises all about?"

"It's a nice, lovely ride along the coastline in my sailboat *Aukai*. She's my baby." Mr. Yepp picked up a fork and speared a chunk of pork. "Very romantic. Especially nice for lovers and honeymooners like yourselves. We serve dinner and drinks, too. You folks like ballroom dancing?"

"We do," said Meg.

"We're still learning," said Jon.

"Well," Mr. Yepp shrugged, "you can dance if you want to, but you don't have to. We sail every night, Monday through Saturday. Boarding starts at five-thirty p.m., and we set sail at six. We have room for ten couples, so come early. First come, first served."

"Honey, doesn't this sound romantic?"

Jon glanced at Meg, then at their table mate. "How much?"

"One hundred dollars per couple. Less than any of the others around here."

"We may give it a go," Jon agreed. "We'll be here for two more days."

"Good. Good," said Mr. Yepp in a soft, almost sing-songy

voice. He stayed a while longer, entertaining them with stories of memorable moments from previous cruises. She almost expected that any moment he'd whip out a ukulele and start crooning Don Ho songs. While he regaled them, Meg and Jon laughed along and fed each other french fries.

Her phone vibrated again. She pulled it partway out, peeked at the display. An unfamiliar number with the same area code as her own. *Calif Sys of Higher Ed.*

Something to do with Richie's tuition, no doubt. Well, they could leave a message. She dropped it back into her pocket and nestled closer to her husband, ever the gracious host, making small talk with their new acquaintance.

Mr. Yepp stayed glued to the bench, his gaze fastened just as intently on them. "How did you two meet?"

Were all Hawaiians this inquisitive? Jon related the story with a nostalgic smile on his face. "We met at a parenting support group I used to lead. I waited to ask her out until after I'd stepped down from leadership. The national headquarters would have frowned on me dating a member while I was leading a group."

"It was quite a shock," added Meg with a small laugh, "when he finally let me know how he felt."

"Was it love at first sight?"

A grin pulled at the corners of her mouth. "For me, it was like at first sight." She'd never forget Jon's boyish good humor putting her at ease that first night she walked into a room full of strangers.

She felt Jon's gaze caress her before he replied to their attentive new friend. "It was a growth process. As I got to know Meg, I started thinking she might be the one God had for me." He pulled her closer to his side. "We just clicked. Being around her felt right."

Meg let her grin break free. "I thought he was dating someone."

Jon held her gaze. "And I thought you and Mike were hitting it off."

Perfectly understandable. She and techno-whiz Mike had spent quite a bit of time together, trying to find out who was harassing her daughter Linzee.

It seemed inevitable that Mr. Yepp segued smoothly into the subject of their wedding. She loved nothing more than sharing every romantic detail to whoever would listen. "We wanted to keep it simple," she told him, "yet still beautiful. Would you like to see the photos?" Meg pulled out her phone, noting the one new message. She'd listen to it later.

He studied the photos with interest as Meg briefed him. "This is my daughter and son. They're twenty-three and eighteen." Regal Linzee, Mona Lisa-like in her tranquil beauty, stood next to Richie, resplendent in a black tux. She scrolled to the next photo.

"And these are Jon's two teenage sons." Connor and Tanner were high-fiving Jon, their mouths frozen in mid-whoop.

"Who is this?"

Her gaze followed his pointing finger to Camille's beaming face practically lighting up the stage. "Camille Patterson, my matron of honor," Meg said, "also my best friend."

Mr. Yepp's face held a wistful look as he tapped Camille's photo. "Good-looking lady," he said. "She reminds me of an old love."

"Well, she's married, Mr. Yepp." Meg tried not to laugh. "She and Jon's best man got married in May. I was her maid of honor."

Jon added, "I was his best man."

"She looks good in that blue and purple dress."

"Periwinkle and plum, to be exact."

Jon squeezed her waist. "Meg is an artist. She knows her colors." He tapped her phone. "Show him your painting gallery, sweetheart."

She obliged, opening a photo album displaying her favorite paintings. Her heart still twinged at the sight of

Tornado in Z Minor, which she'd painted last year while her world fell apart. She'd sold it at an art fair, but kept the photo as a reminder of God's grace sustaining her in the midst of the storm.

Mr. Yepp gave a good-natured nod at her handiwork. "You're a talented lady, Mrs. Paulson. And a beautiful bride." He stretched his arms high and got to his feet. "Time to head back to my boat," he told them. "It sure was nice meeting you folks. Mahalo. Thanks for sharing your photos with me. I would be delighted to have you as my guests." He stuck out a hand. "See you later then?"

"Nice meeting you too." Jon shook their new friend's hand. "Maybe we'll see you tonight."

Mr. Yepp saluted and walked away, and Meg stared after him, biting her lip. "Are you going to tell him yep, or nope?"

Jon laughed, and Meg thought back to her life last year before Jon invaded her heart. God had blessed her beyond her wildest wishes with a fine, funny man, a man she looked forward to spending the rest of her life laughing with.

They soaked in the intoxicating ambiance for another half hour, talking about everything and nothing. Meg kept glancing at the solitaire diamond sparkling on her finger, then at Jon's gold band, her heart swelling.

At last Jon took her hand and gave it a gentle squeeze. The tenderness in his gaze stilled her laughter, quickened her heart rate. "Let's get going. I'm ready for some real dinner." He tucked her hand into his elbow, and they headed across the green lawn toward the lavish resort hotel, all coral stucco, and shiny glass. Red and yellow plumeria broadcast their scent to the far ends of the grounds. Bistro tables and chair sets dotted the cobblestone patio, and a large asymmetrical swimming pool spread out to their left.

The air-conditioned, chrome and marble lobby lost nothing in luxury. She rested her head on his arm and tucked her hand around his waist as they passed the front counter. A small crowd had gathered around the TV behind the counter, intent on some sort of breaking news.

She slowed, torn between curiosity and haste, then resumed her brisk pace. The breaking news could wait. In the elevator, alone with him, she leaned into the steadfast strength of his chest and ran her fingers through his thick chestnut strands. "What are you thinking?"

He smiled and winked. "Which shall it be? A dinner cruise with Mr. Yepp, or dessert in our room?"

Bless that man's amorous heart. He knew how to make her feel like the most cherished woman on Planet Earth. He even loved her morning face, all droopy-eyed and unadorned. "I'm ready for some food. How about that cruise?"

Jon pulled her face close to his and kissed the spatter of freckles across her cheeks. "It's almost five now. By the time we change and drive to Lahaina, Mr. Nope, I mean Mr. Yepp, will be out to sea."

"Can we put Mr. Yepp on our to-do list for tomorrow?"

His gaze probed hers. "We can." His soft expression added a layer of meaning to the simple words.

The spell snapped when the elevator dinged at the eleventh floor. Jon quickened his pace as they strode the hall to their oceanview suite. "We could have dinner at that place we saw last night."

"The cute seafood place?" she said. "Sounds yummy. I just need a quick shower."

Jon's eyes lit up, and he lowered his voice. "A shower for two sounds yummy to me."

"More yummy than a seafood dinner?" Breathless anticipation gripped her. "You Mr. Romantic, you."

Still in stride, he bent over and pressed a kiss on her, then fumbled to open the suite door. Pulling her inside, he wrapped his arms around her like a koala bear. Pressed against him, she relished his irresistible scent, his snug embrace. Thoughts of food and dinner fled like rabbits from a forest fire.

Her phone vibrated in her pocket. Without looking at it, she pulled out the pesky intruder and tossed it on a small table. Jon's lips whispered against her hair. "All of a sudden, I'm not in the mood for seafood anymore." His grip tightened around her waist while his foot found the door and shoved it closed with a decisive thud. Then his fingers found the deadbolt and flipped it firmly into place.

~~~~

The shrill ring of the room's phone woke Meg from a deep sleep.

She couldn't think of a single favorable reason anyone would call in the middle of the night. A rising sense of unease peaked in an adrenaline rush, jolting her fully awake. She groped around, feeling for the phone's hard surface. Then she remembered. The phone was on Jon's side of the bed. She'd have to crawl over him.

Jon stirred, but faint snores still floated from the adjacent pillow on the king-sized bed as she launched herself over his prone body. It was nearly midnight, the clock radio informed her. Nearly two o'clock at home.

The portable phone rang twice more before she managed to get it to her ear. "Hello?" she croaked, grabbing her robe and scurrying into the front room so as not to wake Jon.

"Mom?"

"Linzee?" A flickering glow pulsed through the large room. They'd forgotten to turn off the TV. On the screen, a patrol car's red and blue lights rotated next to a palm tree, the scene superimposed over a concrete building in the background. A cop show midnight rerun?

"Where've you been?" The panic in Linzee's voice set her heart to pounding.

"In Hawaii. Enjoying marital bliss." Did Linzee really expect details?

Linzee clicked her tongue. "Well, duh. I mean, we've been calling and calling your cell phone. Why haven't you answered?"

"Who's we?" Alarmed by Linzee's tone, she went to the table near the door and picked up her phone.

Twenty missed calls.

Ten new messages.

What in the world?

"Oh my goodness," she whispered. "What is going on?"

"Richie was shot, Mom. Last night in his college class …"

Meg's knees buckled. "Shot? Why? How?"

The cop show on TV—not a rerun then, but something far worse?

She grabbed the remote and turned up the volume on ABC News. Ambulances, police cars, a million strobe lights turned the scene into a macabre dreamscape.

Linzee kept talking over the chaos. "It's been all over the news. I can't believe you didn't see anything."

She and Jon hadn't paid attention to the TV.

"They finally called Dad at nine o'clock since they couldn't get a hold of you …"

This was a nightmare. Had to be. Any moment, she'd wake up and …

Jon wandered in, wearing only plaid boxer shorts and rubbing his eyes. "What's going on?"

She could only make frantic jabbing motions with her finger at the TV. He cast a confused look at the nightmarish scene.

Linzee's voice screeched in her ear. "Mom, you need to come home."

Flickering colors played over the walls and furniture as if she were in some amateur haunted house. A somber-faced male newscaster standing next to a sign stared at them. "We're back in San Rafael, California, at the scene of the latest school shooting. Another random shooting. More casualties. When will it end?"

"Casualties?" she whispered, lowering her shaking body to the couch. The camera panned to the sign: Ignacio College.

Her knees knocked uncontrollably as Jon sat next to her and held her against his chest. His steady breathing calmed her own. Did he realize yet what he was seeing?

"Is ... is Richie ..."

"He's still alive, Mom, but in critical condition. I'm calling from the hospital. Dad's here with me."

Critical condition. She crumpled against Jon, her trembles surely infecting him with fear. In silence, they watched the scene unfold.

"A teacher, Geoffrey Hope, is dead." The newscaster's voice rose over a siren in the background. A photo popped up in the upper right corner—a candid shot of a thirty-something African-American gentleman in the act of speaking.

Her unsteady hand knocked the phone against her ear. "That's Richie's Spanish teacher."

"Three students are dead, two critically injured. Their names will not be released until their families are notified."

The twenty missed calls.

"At six-thirty yesterday evening, the gunman walked into Mr. Hope's classroom and opened fire, then turned the gun on himself ..."

Linzee said something, but Meg no longer listened.

"The gunman was identified as nineteen-year-old Coby Michael Jarrett, son of the Rio Rancho couple found dead from gunshot wounds earlier today."

Three faces appeared on the screen—a thirtyish couple and a teenage boy, dark-haired, olive-skinned. The dad, a John Denver lookalike, wore wire-rimmed glasses like the singer. The attractive brunette woman offered a carefree smile at the camera. "Investigators believe Coby Jarrett shot his parents, Robert and Roseanne Jarrett, then drove to Ignacio College, a two-year institution in San Rafael. His motive for targeting the college, if any, is not known at this time. Investigators have found no connection with the shooter to Mr. Hope, the college, or any of its personnel or students. It appears to be completely random.

12

"Neighbors and friends of the Jarrett family describe the young man as 'troubled', 'withdrawn.' One source, who requested anonymity, said Coby Jarrett had been under psychiatric care for schizophrenia after suffering a breakdown last year."

Meg sucked in a breath. Her son had had a run-in with some crazy psycho.

"Mom? Mom!"

Meg jerked. "What?"

"When are you coming home?"

She tipped her head, met Jon's distressed gaze. "Right now, Linzee. We're catching the next flight home."

Chapter Two

The longest five and a half hours Meg could ever remember ended at eight a.m. Pacific Time when the plane touched down in San Francisco. She and Jon hadn't talked much since they boarded. Something dark and terrifying floated around them, curled around her heart, threatened to invade their marriage. She marveled he'd slept at all. She couldn't sleep, couldn't read, could only pray and clutch Jon for the entire flight.

She couldn't tell him guilt gnawed at her. Last night, while the two of them stayed wrapped up in their own little bubble, danger stalked her son. And she'd deliberately, selfishly, ignored the school's persistent calls. He could be dead before she reached him.

The rational part of her brain reminded her she hadn't done anything wrong, and she couldn't have done anything to prevent yesterday's tragedy. Yet how selfish it felt for her to enjoy marital pleasures while her son suffered. She cringed, remembering the repeatedly vibrating phone and her irritation at the interruptions.

Did Jon share her remorse?

She reached under the seat and retrieved her bag. "Why is God doing this?"

Jon shook his head. "I don't know." His biceps flexed as he lifted their suitcases out of the overhead bin. "But I haven't stopped praying since we heard the news." His face stayed solemn as they deplaned and made their way to the long-term lot. Not a hint of a smile cracked his stiff countenance. When she first met Jon, she'd been drawn not only to his profound wisdom but to his upbeat good humor, his way of lighting up a room with his very presence. His curved-up mouth always poised to break out in a smile.

Who was this worried, grim man by her side? What was going on in his head? Anger that they'd had to cut their trip short? Exasperation that calamity had once again visited Meg's family? *God, I hope you aren't planning to take Richie. Wasn't Linzee's kidnapping last year trial enough? My brand-new husband must be getting tired of all this drama. Most men would.*

His snug grip on her hand brought a sliver of light into her heart. She searched his face as they pulled their suitcases along behind them, past restaurants and souvenir shops, past hordes of other travelers, many babbling in unfamiliar languages. In every bar, a TV replayed the tragedy, over and over. The same appalling images kept assaulting her senses. People gathered around the screens, gaping, no doubt horrified that this time the violence had struck so close to home. She ducked her head as they hurried past each TV, even though nobody knew her connection to the tragedy.

Numerous text messages awaited her. Apparently, Camille and Bill and the entire prayer chain had heard of the tragedy. Linzee must have told them.

On the northbound 101, Jon let out an exasperated oath when the traffic slowed at San Bruno. The morning rush hour threatened to impede their progress to San Rafael, typically less than an hour from SFO. A tense silence enveloped them, broken by an occasional text from her daughter.

"Linzee says he's hanging in there, wonders when we'll be there."

"Still half an hour away."

She did a double-take at Jon's uncharacteristic terse tone. He was taking this as hard as if Richie were his own son.

"Jon, talk to me."

He glanced over. "Hard to know what to say without sounding lame."

"I hate this ... this silence between us. I already feel so terrible that I didn't find out for six hours. Are you angry?"

Jon swerved into the right lane, maneuvered into a tight

space between a yellow Saab and a silver Mercedes. "Why would I be angry?"

"Well ..." She looked at her fingers twisting together, heard her tone rise toward hysteria. She swallowed hard. "I could have found out right away if I'd answered the phone. But we had other things on our minds." Her face flamed, the precious memories from last night now tinged with shame. "Today you seem ... mad at me."

"I'm not mad, Meg."

She listened carefully for traces of sarcasm or regret but heard only sorrow.

"It's just that, what happened last night was huge. Quite a lot to wrap our brains around."

Her eyes burned. She didn't trust herself to speak.

"To make matters worse, I have no clue what God is up to."

She sniffed, composed herself. "Neither do I. I just don't get it. Why didn't He protect my son? Why didn't I answer my phone! I should have known something was wrong."

Jon pushed the radio on. "I hope you're not blaming yourself. I was a willing participant, too."

She sniffed and switched the station. "This is KRQA, playing your favorite Christian hits." She let Matt Redman's smooth voice sink deep into her spirit. Little by little, the soothing vibrations eased the tension away.

When the song ended, a newscast began. "Investigators in San Rafael, California, are still searching for clues to yesterday's shooting at Ignacio College, where a teacher and three students were killed and two students critically injured, just a day after another random shooting killed Cassandra Milliken of San Anselmo. Nobody knows yet why Coby Jarrett targeted the college, or Spanish teacher Geoffrey Hope. Police are still digging into his background for any thread of connection. The gunman's computer and several other electronic devices were seized from the home of his parents in Rio Rancho, who were—"

Meg punched the radio off. "I've already heard this. Way too many times. I'm still waiting to learn, why Richie? What did he ever do to deserve this?"

When they arrived at the hospital, Meg warned him, "Just FYI that Phillippe is here."

Jon nodded at the mention of her ex-husband. "Not a problem for me. Hopefully not for him, either."

Memories flashed through Meg's mind—that brief span of time last year when she'd felt torn between two men—her ex-husband and Jon. Until God made His plan clear. "Phillippe will be fine with it. He says he saw it coming." At Jon's baffled expression, she rushed on. "You and me, I mean. Not the shooting. I told him ..."

She stopped, her jaw dropped. News vans, covered with impressive, high-tech equipment, filled the lot. Hospital personnel shouted at the hovering reporters. Jon took her hand. "Just look casual. Don't let them see you sweat, or they'll be all over you."

Her wise husband was right. She pasted on an upbeat expression and swung Jon's arm back and forth, casting curious glances at the furor as though she had no clue what was going on. Couldn't those sharks tell she was faking it? But they made it inside without incident. In the elevator, Meg released her pretend smile and let herself droop. As they sped upwards, Jon pulled her to him and nestled her head against his sturdy chest, caressing her hair. They stayed like that for four floors, ignoring the other two riders, her anxiety quieting with each ding.

"But God works for the good to those who love him and are called by his name," a voice whispered to her. But if her son didn't survive, how could God bring good out of that? How could *she* possibly survive?

She hesitated outside Richie's room, her heart fluttering, stomach clenching, the coffee she'd drunk on the plane turning her stomach into a pool of burning acid. Latching her gaze onto Jon's stubbled face, she searched for reassurance.

17

Buoyed by the love in his chocolate-brown eyes, she stepped into the room.

The hum of machines and soft voices whirred around them. Phillippe, Meg's ex-husband, and Richie's ashen-faced girlfriend, Kassidy, bent over a shroud on the bed, tubes sprouting from it like octopus tentacles. Linzee, her back to them, hovered next to it.

Avoiding Phillippe's accusatory gaze, she eyed the lump under the blanket. Richie?

"How is he?" Jon's voice boomed over the background noise.

Linzee jumped, then clutched her heart. "Oh, I'm so glad you're finally here. The surgery is done, and he seems to have stabilized."

Phillippe lowered himself into the vinyl chair, his bulky frame dwarfing the seat. "The cops were here. They left about an hour ago."

Cops. Of course. "Why were they here?"

"Asking questions, naturally. Wanting to know if Richie knew the perpetrator. I told 'em we had no idea." He handed Meg a slip of paper. "They want you to call when you get home."

She stared at the paper, the figures blurring. Not only would they face a media storm, but an interrogation from the authorities as well. And this was just the beginning.

Meg slipped the paper into her pocket and hurried to her son's side. His face held a slack-jawed look, as though he were merely sleeping. A tube, connected to a humming ventilator, injected oxygen down his throat and into his lungs.

"Richie," she whispered, her face crumpling. He didn't stir. Not that she'd expected him to.

The high-tech monitor behind him emitted steady beeps. She beckoned to Linzee, who followed her to the hallway.

"I want to know everything. What's his prognosis? Where was he injured and how bad?"

"I told you all that on the phone."

She'd been fixated on the news. "Please, tell me again."

Jon joined them, and she nestled at his side, drawing strength.

"One of the bullets grazed the side of his head. He'll probably have a permanent scar." Her voice hushed, Linzee pointed to a spot above her right ear. "But the more serious issue is, he fell and hit the side of his head on the professor's desk. That's what sent him into the coma. The doctors have no idea when or if he'll ever come out of it. They have no clue if he'll be back to his normal self, or if there will be any residual brain damage."

A whimper flew out of Meg's mouth. Would she and Jon be burdened with a disabled son for the rest of their days? Would God really do that to them?

"I still can't believe you didn't see it on the news."

Meg squirmed under Linzee's knowing smirk like a guilty teenager sneaking home late.

"You can't have not been around a TV all night."

Meg's face grew warm. "We—well, we just felt like staying in for the night. We had dinner delivered to our suite, then went to bed."

Linzee's blue gaze pinned Meg. "But your phone. The school called you, Dad and I both tried calling you—"

Jon broke in. "We're really sorry about that. We'd put our phones to bed for the night."

Meg squeezed his hand, thankful he'd gone to bat for her. "Excuse me, ma'am?"

Meg spun around. A blue-smocked nurse, petite as a pre-teen, stood there, waiting for them to move. Meg jumped out of the way, and they followed the woman inside.

At Richie's bedside, the nurse faced her. The name badge read Quan. "Are you Richard's mother?" she said in a soft lilt.

"I am." Meg held out her hand and made introductions in a quavering voice.

"So glad you could make it back. I understand you were vacationing in Hawaii?"

Meg nodded, then forced out the question she was afraid to ask. "Has there been any change in his condition?"

Quan pushed a shock of black hair out of her eyes, and then placed a tiny hand on Meg's arm. "I will ask the doctor to speak with you." She lifted Richie's arm and began to rub vigorously.

Richie's chest rose and fell with each precious breath. Looking up, Meg met Phillippe's agonized gaze. Kassidy, still beside him, wrung her hands, her already thin face taut as a drum, her wide gray eyes fixed on Richie.

Meg bent over her son, her mouth near his ear. "Richie," she murmured. "It's Mom. Can you hear me?"

He remained motionless except for his rising and falling chest. Compression socks on his lower legs created their own rhythm as they squeezed, then released, keeping the lifeblood flowing in Richie's limbs. The others fell silent as if sensing the gravity of the moment.

She rubbed the only bandage-free spot on his head, his hair downy-soft beneath her fingers. "You *can* survive this. But you've got to fight. Just like you did on the football field against Novato last year, when that three-hundred-pound linebacker knocked you out. Remember? You got up, you kept going." She squeezed his shoulder. "Don't let the shooter win. Don't ..."

Gasping, her voice wobbled, hitched, and the next moment, her head landed on his chest, tears streaming from her eyes, leaving wet tracks on the drab blanket. She sobbed and wailed until Jon pulled her off her son and gently led her from the room.

Chapter Three

The early morning sun shone through Dr. Nguyen's office windows as Meg leaned in, staring at him across a faux-wood desk. Jon's warm hand rested on her knee. Phillippe, on her left, crossed his legs and gripped the armrest.

"I'll be honest with you. The full recovery rate for a lengthy coma is not high."

Dr. Nguyen's words stabbed her. "You have no way to predict if … when he'll, um, recover?"

The thirty-something doctor lifted one shoulder, held it for a moment. "We just can't say for sure. Your son, apparently, fell onto the desk when the bullet grazed him. He hit his temple, which caused a subdural hematoma of the brain, resulting in a coma." He clicked on the laptop in front of him, then turned it to face them. A cloudy skull image seemed to grin at them from the screen. "This area of the head right here, just above the temple …" He traced a path along the side of the bony mass, "is the most fragile, and an injury there can be life-threatening."

"Can you explain what a subdural hematoma is?"

"Bleeding inside the skull but outside the brain, to put it in layman's terms."

She couldn't hold back a cringing shudder.

"Best case scenario is, he awakens within a month. The odds of full recovery are highest in such a case. But if he doesn't …"

"What?"

"If the coma persists for six months, the patient's odds for recovery are slim. Worst case, he could require chronic care the rest of his life."

She grabbed and vice-gripped Jon's hand as the words

sunk in. Her gaze passed over the painting on the wall behind the doc—a golden Buddhist temple—to the framed family photo gracing his desk—smiling wife, two preschoolers. Four happy faces grinned at her, not a single one of them comatose.

"If he does come out of the coma sooner, he'll still require months of therapy. He'll need to relearn everything. Walking, talking, riding a bike. In the meantime, your son is getting the best possible care. We inserted a brain pressure monitor, and the latest reading was five. Yesterday it was eight. Anything under ten is good. We are constantly watching it, as well as his brain activity. As long as his brain shows some activity, we will remain hopeful."

She sought Jon's eyes, desperate for his steely strength to reassure her. But he still stared at the doctor, brows in a frown. She could almost see the thoughts churning in his mind … identical to hers. Enormous medical bills. Uncertain future. Months of stress.

"Thank you, Doctor." Jon's even tones calmed her heart rate, but she could hear the emotion hiding underneath.

Dr. Nguyen picked up his clipboard. "Any questions?"

Yes. How do I do this? "No." She shook her head. Her heart had fallen somewhere to the region of her toes, and abruptly she pointed her feet toward the ceiling as if she could coax her heart back into place.

Jon stood and offered his hand. She pulled herself to her feet, barely registering the goodbyes they exchanged with Phillippe, then she and Jon shuffled back to Richie's room.

"He didn't make it sound very hopeful."

Jon wrapped his arm around her shoulders. "He's just trying to be realistic."

She didn't want realistic. She wanted her son back. Her steps quickened. "I blame that college. They had absolutely no security in place. In fact …" she stopped and fumbled for the phone in her bag, "I should call them right now and give them a piece of my mind."

The roar in her head crescendoed like an incoming tide,

nearly drowning Jon's voice. "Meg."

She unscrunched her shoulders and met his steadfast gaze.

"Don't do anything while you're upset." He grasped her upper arms. "Don't you think the college personnel are just as upset as the rest of us? Come on. Breathe."

She complied, pulling in cool rivers of air, again and again, like a swimmer rescued from the undertow, until the roar ebbed away. She'd lost complete control over her facial muscles, and now they wavered between angry frowns and teary-eyed blinks. Her husband stayed rooted in front of her, an oak tree in a storm keeping her from sailing over the cliff like a fragile leaf. As long as she clung to him, she could almost believe in a happy ending, believe that everything would be all right with her son.

~~~~

With persuasion from Jon, Meg went straight to bed when they arrived at their San Rafael home. Jon held her as she cried herself to sleep.

She awoke to him jostling her. "Sorry, my love, but some police officers are here to talk to us. I tried to tell them to come back later, but they wouldn't take no for an answer."

"The police?" Reality crashed over her. She sat up so fast, Jon lurched back. "What time is it?"

"A little after two. You slept a good four hours."

She groaned and rubbed her eyes against the sun streaming through the window slats. "Has the hospital called?"

"No. We can assume that means no change. They promised to call if Richie's condition changed."

She shook tangled hair from her eyes and the cobwebs from her mind. "Why are the police here? We're not the criminals."

"They were pretty vague." Jon's rueful tone told her he understood her trepidation.

She reluctantly followed him into the living room, where

a man and woman waited. Jon introduced her, and the woman offered her hand. "Detective Mary Lethbridge." She nodded at the baby-faced man towering beside her, who looked barely old enough to drink a legal beer. "My partner, Detective Tucker."

Tucker glanced around. "Does your daughter live here with you?"

"Linzee? No, she has her own place," Meg said. What did he want with Linzee?

"Oh." The detective's expression revealed nothing, but two red spots appeared on his cheeks. "We may need to ask her some questions, too."

Meg squelched a smile. From his averted gaze and cherry-red cheeks, she suspected Linzee had piqued his interest when he'd met her at the hospital.

She sobered when he added, "May we sit down?"

She and Jon settled hand-in-hand on the smooth brown-vinyl loveseat, and the detectives took the adjacent matching sofa. Detective Lethbridge lowered the notebook she was clutching to her lap. An unmistakable air of authority hung over her and Detective Tucker, despite his youth and good humor.

The atmosphere around them seemed to thicken and stand still.

"What can we help you with?" Jon's voice matched Tucker's somber tone.

"There are certain points in this case that make us wonder if Mr. Hope or your son knew the shooter," Lethbridge began. "Witnesses say it looked like he intentionally aimed the gun in Mr. Hope's direction as if he were at target practice. But your son and the other injured student were standing right next to the teacher. We're trying to find out if the shooter was targeting any of them."

"Did the shooter have a connection with the students who were killed?"

"We haven't found one yet. After Mr. Hope, your son,

and the other student collapsed, the gunman walked around shooting at random. By this time, most of the students were either running from the room or were hiding under their desks."

Meg shook her head. "Why would anyone purposely shoot my son? He has no enemies. Everyone loves him. I think he just happened to be in the wrong place at the wrong time."

Lethbridge nodded. "That's what we believe, too. But some of the evidence makes us wonder."

Before she could ask what evidence, Jon asked, "How many were in the room?"

The detective glanced at her clipboard. "A total of twenty." Her gaze probed Meg. "Did your son ever spend time in Rio Rancho? Say, with friends, or social connections, where he might have run into Coby Jarrett?"

"Not that I'm aware of."

"Okay. Then our next step is to obtain your permission to search your son's computer for any link to the shooter, no matter how small."

She chewed on her lower lip. "Why do you need to know this?"

"We've obtained Mr. Hope's computers already, and found nothing on it that indicated he knew the killer."

"We're baffled by the randomness of it, considering the distance the killer had to drive to get there," Detective Tucker said. "Normally, when these mass shootings happen, the gunman chooses a location he's familiar with. Think back on the recent mass shootings. Sandy Hook, for example. Lanza chose the local elementary school. And the community college shootings in Arizona and Oregon. The shooters had attended classes there. The mall shooting in Oregon. It was close to the shooter's home."

Meg nodded. "I see what you're saying. This guy drove thirty miles from Rio Rancho, clear across the bay from San Rafael—"

"When he could have chosen a closer location," Jon

finished, echoing her thoughts.

"Yes." Lethbridge tapped her finger on her clipboard. "It's not typical behavior for a mass shooter. So we think there was a method to his madness. For some reason he selected Ignacio. We're trying to find out why."

Chapter Four

"A method to his madness." The words carved a hole in Meg's heart. She leaned against Jon after the officers left, her emotions in shreds, letting random thoughts drift through her mind.

The next moment she leaped off the couch, certainty in every tense muscle. "The college! I have to go talk to them."

"Wait, sweetheart."

She whirled, gesturing Jon to her side. "Please come with me. I need you there."

His face held a puzzled expression. "The college is closed, Meg. The place will be crawling with investigators." His hands caressed her back while his voice caressed her spirit.

"I don't care. Somebody needs to take responsibility for what happened to my son!"

The ringing doorbell made her jump. Too startled to answer it, she stayed frozen while Jon rushed to open the door.

Bright crimson hair announced Camille's arrival. Bill followed on his wife's heels clutching a bag as Camille rushed to Meg and squeezed her in a shoulder hug. "Girlfriend?" Camille stepped back and studied Meg's face.

Meg searched her best friend's eyes, hoping to see reassurance, a promise that Richie would be okay. But even Camille's always-jolly expression now resembled that of a funeral attendee.

"I've been calling you all day. We've been so worried. Are you okay?"

Meg felt her face crumple as the men stood helplessly by. "No," she whispered, dropping her forehead to Camille's steady shoulder. "I'm not okay."

"Sorry. Stupid question. Of course, you're not." She ran her fingertips along Meg's back, injecting steely calm into Meg's nerves. "Linzee's been keeping us updated." Her breath tickled Meg's neck. "I know it sounds serious, but praise God he's stabilized. Right?"

Meg nodded at her optimistic friend's feeble attempt to look on the bright side but inside fought back annoyance mingled with despair. "Stabilized" only meant her world had stopped turning upside down, and now hung suspended, trying to decide which way to spin. Life, or death. Restored health, or helpless disability.

"Are you hungry? We brought sushi."

Her stomach rebelled at the images of sushi. Food would only stick to the roof of her dry mouth. "No thanks."

"You could always write a blog. On Facebook, for example. 'Pray for Richie.'"

A blog? Sounded like a big energy suck.

"Think how many people will be praying for him once it gets out there. Millions!"

Meg sniffed, the fresh scent of detergent in Camille's sweater filling her nose.

"Right, Jon?"

Of course, Camille would call in reinforcements.

"She's got a point, sweetheart."

"I'm a painter, not a writer."

"You don't have to be a professional. Just pour out your heart and let the world in on your son's journey."

"I agree." Camille lifted her gaze toward Jon. "By the way, have you two heard the latest news?"

Meg shook her head, steeling herself against more bad news.

"They're about to announce a new discovery in the case."

Jon sprang to action and clicked on the TV. Meg reluctantly let Camille push her to the sofa. She sighed and sank into its depths as a wooden-faced newscaster shuffled papers on the TV screen.

Every muscle in Meg tensed when he eyed the camera. "Good afternoon, we're Jerry and Jenny bringing you a breaking update on yesterday's shooting at Ignacio College." Marin Hall, a squat, stucco building, appeared in the background, barricaded with yellow tape. "Investigators have found a possible connection to the shooting Monday evening of Cassandra Milliken of San Anselmo, whose body was found in her garage." A wispy-haired woman appeared in a photo box, her plump arms wrapped around a toddler on her lap, a Madonna-like smile on her bespectacled face. "San Anselmo police have released information that the bullets that killed Mrs. Milliken were the same caliber used to kill Coby Jarrett's parents and the three Ignacio victims."

The man turned to his female counterpart, who added, "The mystery deepens. Now investigators are asking, are the murders of the San Anselmo woman and the college professor and his students somehow related? Did Coby Jarrett also kill Mrs. Milliken? If so, why?"

"Six degrees of separation," Jon muttered, popping sushi into his mouth.

"What?"

"You know the saying. Every person in the world is separated by a chain of six acquaintances." He rubbed her knee. "So all they need to do is figure out the six people separating the killer and the victim."

"You make it sound so easy."

The camera panned to the college again where uniformed bodies swarmed. "There are still many unanswered questions, Jenny," Jerry's disembodied voice intoned. "Ignacio's president George Hales held a press conference earlier today and attempted to answer some of those questions. Here's what he had to say."

Meg tuned out the president's speech. She didn't want to hear a string of meaningless platitudes. Of course, he was grieving with the rest of the community over this heinous crime. Of course, he was shocked and outraged that violence had visited his campus. Nothing he could say would make up for the grievous lack of security. Or restore her son to his former carefree, energetic self.

~~~~

Linzee's phone rang just as she was getting ready to leave for the hospital. She frowned at the name displayed — *San Rafael Police Department* — then sighed, knowing her visit to Rich would have to wait. "Hello?"

"Ms. St. John?"

"Yes?"

"This is Detective Ken Tucker of the San Rafael Police Department." She heard loud male laughter in the background, and a mental image presented itself — an unsightly room full of grizzled, beer-bellied cops guzzling soda and telling off-color jokes.

Then she stopped herself. Last year after she left the gay lifestyle, she promised God she'd try to quit demeaning men in her thoughts. God continued to gently remind her of her promise whenever she fell back into old habits.

The man continued in a pleasing baritone, "You met my partner and me in your brother's hospital room."

A vision of a kindly young giant rose in her mind. "Oh. Right. I remember you." The one whose name sounded like Kentucky.

"We have some questions we'd like to ask you. May we drop by for a few minutes?"

"What kinds of questions?"

"Regarding your brother."

She didn't even know Rich that well anymore and told him so.

"We'd still like to ask. Sometimes people know things they don't know that they know if you know what I mean."

She reluctantly agreed. Fortunately, the Carlitos, the church family she lived with, was out of town for a couple of days. They'd never have to know cops dropped by.

But now she couldn't escape the bubble of anxiety circling her. She paced to evade the disturbing images of gunfire and chaos battling in her head. Despite the rare contact she'd had with her brother, this had hit her hard.

Detectives Tucker and Lethbridge arrived within five minutes in an unmarked car, for which Linzee was grateful. As they stepped over the toddler's toy cars on the floor, she caught Tucker glancing around at the family photos on the mantle, the wall-mounted TV, its shelves beneath crammed with game components and DVDs. He snuck a quick glance at her as if he wondered what she was doing in such a kid-infested environment. "Your mom said you're a nanny for this family?" His voice rose at the end as if doubting he'd heard right.

Was her history that obvious to this guy?

"That's right. They knocked my rent down in exchange for babysitting."

"How old are the kids?"

"The girl is eight and the boys are two and six." She offered them a seat on the flower-print sofa.

"Good deal. Rent rates have gotten unreal." His eyes crinkled at the sides, reminding her of Mom's new husband.

By the time they'd seated themselves, Linzee had decided Detective Tucker's face was as kind as his voice, though his height and bulk might make him appear intimidating to a crook. Maybe he wasn't so bad. For a guy. Not so much the lady cop, whose deep lines around her mouth gave her a perpetual scowl.

The woman spoke for the first time, in a voice surprisingly high-pitched for such a stocky, metal-bedecked woman. "What can you tell us about your brother's friends and associates?"

Linzee shrugged. "I know almost nothing about his personal life."

"Do you have reason to believe he knew the shooter?"

Linzee widened her eyes. "Knew the shooter? I doubt it."

The questions kept coming, rapid-fire and emotionless, none of which she had answers to.

Tucker was leaning forward, seemingly intent on her non-replies. "We think the shooter was after someone specific in the classroom."

Linzee shuddered. "You're saying it wasn't your usual random school shooting?"

Tucker nodded, his expression hardening. "Correct. We think it was deliberate and premeditated. We just don't know who the intended victim was."

She plunged in with the question that had nagged her since yesterday. "How did he get hold of the gun? I bet it was legally purchased and registered, wasn't it? Don't all these shooters somehow obtain legal firearms before they go out and commit mayhem?" Her nostrils flared with suppressed outrage. "How can you people allow it to continue?"

"Wait, wait." Tucker held up his hand. "We're the ones trying to keep you safe."

"Yeah? Where were you yesterday when that guy walked into my brother's classroom?"

Something flickered in Tucker's eyes. Had her harsh words hurt his feelings?

She ran the toe of her sandal along the slate-gray carpet. "Sorry. I'm just so upset. These shootings keep happening."

Lethbridge's frown deepened, but Tucker's face softened. "We hate it too." He dug into his breast pocket and took out a business card. "Here."

She took it from him. *Kenneth Tucker, Det. San Rafael Police Department.*

"Anytime you need to talk, don't hesitate to call. Trust me, we're on your side."

If you say so, Kentucker, she added silently.

She nodded as they let themselves out, then stood at the front window, watching Detective Tucker fold his long frame into the passenger seat, baffled at this new sensation inside her. She was actually sorry to see him go. Something about him felt safe and solid, as immovable as Mt. Shasta during an earthquake. Like that sweet cop who rescued her from her basement prison last year.

She didn't know where all this was coming from, and she wasn't sure she wanted to know.

He glanced over from behind the glass and caught her eye, and she hastened away from the window before he could figure out she'd been spying on him.

Chapter Five

A candlelight vigil for the shooting victims was planned at Lagoon Park that evening. When Jon asked Meg if she wanted to go, she shook her head, shuddering at images of disconsolate faces crying oceans of tears. "I'm carrying on my own private vigil right here," she told him, placing her hand over her heart. And, starting tomorrow, she would continue it beside Richie's hospital bed. She'd failed him once. No way would she fail him again. This time, she'd be there for him when he woke up.

When—not if.

A sobbing woman on the TV, her face deliberately blurred, captured Meg's attention. "I remember him. The shooter," the anonymous woman cried to the female reporter, who held a microphone to the woman's face. "He smelled like he needed a bath. I thought nothing of it when he asked me how to find the Spanish class." Her voice crackled. "I asked him if he knew the room number, and he said, polite as can be, 'I believe the teacher's name is Mr. Hope.' And I told him where to find it!" Her wail peaked before she broke down again. The reporter murmured sympathetic noises into the mike.

When the woman composed herself, she sniffed and continued. "If I'd only known that guitar case had a gun inside, I never would have told him."

The camera switched again to the newsroom. "From the cafeteria worker's testimony, it now appears evident Coby Jarrett deliberately targeted Geoffrey Hope's classroom," Jerry continued, as a photo of the teacher flashed next to him on the screen.

"Dear God," Meg murmured, curling her fingers around

Jon's. "Why?"

Camille, on her other side, sucked in a breath.

Jerry's face grew even more somber. "Many people in our community are struggling to come to terms with this tragedy. Many of you either knew or knew of, the victims. In light of this, First Baptist Church in San Rafael is opening up their grief support group to anyone in the community who would like to drop by."

Meg slid her gaze to Jon. Was he too remembering the first time they met at First Baptist Church? He met her eyes and squeezed her hand, his thoughts in apparent synchronicity. She'd often wondered what happened to the FOGY group they'd all attended there each Monday evening. Camille was reminiscing too, judging by the elbow nudge on her right.

The familiar brick building, the site of so many precious memories, brought a smile to her heart, if not her face. "The group meets Thursday nights," Jerry explained. "If you need someone to talk to, they begin at seven p.m. at the church."

"I'd like to go," Jon murmured. "I think it will do us good."

She nodded, remembering the life-changing events the last time she joined a support group at the church. Maybe this one would prove as cathartic.

"We're heading for a short commercial break, but don't go away. Up next, we'll be broadcasting the president's speech from the White House earlier today. He offered his response to the tragedy and some common-sense solutions to our nation's pervasive gun violence." The scene faded and switched to a pharmaceutical commercial.

Bill rubbed his hands together, his mouth in a scowl. "Here we go. Another speech from the president about gun control."

Camille nodded. "Making gun owners feel guilty about exercising our Second Amendment rights."

Meg got to her feet, her chest seizing. Her son hung

between life and death, and everyone wanted to turn his tragedy into a political debate. "I don't want to hear the president's speech." Her voice choked as she gestured at the TV. "You guys feel free to watch, but please excuse me."

Camille rose as well, her eyes casting compassionate beams. "We'd better go too." She grabbed Meg in a tight hug. "Just know that hundreds of people are praying for you."

Meg could only nod as she waved goodbye to her friends, then hastened toward her painting studio. Her fingers itched to unload all her angst on canvas.

But before she could reach her sanctuary, Jon came up behind her and eased her around to face him. Worry lines creased his brow, and his gaze bored into her. "What's wrong?"

She shook her head at him, her brave façade crumbling. "I can't listen to any more. It's all too much. I'm afraid to go on social media or answer the phone." Tears made tracks down her cheeks. "This—" she gestured vaguely toward the outside world— "all this discussion, debate, only makes me angrier. Easy for them to go on and on about it. It's not *their* son lying in the hospital!"

He gathered her to his shoulder as she wept, stroking her back as if she were delicate china. While she huddled inside Jon's embrace, his kisses soothed the storm in her heart, sweeping her away to a place where violence, madness, and death ceased to exist.

Her husband's love could almost make her forget the grim reality waiting for her.

~~~~

Unable to sleep, Meg finally threw off the covers at midnight and rolled out of Jon's limp arms. Pattering to the kitchen in her robe, she heated some milk, added vanilla and cinnamon, and carried the warm mug to her studio, sipping as she went.

She placed a pad of paper on the easel and turned on its soft overhead lighting, her brain racing. Which medium would best serve for self-therapy? Oil and acrylic would render every gritty detail. Or watercolor, for a modern flair.

No. She picked up a charcoal stick, to reflect the gray shadows and dark valley her life had become and started with a broad stroke across the paper.

As always when she created art, she disengaged her head and let her heart take over. After many mindless strokes, a shape emerged. Stepping back, she tilted her head to examine the flower-like creature on the canvas—a rose on one side, its petals drooping to the ground, a dandelion on the other, its spores reaching to the sky.

The rose needed color, so she picked up a watercolor brush and filled in its petals with the same crimson shade as the dozen roses Jon brought her the night he proposed. As if she'd summoned him, a knock sounded, and the man dominating her thoughts peeked in as she completed her final strokes.

"I thought I'd find you here." Jon was at her side in seconds. She watched the shifting expressions on his face as he squeezed her shoulders and peered at the canvas. "Fascinating contrasts. Tell me what you did here."

She sighed out the tension under his massaging fingers, her deltoid muscles melting like warm tar. "The beautiful rose is you and me. But an ugly dandelion has invaded and wants to choke the life out of us."

"We need to pray, then." He swiveled her around into his embrace and stroked her hair. "I haven't even suggested we pray, and I'm supposed to be the spiritual leader." He brushed the hair from her forehead and kissed her brow. "Let's do that right now."

She smiled, her first in hours. "I love you, you know that?"

He smiled back. "I love you too, sweetheart."

Chapter Six

The one remaining news van in the hospital parking lot had Meg detouring through the emergency room the next morning, and nobody stopped her to inquire about her business there. Weak with relief, she made her way to Richie's room, where he lay as still and quiet as he had the previous day. The splashes of color from numerous flowers provided relief from the grayness. From the odors of sickness and disease. There must be ten bouquets so far, with more being delivered every day.

She breathed in a recipe of mingled scents. Meg had hoped for some tiny increment of improvement, but, according to Quan, Richie had not responded since his arrival. "You're his first visitor today," she told Meg.

"His dad and sister will be here this evening."

"And your husband?"

"He's spending the day moving his belongings out of his house in Sausalito and into mine, so we can be closer to my son." They'd decided to reverse their original plan to move into Jon's house and rent hers out. She'd been looking forward to the shorter commute into the city and her job at Noelle Marquette. Now, not only was she facing the same long commute, but Jon would be farther from the Sausalito boat shop he owned. "He's going to try to stop by tonight."

Quan studied the beeping instruments as she examined Richie. "How long do you plan to stay today?"

"All day, every day. Until he wakes up."

Quan lifted her brows but made no reply. No need to tell the nurse she already emailed her boss for extra leave time.

"How're his brain pressure numbers? Any improvement?"

Quan examined the chart. "Holding steady. We're hoping to remove the port from his skull in the next day or two."

Which sounded promising, even if she didn't know what it meant. "Anything else?"

"Well, his blood pressure is elevated, probably due to the pain, so we're increasing his pain meds. His electrolytes are down, so we added sodium to his IV."

"I see." She didn't understand the mysterious world of medicine, but she was grateful Quan and the other pros here did.

"This afternoon the neurologist will decide if he needs additional surgery."

Please, God. Please.

The hours dragged, nurses came and went, but she stayed by Richie's side, reminiscing aloud on favorite memories from his childhood. Whatever it took to prod his brain back to life. Occasionally she took a food break in the cafeteria, or a fresh air break out in the graveled courtyard, perched on a succulent terra-cotta planter. Hoping for a distraction, she opened Facebook on her iPad. Eighty-three new messages awaited her … messages of horror and sorrow, encouragement and support. Her heart clenched. Although they warmed her, they did nothing to get her mind off reality.

Her email list was twice as long. Ignoring several messages from national publications asking for interviews, she soon gave up wading through all of them and headed back to Richie's room. As she passed one of the waiting rooms, a newspaper headline jumped out at her: PRESIDENT CALLS FOR TIGHTER GUN CONTROL LAWS IN WAKE OF SHOOTING. An irresistible urge pulled her feet closer. As she picked it up, she gasped at the headline below it: JARRETT STALKED HOPE AND MILLIKEN. She carried it to the room on trembling legs and squinted at the fine print.

"A break in the Ignacio case has investigators hopeful they are getting closer to finding answers. Despite Jarrett's obvious efforts to wipe his hard drive clean, police technicians have uncovered enough history on the young man's computer to convince them that he deliberately drove to Ignacio College Tuesday with the intention of killing forty-three-year-old Geoffrey Hope."

Meg's mouth went dry, but she made herself keep reading. "Starting in January of this year, Jarrett's search history shows he conducted numerous online inquiries on Hope, including college transcripts, previous employers, and cities of residence.

"Police also found nearly as many searches of Cassandra Milliken, nee Martin, the San Anselmo woman shot Monday evening. The latest evidence points to Coby Jarrett, but police have yet to discover anything that would point to a motive for the shootings.

"They continue to dig into the lives of Jarrett and his parents for clues to the troubled young man's psyche. They've found no indication the family knew or had any association with Mr. Hope or Mrs. Milliken. Records show Coby Jarrett had attended Rio Rancho High School through his sophomore year but had a psychotic breakdown early in his junior year. From that time on, he was in and out of psychiatric care. But friends and neighbors of the family say that his medication seemed to be normalizing him over the last few months.

"When neighbors in the Jarrett's middle-class Rio Rancho neighborhood were asked if the events of Tuesday took them by surprise, or if they'd seen it coming, the replies varied. Melissa Alex, 47, expressed shock. 'My husband and I have lived next door to Coby since he was five. He was a sweet little boy. Very inquisitive. I don't know what went wrong. Bob and Rosie were great parents. But something happened to him in high school. It's like the wiring in his brain just got all tangled up.'

"Another neighbor, who wished to remain anonymous, claimed the shooting did not surprise him. 'Coby used to

40

shoot his BB gun at my dog. Just for fun. Looks like he was practicing for bigger things, wouldn't you say?'"

Meg tried to swallow the fist-sized lump in her throat. "Coby was the Jarrett's only child. Robert Jarrett, a shift supervisor for Shell Oil refinery in Martinez, and Rose Jarrett, a substitute teacher for Rio Rancho School district, were well liked and respected in the community. Both were forty-five at the time of their death.

"Mrs. Milliken, 37, known as Sandy by friends and family, was a licensed day-care provider, and leaves behind a husband, Christopher, 38, and two sons, ages 9 and 4. Mr. Hope had been employed by Ignacio College for two years and is survived by a wife, Courtney, and a 14-year-old daughter."

The paper slid to Meg's feet. The chair arm's metal dug into her fingers under her vise grip as relief wrestled with horror … relief that Coby hadn't been aiming for Richie, but horror at his vendetta against those poor people. Had either of them had any suspicions someone out there stalked them? What had they done to Coby to deserve such a fate?

~~~~

Judging by the crowd's shouts outside the college, the gun control rally was well underway. Linzee held up her sign plastered with photos of Richie smiling his carefree grin, as she searched for her friends. "What if he were YOUR brother?" the sign asked. A couple of signs showed X-ed out photos of guns, others displayed sentiments like "End the Violence Now!" A few Second Amendment folks, evident by their signs claiming that guns don't kill people, people do, walked the fringes. News vans lined one side of the street, cop cars the other.

Her two friends waited near the yellow crime-scene tape. Behind the tape, the site was mostly deserted. Whitewashed Marin Hall reflected sunlight, a still life painting putting on a brave front.

"Hey-a," she greeted the duo. "Have I missed anything

exciting?" A swift gust of the cool breeze off the bay sent her sign colliding with Ian's, and she shivered. She should have worn a jacket.

"Not really. How's your brother?" asked Claire, her green eyes glaring at the cops swarming the opposite sidewalk, all no-nonsense in their spiffy uniforms and gleaming medals.

"He might as well be dead," Linzee bit out.

Claire swiveled her gaze away from the cops and widened her eyes at Linzee. "Serious? He's still under?"

Linzee winced at the poor choice of words, then told them all she knew.

A loud altercation to their left sent two cops running at a pro-gun protester screaming in someone's face. Two journalists sprinted in the same direction, their tablets leading the way, followed by a cameraman.

Linzee gestured to her friends. "Let's get over there. If I can snag an interview and tell my brother's story, maybe people will start taking this seriously." She inched closer so as not to draw attention from the cops.

Moments later, one of the reporters noticed her sign. He left his partner and headed her way. "Miss, may I ask you a few questions?"

At her nod, he asked for her name and pointed to her sign. "I'm Ted Corban of the San Francisco Chronicle. Your brother is one of the victims, I see." By now, everyone in the world must recognize her brother's face.

"Yes." She drew herself up to her full five-foot-seven. "He's lying unconscious through no fault of his own because of a deranged maniac with a gun. And I'm here to help raise awareness. We want to be catalysts for change." Another swift breeze tipped her sign sideways. She wrestled it upright. "The kind of change that will keep guns out of the hands of deranged maniacs."

"California already has the most restrictive gun laws in the country. What more do you think we need to do to keep guns away from deranged maniacs?"

"Nobody should be allowed to buy a gun until they've passed a mental health evaluation."

"Mental health tests are already required by law."

"But anyone can buy ammunition without a background check."

A small crowd had gathered, their cheers and applause punching the air, depending on which side they agreed with. Linzee sought support in Claire's approving gaze. "Someone's letting the crazies slip through the cracks. That guy shouldn't have had a gun."

"From what we understand, the shooter had access to an unregistered shotgun that belonged to his grandfather."

He wanted to play devil's advocate, did he? She could play that game, too. "Then the grandpa should've reported it stolen. Maybe we should prosecute him, huh?"

"Do you feel that holding gun owners responsible for reporting lost or stolen weapons is the answer?"

She bobbed her head, accompanied by nods from half the onlookers. "I do. Believe it or not, gun owners are not required to report them in those situations." The crowd applauded as though she'd offered the wisdom of Yoda. The cameraman zoomed in for a close-up, and she gave the lens her most earnest look. "With all of us working together, we can turn this tragedy into a positive force for change."

She faltered when a dark suit in the distance caught her attention. The suit was closing the distance between them, and then the face belonging to it clarified.

Detective Ken Tucker was on his way over, his eyes fixed on her. Words fled her mind, carried away by the gust of wind. *Oh, no. It's Kentucker.* Linzee, gasping, slid her gaze sideways, but the crowd pressed in on both sides.

Regaining her poise, she focused on the reporter. "Thank you for letting me speak." She spun, an unseen force sending her legs in the opposite direction from Tucker.

"Hey," Claire called. "Wait up."

Linzee kept her gaze on the approaching yellow tape and her two hands on the buffeting sign's wood handle. Claire materialized, panting, by Linzee's side. "You did awesome, my friend. Can't wait to see it on the news. I bet it'll go viral."

"I didn't do it for my fifteen minutes of fame."

"But you'll probably get it anyway." Claire chortled. "You're going to be the next big YouTube sensation."

Linzee shook her head and opened her mouth to protest.

"Ms. St. John?"

She whipped around to see Tucker coming at her as though she'd already surpassed her allotted fifteen minutes of notoriety and now he was going to have to ticket her.

"Can't you call me Linzee, like everyone else?" As she freed one hand to flip the hair out of her eyes, another gust chose that moment to swing her placard edge-first right between the detective's eyes.

"Yow!" he yelled.

She jumped back, tossing the errant poster to the ground as he swiped at the red spot growing on his brow. Claire backed away.

He glared at Linzee. "Do you have it in for me, or something?"

"No, no, I'm sorry!" What an idiot, to hit a policeman, for heaven's sake. "It was an accident! Are you okay?"

He nodded, still rubbing, but his glare had faded to wary scrutiny. So far, no blood. "I just came over to say hi." He shuffled his feet. "And to ask how your brother's doing."

"And then you got hit by a sign." A giggle sputtered out.

His eyes crinkled, and his hearty laugh joined in. "No harm done. You only missed my eye by a millimeter."

"Blame it on the wind." She flung a hand toward the bay.

"Right. So …" He gestured around at the dispersing crowd, law-enforcer aura back in place. "Everyone's leaving. It looks like you guys made your point." Then his face transformed to shy high-schooler before her eyes. "I really do want to know how your brother is doing. Can we talk over coffee when my shift is over?"

She stared at him, disbelief crawling up her spine. What would he think if he knew she'd never gone to coffee, or anything else, with a man? Ever.

From the corner of her eye, she thought she saw Claire smirking. If she said yes, Claire would conclude she now swung both ways. If she said no …

An unfamiliar urge took shape in her heart. If she said no, she'd miss a chance to learn what dating a man was like. She wouldn't find out if God could dig deep enough into her heart to transform the soil.

She nodded at the cop kneading his fingers over and over while he waited for her answer.

"Yes. Yes, I think I'd like that."

Chapter Seven

Painting in the Wilderness - Reflections and updates on school shooting victim Richard St. John, by his mother, Megan Shaw Paulson (103 followers)

"O my son Richard! My son, my son! If only I had died instead of you." (Paraphrase of 2 Samuel 18:33)

Picture this: In your dream, a phone rings. You reach for it, you pick up the receiver, but it keeps ringing as you hold it in your hand. Your eyes open, and you realize, this is no dream. The ringing phone is real. Persistent. Annoying. The kind of ring that says, "Beware: Bad news ahead."

It happened to me last week. And it was only the beginning of a terrible twist in this story of my life. Here I was, married less than a week. Honeymooning in Hawaii under a warm tropical sun. But life must have been too easy. Too good. God forbid we get too happy or comfortable here on this earth.

The news on the other side of the ringing phone was even worse than I could have imagined. My handsome, popular, precious son, Richard, had been shot in his community college Spanish classroom and was rushed to the hospital in a coma. You've all heard the news by now ... no need to rehash the details.

Have you ever experienced a tragedy so profound

you felt you were drowning in a dark sea? If you're anything like me, you feel helpless to escape. My usual way of coping when I'm traveling through a desert is to lock myself in my "cocoon" (aka my painting studio) and paint my way out of that wilderness. But this time, it doesn't seem to be effective.

I may not be comatose like my son, but the darkness is surely as powerful as the ocean.

So when you're praying for my son and the other victims, please say a little prayer for me as well. I'm drowning, and I can't find my way out.

Thank you,

Meg

~~~~

Memories rushed Meg's mind as she and Jon entered the basement fellowship hall at First Baptist. The same smell of freon, mixed with the dusty scent of aged stucco, sent her sailing back in time, to the night she and Jon met.

"Bring back memories?" He squeezed her hand, the same memories echoing in his tone.

"Yes, indeed."

Metal folding chairs, about three-quarters of them occupied, were laid out in roughly ten rows. Unlike their FOGY meetings, where the handful of attendees sat in a circle.

"Hasn't changed much."

"Still the same Bible story posters on the walls."

The accordion wall that bisected the room was fully open tonight to accommodate the fifty or so people. A few still stood in clusters, some weeping, others embracing. Bewildered grief hung like gray mist all around. At the front, a solemn, bespectacled gentleman behind a podium scanned the room. Someone blinked the lights off and on, and the hubbub died down. Meg and Jon found seats about halfway

47

back.

The leader introduced himself as Pastor Fred, then opened with a prayer for the injured victims, and the victims' families, a heartfelt cry to God that stirred a cry in Meg's own heart. Then he asked all newcomers to raise their hands. Approximately twenty hands, besides their own, sprang up.

"And who's here for grief support?"

Most hands rose this time.

He grinned. "Just checking that no one was heading for the movie theater ..." he thrust a thumb behind him in the general direction of the mall, "and accidentally ended up here."

A few chuckles echoed before he went on. "For the newbies, I want to thank you for being courageous enough to attend tonight. Sometimes it's hard to admit you're hurting. But after this week's tragedy, I can't imagine any of us not hurting." He continued in a similar vein for a few minutes, and Meg let the words soak into her.

"Many of us are asking where God was Tuesday evening. Why didn't He stop the shooter? Why didn't He save those victims?"

A woman nearby responded with a sob wrenched from her gut.

"These are tough questions, with no easy answers. But I can tell you what God says about tragedy in His word." A projector shone Bible verses on the wall as he recited a passage familiar to Meg. "Second Corinthians 1:3 through 5 says, 'Blessed be God, even the Father of our Lord Jesus Christ, the Father of mercies, and the God of all comfort, who comforteth us in all our tribulation, that we may be able to comfort them which are in any trouble, by the comfort wherewith we ourselves are comforted of God. For as the sufferings of Christ abound in us, so our consolation also aboundeth by Christ.'

"Did anyone count the number of times we see the word 'comfort'?"

A few rows ahead, a man and woman stood, their posture unflinching like stone pillars. The man, his lip curled, clasped the woman's shoulder and hurried her to the aisle, to the exit, and out the door.

The leader paused, unruffled. Maybe he understood that offended folks were an unfortunate hazard of the profession.

Then he stole a glance at the exit. "You might be thinking, 'But I don't want God's comfort, I want Him to keep tragedy far from me.'" Pastor Fred gave a slow, empathetic nod. "I want you to know there's good news. In Isaiah and Revelation, He promises to make a world like that someday. Did you know He's preparing it right now?" He paused a moment to meet folks' eyes as though he were gauging their level of buy-in. "Jesus promised it to his disciples in John fourteen."

He projected more verses onto the wall, then, after he wrapped up, he instructed them to form small groups of five to seven and share with each other how they'd dealt with their grief this week.

Meg and Jon ended up in a group of six, with another couple named Paul and Addy, plus two lone women, Candy and Rachel. The four seemed to naturally defer to Jon as the leader. His self-assured bearing typically inspired confidence.

"How about my wife and I start?" Jon offered. "The shooting affected us personally. I've spent the last couple of days sending a lot of arrow prayers God's way." He paused and met Meg's eye, sending a tingle through her. "Do you care to share, sweetheart?"

She let her eyes stay on him for an extra second, then gazed around the circle at eight curious eyes, her fingers finding Jon's. Might as well get the elephant in the room ID'd first. "My son was one of those injured in the shooting."

The others offered sympathetic murmurs, except for Candy, who gasped, her hazel eyes shimmering. Meg swallowed the golf-ball lump in her throat. "He's in the hospital, still unconscious. But I'm thankful," she squeezed

Jon's hand, "I have a wonderfully supportive husband with a nice wide shoulder to cry on."

Paul and Addy shared a we-can-relate smile.

She sighed. "It's been a tough week. I'm so baffled as to the whys. Yes, I question why God allowed it, but even more so, I question why the shooter did it. The cops told us this week they think he deliberately targeted the college. And I feel if I could just understand why, if I could get into his head a little, maybe it'll speed the healing."

Addy sucked in a breath. "Are you sure you want to know?"

Jon squeezed her fingers. "Tell them about your coping mechanism, sweetheart."

She nodded. "When I'm upset, I paint or draw, although I've spent so much time at the hospital this week, I've only had one chance to indulge in my favorite therapy."

She gave a brief explanation of her art background, then looked at Jon to signal she was finished.

He searched her face and asked, "Mind if I share the story of our aborted honeymoon?"

Before she could reply, the others answered for her with enthusiastic yes's, then responded with suitable chagrin when Jon finished.

Rachel, her brunette hair coiled into a single braid, offered breathy condolences. "I can't imagine what you must be going through."

How could anybody? For the second time in a year, one of her children battled danger. If that didn't require a soul of steel, she didn't know what did.

She caught Candy still assessing her, mouth frozen partway open as though she were watching the dust of Meg's crumbling life settle around her. Meg opened her mouth, but no words came, only an ache the size of a migraine in the back of her throat.

She forced her attention to Paul and Addy, who shared that they escaped to nature when they needed to process their grief. "We drove to Alamere Falls today and hiked," Paul explained.

"It was so peaceful," his wife added, "it was easy to forget the shooting. At least temporarily."

Jon leaned forward, elbows on knees. "Were you connected to any of the victims?"

Both shook their heads, then swiveled when Candy cut in. "I was."

Her self-conscious gaze darted around the circle as they all went still, waiting for her to elaborate.

"I knew Sandy Martin, I mean Milliken, in high school." Her voice went small, like a child's, while her bony fingers picked at lint on her jeans. "We were best friends back then. Everyone called us Candy and Sandy, or just the Andys. But after high school, we gradually lost touch and went our separate ways. When I read about her murder in the paper, I …" She clamped her mouth shut, her wide eyes fixated on some unseen vista.

"You what?" Jon encouraged.

Candy merely shook her head, tears rolling down her cheeks, then sucked in a sniff that rattled like grinding gears. "She was the only one who stood by me when I went through a rough patch. I saw her at our fifteen-year reunion, and we chatted. She seemed happy. But we haven't spoken since." Another ragged sniff. "I should've stayed in touch. She … she didn't deserve to get shot. Why did he shoot *her*?" She broke into a wail and didn't ease up even with Addy's awkward pats on her back.

Candy's bouncing legs picked up speed as she flung her gaze to the ceiling and let her pain erupt through her twisted mouth. The rest of them waited in uncomfortable silence for the anguish to ebb. The woman's grief seemed a little over-the-top. But Meg stopped herself in the act of passing judgment, imagining how she would respond if an old friend from high school were murdered.

She let the scenario play through her mind. Sure, she

would shed some tears in the same situation, but she didn't know if she'd be as stricken as this woman who wept like the mythological Niobe who mourned for the loss of her children.

Jon brought in a measure of normality when he suggested they quietly pray together. So they lifted their voices to God until the meeting adjourned.

Afterward, Candy tapped Meg's arm. "Do you still practice art therapy?" Her fingers were wrapped around each other like tangled rope, and her red-rimmed eyes pleaded.

"I haven't for a while. I needed a steady income, so now I'm a buyer at Noelle Marquette."

Candy's eyes widened—the typical reaction at any mention of the swanky department store. "Nice." Then her face resumed its droop. "Art therapy sounds like what I need."

Meg nodded. "This has been so rough on you. I'm sure creating art will help you get to closure."

"Closure." Candy nodded. "Yes."

Meg scribbled her cell number on a card she pulled from her purse. "Here. Call or text me if you'd like my help."

Her purse chose that moment to vibrate. Someone was calling her cell phone.

It was a nurse from the hospital, calling to tell her Richie's eyes had briefly opened.

She gasped and gestured Jon to her side.

"We'll be right over," she told the nurse.

~~~~

At the hospital, Jon waited in the visitor's lounge to give Meg one-on-one time with her son. So she was alone in the corridor when a bug-eyed gentleman with an iPad blocked her progress.

"Excuse me, ma'am, are you Richard St. John's mother?"

He thrust the device at her, no doubt recording her every move.

She ground to a halt. "Who are you?"

He put out a hand. "Steve Davis from the Marin

52

Mercury."

She bypassed the hand and stepped around him. "I thought you guys weren't allowed in here."

Undeterred, he moved to block her way again. "Has your son regained consciousness? What's his prognosis?"

She turned and retraced her steps toward the visitor's lounge, with the journalist hard on her heels. In fifteen seconds she reached her husband's side.

His brows leaped when he saw her.

"Honey." She took the seat beside him and squeezed his knee, hoping he could read the cry for help in her eyes. "This man is following me and asking me questions."

Jon answered with a glare at the newsman.

The journalist's eyes bulged at Jon. "Are you Richard St. John's father?"

"No, I am not." Jon's mild tone held a no-nonsense edge. "Now, will you kindly leave my wife alone."

"Just doing my job, sir. No harm intended."

Jon nodded, his gaze sending Mr. Davis a clear message to get lost. Finally, the man spun and departed. They watched until the elevator dinged, then swallowed him up.

Meg let out a breath.

Jon took her hand. "Come with me. I'll keep you safe from any more nosy newshounds."

Only standard hospital sounds accompanied them this time. Softened voices from nurses accustomed to chaos. An occasional cry of a patient. Beeps and buzzes from the rooms.

Jon kissed her outside Richie's room, then returned to the lounge. Meg bent over Richie, searching his face and calling his name. After five minutes of this, he remained as unresponsive as a hibernating bear.

In his younger days, when he slept in on weekends, he sometimes needed a few extra jostles before he'd grind open his eyes and glare into a new day. Maybe if she shook him hard enough ...

"Richie?" She placed a tentative hand on his linen-shrouded chest and shoved. Not a budge. She tried again, harder this time.

But his eyes remained shut. A bag of clear fluid dripped its life into him, but couldn't bring him out of hiding. Beeping machines kept track of his active heart like a seismograph. Apparently nothing less than an earthquake could wake up his brain.

Sick at heart, she grabbed his shoulders and rocked them back and forth.

"Hello, are you Mom?"

Meg whirled to see a tall, brunette nurse striding into the room.

"I was told he opened his eyes, and I rushed right over."

The nurse gave Richie a once-over, then eyed Meg with her gray-marble gaze. "Was he shaking? Or were you shaking him?"

"Well, uh …"

"We don't want his breathing tube dislodged."

Meg jumped away from the knifing tone. The nurse whooshed past Meg to Richie's bedside while Meg wished she could crawl inside the tiny cupboard and hide under the clean linen gowns. What was she thinking, shaking him like that?

The frantic actions of a desperate mother.

"He opened his eyes for only a few seconds," the nurse explained in a clipped voice as she checked Richie's blood pressure and pulse, then lifted his right eyelid, her mouth tight with disapproval. "It happens with comatose patients. Sometimes it means they're waking up. We just have to wait and see."

Chapter Eight

Ken Tucker in casual street clothes could pass for a college football lineman. Taller than Dad and Rich. Slightly less bulky than Dad, considerably more so than Rich. He lounged in the wood chair at Gloria Jean's Coffees, his posture far more relaxed than while on duty.

Rather handsome, for a guy. Linzee supposed straight women evaluated men the way she'd always evaluated women. Until last year, when she made her choice to date only men.

She hadn't foreseen how difficult it'd be to follow through. Especially when interesting-looking women showed up everywhere. For instance, that woman with the short red pixie cut at the next table, a ring in her nose, sitting alone. Something about her made Linzee curious. What was her story? She seemed like the type of woman Linzee would like to get to know.

But she had to put those urges aside. She'd promised God, and herself.

Would she ever be able to be "just friends" with a woman she was interested in?

She leaned her forearms on the wood table and forced her focus back to Ken. "You remind me of another cop I know. I met him under very unusual circumstances. You might know him."

"I probably do. What's his name?"

"Well, that's the thing. I never got his name."

Ken's mouth curled up at the edges. "Well, then, how can I tell you whether I know him?"

She grinned back. "He kind of looks like you."

Ken's grin widened. "Okay, so he's super good-looking."

The twinkle in his eye told her he was kidding. There was nothing in the least bit conceited about Ken. A perfect gentleman, in fact. The type of guy who deserved love from a good woman. A totally straight woman, as opposed to conflicted and confused like her.

"And he's probably about your age." Her nonchalance gave away nothing of the turmoil inside.

"What were the unusual circumstances?" he asked, ignoring the steaming pumpkin spice latte beside him. After he'd gobbled down a dense, jelly-drenched raspberry scone, he seemed to have lost interest in his drink.

She threw out her hand with her most theatrical flourish. "He pulled me out of a deep, dark dungeon, where I'd been held captive for many days."

His smile stiffened, and his head tilted. He thought she was messing with him. "Like in a fairy tale, huh?" One of his ears, the left one, sat slightly lower than the other, giving his head an oddly lopsided look. Except when he tugged on his right ear, which, she noticed, he often did, as if he were trying to synchronize them. He would accompany this with an equally lopsided smile.

There was a crooked man ... She grinned at the imagery from the old nursery rhyme. Ken wasn't a perfect-looking GQ guy. Good thing for her. She wouldn't even know what to say, how to act, with a man like that.

His voice, as warm as the steam rising from the coconut-flavored coffee in front of her, gently pulled her back into the moment. "The handsome prince-slash-cop rescued the damsel in distress?"

"You think I'm making this up, don't you?"

He shrugged. "Are you?"

Memories from her captivity chased away the levity. Her fists tightened under the table, out of sight. "No. I'm not making it up. It really happened. I was kidnapped and locked in a basement for four days. Last summer."

Awareness dawned in his eyes. "Wait a minute. I

remember that case." Surprise lifted his entire face as his gaze probed her. "That was you?"

She nodded. "That was me."

"I do know the cop who rescued you. Jason Pope is his name." He finally lifted the neglected cup to his lips and took a sip. She watched his Adam's apple bob as he swallowed. "It must have been a nightmare for you."

"It certainly gave me nightmares for several weeks afterward."

"But you're doing better now?"

"Mostly." She shrugged and gave him a tight-lipped smile. "Is anyone ever one hundred percent better after something like that?"

"I see your point. But at least the perp's locked away for many years and won't be doing that again any time soon."

"To my utter relief."

"Refresh my memory. How'd they figure out where to find you?"

"My fi ... my roommate had her suspicions, and tipped off the police." She bit her lip, having nearly slipped and called Nena her fiancée. She'd bet this manly man facing her wouldn't understand the world of same-sex relationships. If he knew what she'd been, it'd probably be a deal-breaker.

Which meant, if she continued to see him, he couldn't ever find out.

~~~~

Meg opened her eyes with a start. The room felt unusually dark. Moving shadows splayed across the walls like ghosts, jostling flowered curtains and brushing shivery breezes across her bare arms.

She lay very still, certain she'd heard something.

Yes, a series of beeps, urgent and persistent, as impossible to ignore as a fire alarm. Coming from the bed.

She flew from her spot on the floor and rushed to where her son lay. Sometime during the night, the bed had levitated, and now Richie's prone body lay level with her eyes.

The frantic beeping came from the heart monitor.

A flat green line bisected the screen.

Her heart in her throat, she nearly choked on the fear as a white-clad nurse darted into the room.

"Something is wrong with my son," she gagged out.

A tall nurse towered over Richie's bed, the whites around her brown eyes nearly glowing as she gazed down her nose at Meg. "He went into cardiac arrest."

Meg bent forward, gasping for breath that wouldn't come. "Oh, dear God. Dear God." She broke into a sweat as hot waves of alarm coursed up and down her torso. The nurse's movements intensified. The cruel green line stayed flat.

"Hey, what's going on?"

She whirled. Her father stood at the door, his hair shining silver in the weak hall light. She rushed to him, clinging there when somehow, he morphed into an elderly Jon.

"Oh, no. Oh, no." Jon's tone laced with dread, he moved closer, keeping her securely tucked to his chest. She buried her face in his tweed bathrobe as he stroked her hair, murmuring something over and over that couldn't penetrate the roar in her head. Until she finally realized he was praying.

She wasn't sure how long he held her there motionless before the beeping ebbed and settled into a soft rhythm. He released her. "Okay, you can look now, sweetheart."

Meg turned, but couldn't get her voice to work. Only a feeble croak.

Richie's bed had returned to its previous height. He lay perfectly still in his hospital gown, save for the gentle up-and-down motion of his working lungs.

"Ah." She collapsed against Jon, her relief so intense her knees gave way.

He caught her under the arms. "He's alive, my love."

The nurse smiled, her teeth glowing like vanilla ice cream in her cinnamon-colored face. Meg blinked away burning tears and lurched to her son's bedside. A peaceful expression blanketed his features, his chest undulated in perfect rhythm, and his long eyelashes fanned out on his cheek.

Meg jolted awake, and for a whispering moment, the unfamiliar room made her forget where she was. But quiet voices over the intercom, the humming machines, and flowery scents, brought it all back. She was in Richie's hospital room, on a daybed the staff had provided her.

The same beeping monitor that had penetrated her dream emitted a reassuring rhythm. Richie hadn't nearly died in the night. But oh how frighteningly real it had seemed, that dream still fresh in her mind, but fading in wispy fragments. She wanted to curl up in a fetal position with her knees close to her thumping heart, while tides of relief swept away the thoughts that had been running through her mind in recent days. The shameful, ugly thoughts that plagued her—"He'd be better off dead." Because the dream proved as long as he still breathed, so did her hopes.

Her thoughts flew to Jon, who'd been unable to disguise his dismay last night when she explained she wasn't going home with him. "I want to be here when Richie opens his eyes," she'd told him. Various emotions played over his face as he strove to understand. Finally, resigned, he'd kissed her goodbye and exited the room, his silhouette like granite. She needed to hear his voice, the warm one that radiated love.

From the counter beside her, her phone chimed. It had to be him on the other end, wanting to know if she'd slept well. Wanting to hear her voice.

But it wasn't Jon.

"Is this Meg?" the childlike female voice ventured.

"Yes."

"This is Candy Burton. We met last night. At the grief group?"

The lady who'd asked about art therapy. "Oh. Right. How are you?"

"Fine."

After a few minutes of idle chitchat, Candy got to the

point. She wanted to start art therapy as soon as possible. "Today, if that works for you."

So soon? Meg wanted to say no, she wasn't ready. Her mind floundered around for a reasonable-sounding excuse.

"I can pay you."

She shook her head at the unseen caller. "Oh, no, I can't accept money from you. I've let my license lapse. I only practice on myself now."

"Still, I'd love to see an art therapist at work. Would you mind if I observed? You could teach me what you know."

In the face of such unabashed persistence, she finally agreed to let Candy drop by in the afternoon, giving Meg time to tidy up her studio.

A settled peace in her heart told her God was in on this, too.

Chapter Nine

Painting in the Wilderness – by Megan Shaw Paulson (154 followers)

"The sorrows of death compassed me ..." Psalm 18:4

Last night I dreamed my son died. The horror of it was beyond words. I was on the floor in my childhood bedroom. Richie was lying on my old twin bed with the flowered comforter and pink pillow sham, and a nurse was telling me his heart had stopped. At that, my own heart nearly stopped. I remember gagging on my fear, just before I woke up.

There I was, on a real-life cot, in his real-life hospital room. And when I realized it had just been a dream, and my son was lying over there, his ventilator still humming, I nearly choked on relief.

But it got me to thinking about death, and how it would have felt had I lost him. And I realized — he may not have the best quality of life right now. The person he was two weeks ago has vanished. His personality: nil. But oh, how thankful I am that he is alive! I praise the Lord in gratitude that He spared my son, and I trust with all my heart that He's 100% in control.

So thank you, beautiful prayer warriors, for interceding. Continue to pray that his blood pressure will normalize, that his brain pressure reading stays stable. And for wisdom for those hard-working doctors and nurses.

Love to you all,

Meg

~~~~

Candy looked different in daylight. Her twig-like arms stuck out of a sleeveless white blouse, the rest of her just this side of emaciated. Non-descript brown hair was shot through with gray.

But there was nothing nondescript about her deep-set hazel eyes. They carried an ocean of misery. Meg peered into their depths and shuddered. This woman looked like she needed something far more intensive than a grief group and art therapy.

Meg welcomed her in, a sense of inadequacy robbing her of words. On impulse, she gave Candy a five-second hug, hoping the woman wouldn't break, then beckoned her to the hallway.

Candy glanced around at Meg's contemporary living room. "I hope this is a good time."

"It's fine. There's nobody here to disturb us. My husband's at work."

As they passed by the wall of family photos, Candy stopped. "I see you have two kids."

"Yes, my daughter Linzee is twenty-four. And Richard's just eighteen …" Her voice trailed off, her head shaking. "What about you, Candy? Do you have kids?"

Candy flinched, turning her despair-filled gaze on Meg. "I-I do. I did."

Meg caught her breath, waiting for Candy to answer the question she didn't want to ask. But Candy didn't elaborate.

Meg gentled her tone. "Son, or daughter?"

"Son."

"What happened?"

Candy's gaze was fixed on Richie's joyful face. "I-I lost him."

Meg's heart twinged. "Oh, I'm so sorry."

Candy looked away, giving a noncommittal wave of her hand as if to say, what's done is done. But judging from the other woman's darting gaze, Meg knew if she asked any more questions, Candy would bolt like a nervous foal. Meg couldn't blame her.

Candy's next words came out so low, they barely registered. "At least yours didn't commit suicide."

Meg couldn't hold back a gasp. As bad as Richie's injury was, how much worse if he'd done what Candy's son had done. A clammy hand squeezed her heart at the image. The tight hug she gave Candy did little to thaw the ice in her veins.

Words would only sound feeble, so she took Candy's hand and led her across the hardwood floor, Candy shuffling along beside her, and into the studio. Meg showed her the easels, canvases, paints, and charcoals, then encouraged Candy to pick up a charcoal stick and just start drawing.

"When we're troubled, it can mean our subconscious is trying to tell us something important." Meg looked over Candy's shoulder. She'd only drawn a few thick wavy lines so far. "When we give it free rein to create art, sometimes the results can surprise us."

"Hmm. So what do my squiggly lines mean?"

"Not sure yet. Keep going, and I'll give you my opinion when you're done."

Meg stepped away to give Candy freedom to create. The other woman seemed calmer now, her eyes squinting at the canvas, her hand firm and steady. "The name on your card said Megan St. John."

"That was my name before I became Mrs. Paulson last week."

Candy didn't take her eyes off her work. "Does everyone call you Meg?"

"Pretty much. Except for my kids. They call me Mom."

Candy cracked a tiny smile. "Your husband calls you sweetheart."

It was Meg's turn to smile. "Yes, he does."

"You snagged a good man."

"Thank you. He's a wonderful gift from God." Meg walked to the window, the sunlight outside warming her spirits along with Candy's words. "Are you married?"

"Divorced. I married the husband from Hell."

Meg had no reply. This poor woman couldn't catch a break.

"The name Meg suits you," Candy rushed on, as though anxious to change the subject. "I like it." The charcoal scratched over the canvas.

Meg thanked her again, then paced across the room to her painting gallery to give her eyes something to peruse while they talked. "I like your name, too. Short for Candice, I assume? A very pretty name."

But Candy was frowning at the easel and tipping her head to the side as if she hadn't heard. "Okay, come look."

Meg stepped to the canvas. "Oh, my."

A crude waterfall traversed the length of the paper, a crudely-drawn face buried in the cascade, its eyes and mouth wide open as though crying for help.

Candy tapped the simply-drawn face. "Pretty strange, is it?"

"Don't worry, I've seen stranger."

"What do you think it means?"

There was much more going on in Candy's head than her high school friend's murder. How could Meg voice her observations?

Candy filled in the pause. "That's my son, isn't it?" Without waiting for Meg's reply, she grabbed a tissue from the box Meg handed her and patted her eyes. "He was swept away by forces he had no control over." She sniffled, and tears cascaded down her cheeks like the waterfall. Turning back to the canvas, she drew a large stick figure at the top of the falls, then added hair. "See, that's me." Gasps punctuated her sentences. "I'm watching him go over, and I can't do a darn thing about it."

"You feel helpless."

"I ... I had no clue. No clue ..." She stopped, refusing to say any more.

How odd she hadn't known her son was suicidal. In most cases, suicidal people left unmistakable clues. Meg floundered for the right words. "Sweetie, you need more than what I can offer you. Have you tried a therapist?"

Candy, hiding her face in her hands, shook her head. "They ..." her voice came out muffled, "they say time heals all wounds."

Meg found Candy's waist and held tight. "Suicide is far more serious than a wound. I strongly encourage you to seek help. Do you have a pastor you can call on?"

Nodding, Candy eased toward the door with Meg's arm clamped around her. "I'd better go. I wouldn't blame you if you need to go be with your son now."

"I'll call you later to see how you're doing, okay?" They'd reached the front door, and Candy made her escape after Meg wrapped her in one last hug, her own eyes damp with tears.

"God be with you, my friend."

Chapter Ten

Meg prayed all the way to Richie's bedside, in the grips of pounding terror. After last night's dream, she could think of only one fate worse than Richie's — to lose him. Meg had seen how Candy's anguish had enveloped her like a cruel python, destructive and thorough. Her suffering exceeded Meg's by miles.

No newsmen waylaid her this time. Richie's chest still rose and fell, and his skin tone hadn't slid into death's pallor. The compression socks were silent. She glanced around at the unoccupied room. If Richie were conscious, someone would be bringing him dinner right about now.

The absence of human interaction enhanced the room's eerie vibe, unnerving her. She picked up the remote and snapped on the TV, just in time to see a car leap onto an overpass. When the commercial ended, the network switched to the evening news with Jerry and Jenny.

Jerry's unflinching gaze cut through Meg. "Gun control is still in the forefront of everyone's minds. The eloquent young lady we interviewed yesterday, the sister of one of the injured, has already gotten almost half a million hits on YouTube."

Meg grabbed the bed when Linzee's face filled the screen, and for the first time, heard the words half a million others had already heard, saw the poster with Richie's face on it for all the world to see. *Lindsey Saint John*, read the caption below her image.

Those journalists hadn't even bothered to check the spelling of her name.

"Richie?" she whispered. "You're world-famous now. And apparently, so is your sister."

Was that a flicker of response from his eyelids? She leaned her mouth closer to his ear and watched his eyes. "What do you think about gun control? You're probably in agreement with Linzee, aren't you? Especially now." She paused, an idea brewing in her head, then grabbed his hand. "If you can hear me, squeeze my hand."

She held as still as possible, waiting for an answering tug. Nothing.

"Richie? Can you hear me? Squeeze my hand."

The faintest pressure from his hand, as light as a whisper, made her heart leap.

"I felt that! You can hear me, can't you?"

No twinge from his eyelids, but another tiny muscle contraction answered her.

"Praise God. You heard me!" Buoyed with hope, she chattered on. "I'm praying for you, son, and so are thousands of others around the country. Can you feel their prayers strengthening you, healing your mind and body?"

She closed her eyes for a few seconds, visualizing God's mighty hand planted on her son's chest.

"Do you remember anything about the shooter? The cops came to the house, wondering if you knew him. I told them I didn't think so. But now they know he had it in for your Spanish teacher. I wish I understood why. Don't you wish you could ask him, 'What did Mr. Hope ever do to you?'"

The light from the corridor dimmed, and she whirled around. Jon filled the doorway, his mouth curved in a smile, a paper sack in each hand. "I brought food."

She muted the TV. "Thanks, Honey." The fast-food aroma made her mouth water. She hadn't eaten much for three days. She tugged the waistband of her loose jeans testifying to her lack of appetite.

He took her in his arms and stroked her hair. "I missed you." He pressed a kiss on the top of her head.

"Ditto, hon." She lifted her head for a proper kiss.

It was over too soon. He stroked under her chin, a

hopeful gleam in his eyes. "Does that mean you're coming home with me tonight?"

How she wanted to. But she couldn't abandon Richie now, this close to a breakthrough. His brain was awakening. She could sense it.

The hope in his gaze vanished. "I take it your silence means no."

"Jon, he can hear me." His probing stare stirred up her defenses. "He was actually responding to my voice."

His arms dropped to his side. "I'm glad to hear it. But you know the hospital will call you right away if his condition changes." His soft, reasonable tone couldn't hide the edge.

"He's about to wake up. What if nobody's here when he opens his eyes? He'll freak out."

A nurse bustled in, aborting the argument about to erupt. "Oh, hello." She barely glanced at them as she moved to Richie's side and lifted his arm.

"I think he's waking up." That should get the woman's attention.

"Really?" The nurse paused and turned a curious gaze on Meg. "What makes you think so?"

Meg told her, then drooped when the nurse replied, "I've seen comatose patients act responsively when it's really just a muscle reflex. But sometimes it can be a positive sign. Keep your chin up."

No one said anything for several seconds. Meg was afraid to look at Jon. Up until now, he'd been so understanding. His patience tank must be running low.

She ventured a peek at him. Jon was rubbing his head with both hands, a sure sign he was agitated.

Sighing, she plopped in the vinyl chair and took out the burger, her mouth suddenly dry again. But she forced herself to take a bite. As she feared, the food stuck to the roof of her mouth. Even gulping water didn't make it any more edible.

Jon sat also, and they shared a silent meal, broken only by the nurse's quiet comments, the rustling of fast-food wrappers, and the battle waging inside her.

Her husband needed her.

But so did her son.

There was only one of her, but two of them. One able-bodied, the other comatose.

A no-brainer choice.

Jon stood up to leave, his eyes beseeching her. "He might not wake up anytime soon. I don't think it's good for you to wait here 24/7 until he does. He's in good hands." His gaze held hers like a magnet.

Tears formed in her heart. "I guess you're right," she whispered. "But I don't feel right about leaving him."

He gave her one last, long look before he walked out the door. "Let me know what you decide. I'll be at home. Waiting."

He disappeared, but the vision of his tight mouth, the unhappy sag of his shoulders, made her change her mind and rush after him. "Jon?"

But he was gone.

~~~~

After Meg had shut herself in the bathroom for a long cry, exhaustion set in, and she crawled onto the daybed. She needed some overnight supplies and started to text Jon.

No. He would not be receptive.

But Linzee might. She called her daughter, who agreed to help.

Meg must have dozed, because the next thing she knew, Linzee was shaking her.

"Mom?"

Meg sat up, and Linzee blanched when she saw her face. "Have you been crying?"

Meg nodded. "Jon's upset that I'm staying here instead of at home with him."

"Your first marital spat, huh? I'm sure it won't be your last."

Trust Linzee to make light of it. Meg pointed to the bag

in Linzee's hand. "Thanks for bringing my stuff. You can set it in the chair." She stretched her arms to the ceiling and updated Linzee on her earlier interaction with Richie, adding, "But the nurse doesn't think it means anything."

"Oh, Mom." Linzee pushed out her lower lip like she did as a child when she received bad news. She went to Richie's bedside and studied him. "He looks exactly the same to me. Are you sure it wasn't wishful thinking?"

"I don't want to believe that."

"How weird it must be, to be in a coma. I wonder if he dreams, and if he can sense activity around him."

"I'm sure he's blissfully unaware of everything."

"Dad hasn't been to see him since that first day. Neither has Kassidy."

"Poor Kassidy. I hope she waits for him. I can see them married someday." Assuming he woke up. And that he woke up as the old Richie. Otherwise, she couldn't foresee any grandchildren in her future. Unless Linzee ...

Meg hopped off the bed. "I've been meaning to ask you. Did the cops come and talk to you?"

"The cops?" Linzee cast her an odd look. "Yeah, they did. A couple of days ago. Why?"

"They said they needed to ask you some questions. What did they want to know?"

Linzee repeated the conversation, the same strange expression clinging to her features.

Meg tilted her head, as though appraising a painting. "What?"

"What?"

"What's up with that funny face?" The nice young man who'd blushed at Linzee's name ... surely he wasn't responsible for her expression.

Linzee's face snapped back to neutral. "What do you mean?"

Meg chuckled. "I got the impression one of the cops wanted to get to know you better."

"I hope you mean Kentucker, not Mary."

Meg laughed for the first time all day. "Kentucker, huh? You're already on a nickname basis with him."

"We went out, okay? For coffee. Now will you stop quizzing me about it?" Linzee pressed her lips tight together, but not before Meg caught a tiny smile trying to escape.

"Do you like him?"

"Mom!"

"Just one more question?"

"I like him fine."

"Are you going out with him again?"

"That's two questions."

"I'll take that as a yes."

Linzee shrugged as though it made no difference to her, and punctuated her disinterest by flipping a thick golden tress over her shoulder. But she kept her face carefully turned away from Meg.

A sliver of light wormed its way into the darkness in Meg's heart. Her daughter's dramatic conversion last year had come full circle. *Lord, let this work out for Linzee.*

"I saw you on TV at that rally yesterday. You did great."

Linzee whirled. "My friend Claire warned me it might go viral. Sure enough ..." She stopped, fists on hips, face scrunched. "Wait a minute. You probably disagreed with everything I said."

It was Meg's turn to shrug. "You still expressed your views effectively. I was proud of you."

Linzee's puzzlement morphed into a smile. "Well, thank you. I was taught by the best."

"Who would that be?"

"You, of course."

Meg felt her brows leap in surprise. "I didn't know you felt that way."

"I mean, you're a lot more conservative than I am, but that doesn't mean I can't borrow your techniques."

They shared a grin, then Linzee came over and wrapped

her arms around Meg's shoulders. "Feel better now?"

"Yeah."

"Good. That man is too crazy about you to stay mad." Linzee's breath sent puffs of warm air into Meg's neck. "He's probably just very hurt. He only wants to be with you because he loves you."

Meg couldn't bear the idea she had hurt Jon. "I know."

"Don't take his love for granted."

"You're very wise, daughter of mine. Someday, you're going to make a great wife to some lucky man."

"We're not going there."

Meg pulled back and searched Linzee's eyes. "Do you think I'm making the right choice?"

"What, choosing to be with your son instead of your husband?"

Meg winced, but Linzee didn't let her reply.

"I don't think I'm the best person to ask. I've only had one date with a man my whole life."

Meg gathered her in her arms. "And I wish you many more."

Chapter Eleven

Painting in the Wilderness – by Megan Shaw Paulson (1134 followers)

"In thy presence is fullness of joy; at thy right hand there are pleasures forevermore." Psalm 16:11

Dear friends,

I am so warmed by all your kind comments and sweet gestures. The fact that so many loving brothers and sisters in Christ are following our journey and sending encouragement, well, you just make my day.

Today I distinctly felt the Lord's presence in Richie's hospital room. My daughter Linzee and I held hands around him and prayed, and when the Holy Spirit invaded, I could've shouted "Glory Be!" Richie is still utterly helpless. Machines still perform all his bodily functions for him. Yet the Lord was reminding me that He knows Richie's future. He's just not going to tell me what it is. I have to trust Him.

Amen, Lord Jesus.

Meg

~~~~

So much for "only one date with a man." Tonight she'd break that record. Wouldn't Mom be overjoyed? Linzee eyed Ken's young-Joe-Montana profile as he drove them to Skylight Theater in his conservative white sedan that evening. A strange, weird, unfamiliar sensation, generated after he told her she looked nice tonight, still lingered in her heart. Mom had promised God could change her heart if she asked Him to, yet she hadn't really, entirely believed it.

"How goes the investigation?"

He glanced over before returning his gaze to the boulevard. "Slow but steady. We're learning new things about Jarrett every day."

"Has anyone figured out his motive yet?"

"Actually, our techs found something really fascinating when they searched his online history." Ken slowed, then braked at a crosswalk where a woman with a stroller waited on the curb. He waved them across, watching with maddening patience as if to ensure they made it safely to the other side.

Linzee, chewing on her thumbnail, tapped her toe to the hip-hop playing on the stereo. "What did they find?"

He didn't move forward until mother and baby reached the opposite curb, the cop in him on full display. "He did a lot of research on crack babies."

Not what Linzee expected to hear. "Crack babies? Whyever for?" Maybe Jarrett had gotten a crack addict pregnant.

"He apparently wanted to know the effects a pregnant woman's drug use has on her unborn baby. Particularly on its long-term mental health."

"I thought that was common knowledge. I wonder why he needed to research it."

"More specifically, if drug use by a pregnant woman is linked to schizophrenia in the child."

Linzee gasped. "Is it?"

"I'm no expert, so I wouldn't know if there's a direct cause. But Jarrett seemed to be looking for one."

"Maybe he was researching for a class project."

"Not likely, since he wasn't enrolled in any school."

"Then … then why?"

"We think …" His tone turned rough as sandpaper. "He

may have discovered his mother took drugs while she was pregnant with him, and he wanted to know if it caused his mental disorder."

"Was he a crack baby?"

"We don't know yet. We hope to find out when we interview Rose Jarrett's family members."

Linzee grimaced at the idea of being interrogated at such a painful time. "You'll be nice, won't you?" She forced a teasing note but meant every word.

He obliged with a grin. "But of course. I was nice to you, wasn't I?"

"You were most definitely Mr. Nice Guy."

He cleared his throat. "Here we are." Turning into the theater parking lot, he added, "From what I know of the mother, she didn't seem the type to have ever used drugs."

Linzee shrugged. "You never really know the secrets people hide about their past." Including herself.

He pulled into a spot near the walkway. "No, you don't. But if we find out she did, we'll be that much closer to determining a motive."

"You mean, maybe he blamed her for his mental issues?"

He made no move to open the door but turned to face her. "That's what it looks like."

"Still, to shoot your own mother ... and it still doesn't explain why he shot his father."

"He may have wanted the father out of the way in order to accomplish his goal."

Linzee shuddered at Ken's matter-of-fact tone. "In other words, you think my poor brother was shot by a loony tunes with parental issues."

Shoving the door open, he said, "There are a lot of 'em out there. And more of 'em popping up every day."

~~~~

On the second morning of Meg's vigil, Jon's number flashed on her phone. For a moment, she wondered what day it was. Then she remembered. Saturday. Four days after the shooting.

She snatched up the phone before it finished the second ring.

"Morning, honey." She made sure to put a lilt in her voice.

"How's Richie?"

She flinched at his uncharacteristically terse tone. No "Hi, sweetheart," or "I missed you."

Uneasy, she glanced at her motionless son. The nurse should be here any moment. "No change."

"Did you sleep well?" Finally, a hint of concern in his voice.

"Not really." She'd tossed and turned on the hard cot, unable to get Jon off her mind. "Did you?"

"Nope."

She waited for him to go on.

"I did a lot of thinking and praying." She listened for anger or irritation, but only a weary sigh intruded. "I prayed all day yesterday and all night, asking God how He wanted me to respond when my wife put her son ahead of me …"

"No, Jon …"

"Please hear me out. I didn't hear a word from the Lord. I figured I wasn't listening good enough. Finally I realized my prayers were being blocked because of my selfishness, so I had to repent."

She pressed the phone tighter to her ear as if by doing so, his words could bypass her head and find their way to her heart.

"Anyway, we need to talk. Can you meet me at home?"

She glanced again at the immobile shroud on the bed, her heart twisting. Richie hadn't moved all night. Discouragement set in. No telling how long before he opened his eyes again, how much of her marriage she'd have to put on hold until then.

She needed Jon like she needed water. She missed him with a dreadful ache in her gut. Yet she'd set him aside to tend her son, who already had the best care available. Her grief and worry had skewed her judgment, made her forget her vow to forsake all others.

She agreed, then flew from the building and jumped in her car, reaching her driveway in ten minutes. Jon must have been watching for her because he waited on the front porch.

"Honey." She wasted no time planting a long kiss on his lips. His surprise showed in his hesitation, then he chuckled and squeezed her tight, fastening his lips on hers.

They made it through the front door before he released her, the beloved crinkles next to his eyes in full bloom.

"If you're trying to tell me you missed me," he lowered his voice to a husky whisper, "I got the message loud and clear."

She grinned and cupped his head in her hands. "What was it" she whispered between kisses, "you wanted to talk about?"

He kept his face inches from hers. "I love you." More kisses. "Please come home."

"I'm here."

"For good?"

"For good."

He squeezed her again and lifted his face to the ceiling, his mouth forming words. "Thank you, Lord."

~~~~

After Meg had showered and changed, she checked her phone for messages.

I know this is short notice, but can you meet for lunch today?

Candy had sent it at ten, an hour ago. The poor woman must still be struggling. Meg couldn't think of any reason to say no. She hadn't made any plans except to be with Richie, and Jon planned to spend the day hauling belongings from his Sausalito house.

With a plan brewing in her mind, she asked Candy to meet her at the Grapevine Café in Novato. *There's someone I'd like you to meet.*

When Meg set off the door chime at Grapevine twenty minutes later, Camille, silver coffee pot in hand, stopped in mid-pour, her sassy smile lengthening.

"Girlfriend!" Her enthusiastic greeting attracted attention from the couple in cowboy attire at her table, who stared at Meg as though Shania Twain had walked through the door.

Candy walked in seconds later, and Meg made speedy introductions. They followed Camille to a table beside a window sporting frilly gingham curtains, overlooking a vast asphalt desert and distant, tree-studded hills.

"Do I know you?" Camille narrowed her eyes at Candy, the silver pot motionless in her hand. "You look familiar to me."

Candy returned her stare. "I don't recall that we ever met."

Meg cut in, "Camille has a photographic memory for faces."

"Pfft. Not anymore. The little gray cells aren't what they used to be. I can't even remember what I had for breakfast."

Meg turned the white ceramic coffee cup right side up. "You don't eat breakfast."

Coffee sloshed into the cup. "You see? There's nothing to remember."

Candy observed the exchange with an amused smile, then lifted the menu. "Do you have a lunch special?"

"Our lentil soup with smoked sausage is only 4.99 today."

Candy ordered the special, and Meg lay her menu to the side. "I'll have my usual Nicoise salad."

Camille kept eyeing Candy, tilting her head to the right, then the left. "I know I've seen you somewhere before. Do you attend Church on the Rock?"

"No, First Baptist."

"You lived here a while?"

"Born and raised in San Rafael. Would have graduated

from Terra Vista High School in 1996, but …"

"My alma mater too," Meg told her. "But I was six years ahead of you."

Camille shrugged one shoulder. "It'll come to me." Stepping backward, she smirked and added, "A nice hot cup of peppermint tea will whip those little brain cells into action." Waving, she returned to the kitchen.

Meg leaned toward Candy. "I wanted you to meet her because she has a way of brightening everything and everyone around her. It's hard to stay depressed in Camille's presence."

"I can see why. It's weird she thinks she knows me. I'm quite sure I've never seen her in my life." Lifting the glass of water to her lips, she sipped. "Anyway, how's your son? Is he any better?"

Meg shook her head and relayed the previous days' events over soup and salad.

Candy's frown intensified. "When you go back to see him today, may I tag along?"

Meg, downing her last bite, couldn't imagine why Candy would want to accompany her to see Richie. "Do you think it's wise? Wouldn't it remind you of your son?"

Candy lifted a shoulder. "Maybe. But it might be good for me to offer someone else support for once, instead of me always leaning on others."

Meg agreed to let Candy follow her to the hospital, and after telling Camille goodbye and leaving a generous tip, they set out.

Only one news vehicle remained in the hospital lot, lonely and unoccupied at the far north end. Meg gestured toward it. "At least most of the news people have left. They've been nothing but a pain."

"I can imagine." Candy stepped onto the elevator, Meg on her heels. "It no longer seems to be the hot topic on the news anymore."

"Thankfully. Other bad news has taken its place."

Richie's prone form looked precisely the same. Quan bent over him, her fingers digging into his arm muscles, then straightened when Meg and Candy entered. "No change," she told Meg. "So sorry. I wish I had better news."

"At least you still have your son," Candy muttered.

Meg looked at her. True, technically, but he might as well be … No. She couldn't let her emotions take her there. Candy, watching Richie, stood so still Meg couldn't tell if she was breathing. Meg guessed Candy's thoughts centered on her own son.

"What was his name?" Meg softened her voice. At Candy's blank stare she added, "Your son?"

Candy shook her head and aimed her frozen stare at Richie. "I always thought of him by his childhood nickname. Mikey. Till the day he died, he was always Mikey to me."

"How old was he?"

Candy's head jerked back and forth. She still wouldn't look up. "He would have celebrated his twentieth birthday next month."

"Almost the same age as my son."

"Same build, same overall look."

"Really?" No wonder she was so interested in Richie. "Did he play football too?"

She gave a shrug, which mystified Meg, then shook her head with no elaboration. Meg longed to know more. How long ago had it happened? From the rawness of Candy's emotions, Meg guessed fairly recently. But Candy had turned her back on Meg, a clear signal she was through answering questions.

A tense silence fell over them like prickly wool while Quan wrote notes on a clipboard. Meg searched her mind for something to pierce the wall Candy had suddenly erected, settling on, "I'd love to see a photo of him sometime. When you're ready."

"Okay," Candy whispered. She turned, walked toward the door, then stopped beside Meg. "I need to go now."

Meg embraced her friend. "Know that I'm praying for you."

Candy nodded, eyes on the doorway. "Thanks. I'm in desperate need of prayers."

Meg, helpless, watched her leave, anxiety for the broken woman throbbing in her bones. What did she mean by desperate? Not suicidal herself, surely. Alarm bells rang in Meg's head. She didn't want to believe that Candy would follow in her son's footsteps.

Chapter Twelve

Painting in the Wilderness – Megan Shaw Paulson (1201 followers)

"Now unto him that is able to do exceeding abundantly above all that we ask or think, according to the power that worketh in us, Unto him be glory in the church by Christ Jesus throughout all ages, world without end. Amen." Ephesians 3:20-21.

Prayer Warriors - My wonderful husband keeps quoting this passage to me. And today I'm praising the Good Lord! I cling to the belief that Richie is slowly improving day by day. And I know it's because of your relentless, persistent petitioning. This morning Richie is having another MRI to look at the bruising on his brain. We will know the results tomorrow. I am hopeful they will be positive. Please pray the machine will show decreased bruising.

I just peeked in on him. He looks so peaceful, as though he's sleeping. So much better than Day 1, when he had bruises all over his face and tubes everywhere. I can't help but wonder what's going on in that brain of his. Anything? From what little I've learned about comatose patients, I suspect he can hear us, so as much as I can, I'm feeding him encouragement. I tell him he will walk again someday. I remind him he is dearly loved. I update him on his friends' lives, the sports they're playing, the adventures they're getting themselves into. I tell him he'll be hanging with them again, and that this is only temporary.

Sometimes I see his eyelids flutter when I talk to him. Yesterday, I could've sworn he turned his head toward me. Now that was an exciting moment!

Check back tomorrow right here as I share what I hope will be good news.

Choosing hope,

Meg

~~~~

Linzee grinned out Ken's car window. Date number three. Most dates ever with a man. This time, a quick trip to the San Quentin Museum before Ken's shift started at noon. When he'd told her last night he'd never been, she couldn't believe it. "A cop who's never been to the San Quentin Museum? Well, you have to go."

He reminded her he'd only lived in San Rafael for three years before adding, "How about you show me around the place tomorrow morning?"

She'd agreed, trying to make sense of her sudden anticipation. Amazed at how much she enjoyed Ken's company. His droll sense of humor made her laugh, lifted her mood. He never failed to treat her like a lady. Sometimes the strain of keeping her past a secret scraped her nerves, but she maintained her resolve.

She didn't know what she'd tell him when he asked the eventual question about her prior relationships.

"I want to introduce you to my favorite donut shop," he said when she climbed into his car. "Mind if we make a quick detour to Mill Valley?"

She caught her breath. Mill Valley, her former home and the site of her living nightmare last year. She hadn't been back since.

Maybe it was time to face her fears.

"No, I don't mind. What's the name of the place?"

"Lovestruck Donuts. It's fairly new."

"Sounds familiar." She grinned. "And romantic."

He chuckled. "The perfect place to take a girl, right?"

A short drive down the 101 brought them to Throckmorton, Mill Valley's main thoroughfare, where a familiar but unwelcome sight jolted her. She pointed. "Look. See that building? That's Latte Love Shack, my favorite hangout once upon a time."

"Really?" Ken slowed, peering at the off-white stucco building. "It's a donut shop now. Our destination, in fact. Lovestruck Donuts." He steered into the parking lot. Linzee's heart sputtered, and she gasped. He braked and looked over at her. "What's wrong?" A crease formed between his brows, and his eyes searched hers. A honk sounded behind them, and he quickly moved into a parking spot.

She shifted to him. "I'm fine. I ... it's just ... this is the place where I was kidnapped."

"Serious?" Distress edged his tone. "Sorry. I didn't know. We can skip it if you'd rather."

Linzee shook her head. Indulging her silly phobia wouldn't be fair to Ken. Besides, the building looked perfectly harmless. "No, I've been avoiding the place for months. And I'm curious as to what happened to Latte Love Shack. Let's go in."

"Attagirl." They got out and approached the thick wooden double door she hadn't seen for almost a year, still bracketed by potted palms. Ken opened the door for her and placed his hand on her back. A tiny shiver caressed her spine.

She craned her head side to side. A teenaged couple occupied the window table where she and Nena used to sit. A stringy-haired man on the opposite side sipped coffee and perused his iPad. A couple stood at the counter considering their options.

"Wow, it's so different."

"Different how?"

84

"The wall murals have been painted over. The place is brighter, lighter, than before. None of that dark, heavy wood. It looks like a donut shop now instead of a coffee shop."

She eyed the menu, and the mouth-watering displays of donuts, varying from giant to miniature, spanning all colors of the rainbow, and shaped every possible way that dough could be manipulated. A short-haired cashier watched them from behind a high chrome counter. She looked familiar, but Linzee couldn't place her.

"Wow, Ken. This is quite a selection. I don't even know where to begin."

"Since you like chocolate and coconut, I recommend the Cocoa Nut." Ken pointed to a peanut-shaped concoction slathered in shiny chocolate frosting. One look made Linzee's mouth water.

"Looks scrumptious. I'll try it."

"They use only pure, organic coconut."

"Even better."

He turned to the expectant clerk and ordered two. Tray in hand, he led her to a table, and she dug into the most delicious donut she'd had in a long time. Coconut infused the moist cake with the perfect amount of sweetness. She couldn't contain her delight. "Mmmm."

She grinned at his pleased expression. She'd heard somewhere that men slurped up a woman's appreciation like water. Ken downed his donut in five minutes, and she finished hers not long after.

"Don't look now," he said, "but the family across the room has been staring at you ever since we came in. I bet they recognize you from the video."

"Oh no." Linzee, tempted to cover her face, looked at the wall opposite the family instead. "My fifteen minutes of fame has turned into three days. I've gotten emails from People Magazine and Time wanting interviews. I'm not sure if I want to reply."

"How does it feel to be famous?"

"Um ... it feels weird." She pretended to study the cars in the parking lot to avoid the curious stares. "You should see how many views the video has now. Like, almost half a million."

"I know, I watched it. There were so many comments, I couldn't get through all of them. You came across really well and said what you needed to say. Very passionately, I might add." Meaningful pause. "You can look at me now. They're leaving."

"Don't let them stop and try to talk to me."

"No worries, I gave them my best scary-cop face as they walked by."

Linzee chuckled. She couldn't believe she'd never realized how good it felt for a good man to have her back. Nena had been tough, but not physically imposing like Ken.

"Ready to go?"

She nodded. "On our way out, I want to ask the cashier if she knows when Latte Love Shack closed. I never heard anything about it."

With Ken's hand on her back again, she approached the young woman whose name badge read Brianna. The woman was taking a phone order and didn't see her at first.

"Hi," Linzee ventured when Brianna ended the call.

Brianna raised her brows. "Yes?"

"I remember when this was Latte Love Shack. How long has this place been open?"

"About six months."

"Latte Love Shack was so popular. I can't believe it went out of business."

"Well, you know there was that kidnapping that was all over social media."

Before she could stop herself, Linzee grabbed onto Ken's hand. Their eyes met. An invisible signal passed between them.

"The manager got a lot of blame for it. It really hurt the business. The owner finally just cut his losses and sold it."

The squeeze of Ken's hand smoothed over her discomfort.

She shifted back to Brianna. Suddenly Linzee knew why she was familiar. "You worked at the Shack, didn't you? I remember you."

A light dawned in Brianna's eyes. "I did, to the very end. And here I am again." Her chuckle brought a smile to Linzee's face. "I remember you, too." She glanced from Linzee to Ken, down to their clasped hands, back to Linzee. Confusion passed across her face. "But weren't you the one who ... I thought you were engaged to—"

The sudden jerk of Linzee's head stopped the girl from spilling the beans. Barely. She felt, more than saw, Ken's probing stare.

"Well, gotta run. It was nice running into you again." Linzee forced cheery tones from her trembling mouth. "The donut was delicious." She turned and nearly ran for the door, Ken right behind her.

He grabbed her hand as she neared the car. "Hey, slow down. Nobody's chasing you."

Except you.

He opened the door and waited as she settled in, then hopped into the driver's seat. Linzee clutched her denim-clad knees, her nails digging into the fabric. She kept her gaze out the window and waited for the inevitable question.

"You were engaged?" he asked, his tone one of friendly interest, but she wasn't fooled. His ears had practically popped off his head the moment Brianna uttered that word.

"Not exactly," she muttered, a half-truth. If he meant was she engaged to a man, the answer was an emphatic no.

"Not exactly? You mean sort of engaged, whatever that means?"

None of your business, she wanted to say. But their relationship—*friendship*—was still too fragile, too new, to weigh down with conflict.

She sighed and stared at her hands. "I was in a serious

relationship that didn't work out."

He took a right on Throckmorton. "I think that's happened to most of us."

Gratitude at his understanding throbbed through her.

"But I hope you'll tell me more when you're ready."

She nodded, hearing the implication behind the words. *When you're ready.* Which meant, he had the future on his mind.

This time, she'd managed to only kick the can down the road. At some unknown future date, reality would no longer be denied. She shuddered, wishing she could grab time and halt its ruthless advance toward that moment, and inevitable drama. She hated drama. As far as she was concerned, drama belonged in the theater. Not in relationships.

~~~~

"Knock knock?"

Meg, absorbed in wiping drool from Richie's jaw, barely heard the quiet voice from the hallway. She whirled.

"Kassidy!"

Richie's girlfriend stood there, doubt and fear playing across her childlike face. She stepped inside, throwing a hesitant glance toward Richie as if afraid to get any closer. "How is he?"

Meg stepped over to embrace her. "When I massaged his arms today, he wiggled his fingers. All by himself."

Kassidy clung to her as Meg stroked her long brown hair. "Really? Does that mean he's waking up?"

"I fervently hope so."

Kassidy gave a little sob. "I don't understand why any of this is happening."

"Neither do any of us."

"What if he never wakes up? What if he stays like this forever?"

Fear jolted Meg's heart at the ominous words. Helpless and frustrated at her lack of answers, she couldn't reply.

Kassidy bolted from Meg's arms and scurried to the bed.

"He doesn't even look like Rich."

Meg had to agree. He had lost quite a bit of his body mass, and what was left of him had grown frighteningly frail. Between the feeding tube, the ventilator tube, and all the clamps measuring each bodily function, he was more machine than human.

Sorrow glittered in Kassidy's eyes, then transformed to sheer fright. "What will I do ..." her voice cracked, a thin, fragile sheet of glass, "if he doesn't wake up?"

Meg could only stand there, her arm on Kassidy's shoulders—two protruding bones held together by a few inches of skin.

They stood like that for a few minutes, gazing down at the face they both loved. Until a fluttering of his eyelids made them both gasp.

Richie opened his eyes. Blue orbs stared at Kassidy's face.

Kassidy lurched, hand on heart. "Rich?"

He blinked up at her. A guttural sound emerged from his mouth. Kassidy clutched the blanket covering his emaciated frame.

Meg grabbed the call button and jabbed it hard enough to break a nail. In the distance, an alarm clamored.

Richie's eyelids drooped, blinked again, then closed.

"Rich!" Kassidy jostled his motionless form. "It's me!"

"Don't wiggle him," Meg murmured. "I got in trouble for doing that."

A nurse rushed in, her smock askew as though she'd donned it in the dark. "Can I help you?"

Meg, still holding the call button, squeezed it. "He opened his eyes."

The nurse frowned down at Richie. "How long were his eyes open?"

"Only a couple of seconds. But they were definitely open."

The nurse checked Richie's vitals, muttered a few "hmmms," scribbled on a chart, then turned to leave.

"Wait!"

The nurse half-spun, one foot pointed at the door.

"Wh-what did you find?"

"There was a small surge in brain activity, but it's leveled off now."

Kassidy's whimper echoed deep in Meg's heart. How many more disappointments would they have to endure?

Meg sighed, then pulled Kassidy's chin up and leveled a gaze at her. "He hasn't responded to anyone else besides you. Has he done that any of the previous times you've been here?"

Kassidy hung her head. "I—um, I haven't been back since that first day." She looked up. Guilt twisted her face.

Meg patted her arm. "Don't give up on him. Maybe he'll wake up for you."

For the first time since the shooting, Richie's future didn't appear quite so hopeless.

Chapter Thirteen

Painting in the Wilderness – Megan Shaw Paulson
(1276 followers)

"Have not I commanded thee? Be strong and of a good courage; be not afraid, neither be thou dismayed: for the LORD thy God is with thee whithersoever thou goest." Joshua 1:9

Easy for Joshua to say. He didn't have a comatose son whose MRI showed no change. I know I need to be courageous. But I'm not sure what that means, or how to conjure it up out of nothing. Yes, the Lord our God is with us, and with Richie. I know He hears us and loves us. Despite a dismal MRI result, and the loss of hope. We're struggling to walk this rough journey. Please keep praying for us! We're all hanging by a thread, feeling helpless, and we need His comfort again. We need our Richie back.

Grateful for your prayers,

Meg

~~~~

All the way back from the museum, Ken didn't let go of Linzee's hand. She'd never realized how large and strong — okay, nice — a man's hand felt. She decided she enjoyed the feeling. How shocked he'd be to know his was the first male hand, besides her father's, she'd ever held.

He was almost to the Carlito's driveway when he cleared his throat. "Can we talk?"

She shifted, her heart in her throat. One of those dreaded can-we-talk talks. She eyed him, but he was watching the road, not her.

"Um, sure." The last time she'd had one of those talks was last year when she'd ended her relationship with Nena.

But she could hardly call this ... thing ... with Ken a relationship.

She must like him more than she cared to admit.

He cleared his throat again, pulled into her driveway, and checked his watch. "I've got a few minutes before I need to head to work." He shut off the engine and shifted his body to face her, then cradled her hand in both of his. She shifted sideways, one knee pointed at him. A patient stillness descended as he gazed at her for a moment, appraising her.

Finally he spoke. "I just want to tell you I'm really enjoying your company."

"Oh! Thank you." He was off to good start, anyway. "I enjoy yours, too."

"Good. I—" He lowered his gaze to his fingers busily stroking hers. "I like you a lot, and I want to keep seeing you." He raised his gaze to her face, a slight flush tinging his cheeks. "If you're cool with that."

The surge of relief surprised her, and she grinned. "I'm cool with it, Mr. Kentucky."

He laughed. "I've never been to Kentucky in my life."

"Neither have I."

"Well, we'll just have to go visit sometime. Would you like that?"

Would she? A road trip with a man. That brought up all sorts of visions in her head. Did he expect her to sleep with him? The thought terrified her. Not to mention, what would God think?

Still so many unanswered questions. She wasn't even sure if he was a Christian. "Is it okay for you to be seeing me? I mean, you're working on my brother's case ..."

"I don't think it's a problem, but if the chief considers it a conflict of interest, he'll just reassign me."

"I feel like there's still so much you don't know about

me." The understatement of the century.

"But there's a lot I *do* know about you." His eyes went soft. "I know you've had at least one serious relationship. And probably more. I know you like coconut, coffee, and Carly Rae Jepson. And I know you have a great sense of humor because you always laugh at my stupid jokes." He reached out to touch her cheek. "And you're very pretty."

For a moment, she couldn't speak, couldn't look away from his soft gray eyes.

When her brain fog cleared, she blurted the first words that came to mind. "Outstanding, Ken Tucker. You get an A plus for paying attention."

"You bet I pay attention. Now it's your turn. What do you know about me so far?"

"Well …" She grinned. "I know you're a lot older than you look, Babyface. I know you like pumpkin pie and mashed potatoes. And that your favorite Christmas carol is God Rest Ye Merry Gentlemen."

He was nodding. Good.

"And that you played offensive linebacker in high school, you were raised in San Bernardino, and you like jazz. Oh, and I know you look awesome in a cop uniform."

He lifted his palm for a high five, then reached behind her, cupped the back of her head, and leaned in for a kiss. Okay, a quick peck. Still, her first heterosexual kiss.

Was that a stirring in her heart? Or simply wishful thinking?

He lifted his head and smiled into her eyes, his own only inches away. "Do you like baseball?"

She nodded against his hand.

"Giants or A's?"

"A's. You?"

"Same. Niners or Raiders?"

"Niners."

He grinned and high-fived again. "Cal or Stanford?"

"UCLA."

"I should have guessed." He laughed and rechecked his watch. "I've gotta run. Call you later, okay?"

He got out and opened the door for her, then accompanied her to the front door, where he gave her another kiss. A longer one this time.

Again, he gave her cheek a gentle stroke. "Looking forward to getting to know you better."

"Ditto." Emotion thickened her voice. He swiveled and returned to his car, offering her a wave and a smile as he backed out.

She went inside, her heart stirring with something almost too big to comprehend. This dating-a-man business better not put her in over her head.

~~~~

Meg picked up her purse and headed for the door at the same moment Linzee burst into the hospital room. "Mom!" In two seconds, she closed the gap, gave a little cry, and buried her face in Meg's shoulder. "I'm so glad I found you. I stopped by the house, and Jon said you were here."

Meg opened her mouth to ask why she hadn't just called. Then she remembered—a nurse had scolded her for not silencing her phone.

"Is something wrong?" she asked instead as she rubbed Linzee's head, circling her fingers through the velvety strands of hair.

She felt the shake of her daughter's head.

"Something obviously has you upset."

"No." Linzee, her voice muffled against Meg's shirt, let out a half-sob that shuddered through Meg all the way to her toes. And suddenly she knew.

"It's Ken, isn't it? Did he do something to hurt you?"

Another shake, then Linzee slowly lifted her head. Meg searched her daughter's eyes and marveled at the sparkle there. The corners of Linzee's mouth inched upward while her brows did the opposite as if her face couldn't decide what it wanted to do.

"I'm scared."

"Scared of what?"

Linzee bit her lip. "Ken wants a relationship."

Meg's chin dropped. "Baby girl, that's wonderful." She pulled her daughter close. "Why does that scare you?"

"H-he knows nothing of my history. Today, he and I ran into a server from the old Latte Love Shack. She let it slip that I used to be engaged, right in front of Ken. So now he's curious, but I don't dare tell him about Nena." Her voice rose in pitch as she clutched Meg's arms, her eyes blinking over and over. "What am I gonna do? I can't tell him."

"Why not?"

Another guttural cry. "Because. He'd probably never want to see me again."

"You really care about him."

Linzee went still as an unreadable expression crossed her face. "I guess I do. A little." Her mouth twisted. "And not just because he's on Richie's case." She glanced at the bed, then filled Meg in on the new findings Ken had shared last night, her words tumbling as though she couldn't wait to get off the subject of her love life. "At least they think they know the motive for why the shooter killed his parents. But the rest ..." She shook her head. "It's such a bizarro case. Why was he internet stalking Mr. Hope and Mrs. Milliken?"

"I want to know, too. I hope he'll keep you updated."

"I'm sure he will. As long as I don't tell him who I used to be."

Chapter Fourteen

Painting in the Wilderness – Megan Shaw Paulson (1298 followers)

"Peace I leave with you, my peace I give unto you: not as the world giveth, give I unto you. Let not your heart be troubled, neither let it be afraid." John 14:27

There's a plaque in Richie's room with this verse etched on it, courtesy of Richie's youth pastor and family. So many moments, like yesterday, I find myself clinging to it in desperation. For instance, this morning my brilliant husband suggested I play for Richie some of his favorite bands, and see if he responded. So I loaded up my iTunes with some Switchfoot, some August Burns Red ("If screamer rock doesn't wake him up," said my husband, "I don't know what will."), and a couple of tracks from Twenty One Pilots ("Wish we could turn back time, too" Jon mused.) When we got to his room, I turned it up loud. Even Quan was tapping her feet. But not my son. He turned his head in my direction but otherwise gave no sign the music affected him in the least. His blood pressure elevated a little, but his brain waves didn't budge. Before my heart could shatter into a kajillion pieces, my sweet husband pointed me to the plaque. But I turned away, wishing I could shatter it into a kajillion pieces.

I plopped my iPad in front of Richie and streamed one of his favorite football movies, Draft Day. Surely the soundtrack he's heard a zillion times would prod him out of that black hole he's trapped in. But no. No movement, no sound. By this time, Jon was more worried about me than my son, so he took me home, my heart raw and throbbing for the rest of the day.

Thank you for praying, lovely friends. Keep beseeching God for my sanity, and for peaceful sleep. But most of all, that He would have mercy on my son and bring him back to us.

I want you to know, all your encouraging messages keep me going each day. We love you all!

Meg

~~~~

"**M**rs. Paulson!" The bug-eyed reporter from Marin Mercury planted himself in front of Jon and her as they exited the hospital. Where had he come from? He had to have lain in wait for her.

"How do you feel about the new gun control laws being introduced in the statehouse?"

Meg shook her head and stepped around the big feet blocking her path.

"Do you still support the Second Amendment after what happened to your son?"

How could he possibly know her stance on the Second Amendment? "No comment."

"Mr. Paulson, you are a registered gun owner. Has your opinion on gun rights changed since Richard was injured by one?"

"I'm sorry, sir." Jon's voice held an edge of strain. "We really have nothing to add. Particularly if you're hoping to promote an agenda."

"The entire nation is grieving with you and the other families. People are outraged. They're demanding something be done. It's my responsibility as a media person to help communicate the issues."

With her hand in his, Jon said nothing and walked away. The reporter shouted after them, but they didn't stop, didn't even turn their heads until they reached Jon's Jeep. As they climbed in, her husband's face remained uncharacteristically grim. She squirmed in her seat. How unfair all this drama was to him. She couldn't stop a thought nagging her … if he could've seen into the future, would he have still asked her to spend the rest of her life with him?

As if he read her thoughts, he reached over and gave her neck a gentle squeeze. "This isn't going to last forever. The media leeches will eventually move on to the next big story and forget all about this one."

"How do they know so much about us?"

Jon turned left onto the boulevard. "You can find anything on the internet."

"Even my political beliefs? What a scary thought."

As Jon rounded the corner onto Reno Drive, her phone pulsed with an incoming email. She groaned when she saw the sender. "Jon, that pesky reporter sent me an email. 'Dear Ms. Paulson, The Marin Mercury is passionate about our community, and we believe you have an important story to tell, a story that could help right some wrongs. Your willingness to tell the story of your son could help make our world a better place. I know you're enduring a tough ordeal right now, and I understand your reluctance. But I urge you to reconsider your refusal to answer a few questions. You would be doing your community a huge service by letting us get your story out. If you would be more comfortable meeting in your own home, we can arrange that. We want you to be at ease, and we will do whatever we can to make it as pleasant as possible, considering the circumstances. Please call me at your earliest convenience. Sincerely, Steve Davis, Reporter, Marin Mercury.'" Exasperation edged her sigh. "Jon, he makes it sound so innocuous."

Jon braked to a stop in the driveway and hit the garage door remote. "I think you should do it."

"What? You were just as against it as I was."

He rolled into the garage. "I know. But he doesn't sound so bad. And he's right. Maybe your story could help other families who were affected." He shifted to face her. "This would be a great opportunity to share your faith."

"I doubt he'd print anything faith-related. He just wants to promote an anti-gun agenda."

"Maybe." Jon rubbed his palms over the steering wheel while Meg entertained visions of rubbing Mr. Davis' long nose in the dirt. "But I'll be there with you. And we don't have to answer questions about guns if you don't want to."

Meg stared at her twining fingers as each word from her husband's wise mouth melted the ice wall inside her, inch by frozen inch.

"Let's pray about it." He reached over to cover her hands, shattering the last of her resistance. "I'd rather let it be God's call than rely on my fallible human reasoning."

After he lifted up a prayer for wisdom, she offered her own, finishing with, "I already sense God giving me the green light."

"Really? I'm glad because He's giving me the same."

Meg opened the door and swung her feet to the concrete. "I'll call Mr. Davis right now."

~~~~

"WHEN WILL IT END?"

Linzee froze at Walgreen's magazine rack, staring at the question on People Magazine's cover, and the nine innocent faces, including her brother's, on prominent display.

THE LATEST SHOOTING, THE LATEST VICTIMS, said the subtitle. Someone nudged her. "Are you in line?" The barely concealed impatience came from a mother with a preschooler looking at her expectantly.

"Oh no, go ahead." Linzee moved to the side and waved the woman forward. "I'm just looking."

The woman's gaze caught the magazine cover. "So sad about the shooting, isn't it?"

Linzee could only nod. Any minute now the lady would recognize her. She'd exclaim and want to talk about it for the next twenty minutes. Linzee kept her head down, letting her hair conceal her face until she sensed the woman moving on.

She grabbed the magazine, a Sunday newspaper, plus two other news magazines featuring the shooting, and stepped behind the young mother with her little girl to the checkout counter. When it was her turn, the gray-haired checkout clerk tsked as she scanned Linzee's purchases, but thankfully didn't look too closely at Linzee. "These magazines have been selling like hotcakes today. I can understand why."

Linzee made a noise she hoped would convey agreement, then fled. Once in her basement bedroom at the Carlito's, she cracked open a copy of People.

Each victim's photo included a short bio. She fought back tears as each person came alive on the page.

"THE DEAD: Geoffrey Hope, 43, Spanish teacher, husband, and father, was a passionate advocate of his community. When not teaching, he could be found volunteering for Boys and Girls Clubs and coaching basketball at Emerson Middle School. He was born and raised in San Rafael and he and his wife, Courtney, had been married sixteen years and had a teenage daughter."

The next victim's eyes shone with good humor, and her mouth curved into an amused half-smile, as though she were listening to someone's joke and already anticipating the punchline. "Sabrina Anderson, a student in Mr. Hope's class, was a twenty-one-year-old sophomore and hoped to attend law school someday. She lived in Kentfield, and leaves behind a fiancé, a dog, and a cat."

Linzee wanted to punch something over the terrible injustice. The world had lost a bright star in Sabrina Anderson.

The next photo displayed a broad white smile and a determined gaze, a world of light in her eyes. "Tanisha

Jackson was an eighteen-year-old freshman who aspired to be a social worker. She had her sights set on UC Davis when she finished at Ignacio College. She lived in San Rafael with her mom, two younger brothers, and her dog Snoopy."

The ache in her chest threatened to snap her heart in two.

The fourth photo, more serious this time, held a gaze awash with intelligence. "Kevin Phan, 19, was a sophomore and aspiring pediatrician. He'd been accepted into the University of Washington's pre-med program next fall. He lived in Larkspur with his parents and younger sister."

When she saw the heading above the next section, she had to force her eyes to go there.

"THE INJURED: Richard St. John, aged eighteen, was a freshman at Ignacio." A sob built somewhere behind her throat. In the photo they'd chosen for Richie, he wore his high school football helmet, which partially hid his squinting, focused face. Since Mom hadn't answered the magazine's emails requesting photos, they must have acquired this from his high school. "He hoped to collect and restore classic autos someday. During his senior year of high school at Peninsula Christian Academy, he was the star offensive tackle for the Crusaders. On the day this issue went to print, he was in a coma at Marin General Hospital, his prognosis unknown."

Tears flowed freely as she clutched the magazine to her chest. Sniffing back her sobs, she forced herself to read on. "Richard is the son of Meg Paulson of San Rafael and Phillippe St. John of Santa Clara. His sister Linzee, a staunch gun control advocate, recently appeared in an interview which, at this writing, has more than 500,000 views. To view it, go to the link below."

If she hadn't been famous before, she sure would be now. With more notoriety coming her way, she threw the magazine down, unable to handle any more.

Chapter Fifteen

"First of all, I want to extend my deepest sympathy to both of you." Steve Davis relaxed in Meg's Lay-Z-Boy and mirrored Jon's favorite resting position, ankle on knee. "I can imagine how difficult things are for you right now."

Meg opened her mouth but couldn't get her voice to work. Swallowing hard, she nodded.

"I understand you two are newlyweds."

Another swallow, another nod.

"Congratulations. When was the wedding?"

"A week ago, Saturday." Had it really been just ten days ago? She felt like they'd been married forever. She leaned hard against Jon, melding to him, taking comfort in his body heat warming her like campfire smoke.

Davis took a sip of Ecuador Dark from the Cal Golden Bears mug she'd offered him, then fiddled with his iPad for a moment. "The recorder is on, and we are live. Do I have your permission to record this interview?"

She forced a calm nod but inwardly sent a desperate prayer heavenward. "Yes."

"The video will be posted to our social media sites tomorrow morning. The print version will be in Friday's issue."

First he asked them to spell their names, then launched into the questions. "How has your son's injury changed your life?"

Where to begin? "It's been a nightmare." Her foot found Shadow's sleeping form, and she ran her bare toes across his fur. "I look at my son lying there on the hospital bed, so still. *So* still. It looks like him, but he's not there. He almost would've been better off ..." She bit her lip. If she said what she wanted to say, she'd come off as callous. What kind of mom must she be, to prefer her son's death to this limbo he hung in? This living death?

When Davis asked about her son's prognosis, she admitted her uncertainty. She told him about her blog, and the roller-coaster emotions after Richie opened his eyes. For a moment, she forgot who she was talking to. Tears flowed as she poured her heart out.

"Has this tragedy caused you to give thought to current gun control laws?"

She jerked back and swiveled to Jon. She should have known Davis would manage to revisit his favorite agenda.

Jon took over. "We prefer not to discuss that."

"But surely you can see how stricter laws might have prevented this tragedy?"

"Not at all. The perp used a gun that belonged to another family member. Tell me, Mr. Davis. How would stricter laws have kept him from borrowing someone's gun?"

Meg visualized the hunting rifles locked away in Jon's garage in Sausalito. His sons sometimes borrowed them for camping. If either of them purposed to steal one for criminal activity, no law could dissuade him.

Davis frowned at his iPad. "The statehouse introduced new legislation to solve that very issue."

"You mean, the gun turn-in thing? It's a terrible idea."

"Even though it might prevent more tragedies like yours?"

"I don't believe it would. Has outlawing hard drugs prevented overdose deaths?"

Davis' eyes narrowed, his mouth in a hard slit. Meg could almost hear his mental wheels rotating around Jon's words as he tried to think how to reply. "I don't see the two as the same."

"Some people abuse guns, just like some people abuse alcohol. Remember how well Prohibition worked?"

"Gun violence has affected your life deeply. And it's only

increasing. Surely you have some thoughts you can share on how we can prevent future tragedies."

"We can prevent these kinds of tragedies by teaching kids respect for human life." Jon leaned forward, his hands twining together between his knees. "It starts in the family. When I was growing up, it was unthinkable for someone to bring a gun to school and start shooting. Why did that change?"

Davis shifted. "Life is more stressful these days. Schools are trying to do more with less funding. There's not enough money for mental health."

"Not to mention, families are breaking apart. Boys are being raised without fathers. The internet has become a substitute parent. They're growing up with a sense of entitlement and a disrespect for authority."

"Coby Jarrett came from a loving, intact family."

"True. But many perpetrators of gun violence do not. It's a problem you can't just throw money at. Money doesn't fix attitudes."

Meg glanced from her husband's granite face to Davis' protruding eyes. A dark cloud had moved in, threatening to dump cold rain all over the interview.

Davis shifted his laptop to his left hand. "But money can pay for better teachers and schools, which can make a huge impact on kids' attitudes."

"But if they're getting negative messages outside of school, and on the internet, even the best teacher in the world is going to have a hard time counteracting them."

"And how does this stop gun violence?"

Jon stopped, his fidgeting thumbs making circles around each other. Meg could practically hear his prayers flying silently to God's throne.

Lord, please give Jon the words to say.

Jon lifted his head in Davis' direction. "You know the story of the two wolves? A Cherokee is explaining to his son that there are two wolves fighting inside him. One wolf

104

represents good things like kindness, peace, love, generosity, faith. The other represents bad things like hate, greed, arrogance, envy, pride. When the son asked his father which wolf would win, the father said, 'The one you feed.'"

"That's a beautiful sentiment, but real life is not that simple. It doesn't do anything to help innocent victims. Do you have anything to say to those families?"

"To suffering families, I encourage them to pray fervently."

A shadow of a sneer passed across the reporter's face, quickly wiped. "Not everyone believes in God."

Jon nodded. "True. But even if you've never been a praying type, you probably know people who are. And they would probably be happy to pray in your stead." He shifted to Meg, his gaze caressing her face. "My wife and I met at a parents' prayer group last year, just about the time a crisis hit her family. The group met every week, and we all prayed for each other and our kids. We saw God intervene in Meg's family and bring something really positive out of it."

Jon's gaze brought her back into their own little bubble, but Davis cleared his throat again, snapping the spell. She leaned toward him. "You may have heard about my daughter's kidnapping last year? Linzee St. John?"

Davis' eyes lit with remembrance. "So that's why your daughter's name was familiar."

"If not for my faith in God, and the prayers of other believers, I shudder to think what could've happened. The way God intervened was an absolute miracle."

"From what I remember, the police found her in the kidnapper's basement. Why do you say it was a miraculous rescue?"

"The way it came about was a miracle. Her roommate figured out, through sheer brains and determination, who the culprit was, and even found proof. Whereas the police had found no clues whatsoever."

"It was big news at the time, as I recall."

Meg smiled. "If not for God, and my praying friends …" she thrummed her fingertips on Jon's well-muscled thigh. "I would have fallen apart. Despite the stormy circumstances, He still brought comfort and peace to my heart."

"Would you say your faith is also helping you through this rough time?"

Beside her, Jon dipped his head in agreement, and she opened her mouth, but nothing came out. Davis' question swept through her mind, leaving particles of doubt and piercing her heart with conviction. She tried to think back to the last time she'd prayed fervently, the way she had last year when Linzee went missing.

Too long ago to remember.

Instead, she'd requested prayer from anonymous Facebook followers. She'd sought comfort from her husband countless times. But she hadn't sought the Lord's comfort with the same diligence.

Davis still gazed at her, waiting for her reply. She cleared her throat and said the first words she thought of, almost by rote. "I know God's got this." Even as the words left her mouth, an unnatural peace filled her, the familiar certainty she remembered from last year's crisis.

How could she have forgotten that, even now, God cradled her son in His eternal, never-failing arms?

She straightened her spine and slanted a determined gaze at Davis. "If God can do a miracle for my daughter, I know He can do one for my son. And you can quote me on that."

Chapter Sixteen

Meg watched Quan lift Richie's right arm and flex the elbow back and forth, over and over. Then repeat the ritual on the left. She moved to Richie's legs and dug her fingers into his hairy, skeletal right thigh, up and down, in circles, side to side. Time seemed to slow as the nurse continued the rhythmic, hypnotic movements.

Had it only been just over a week ago she'd basked in the warm Hawaiian sunshine with her new husband? Then came home to this? How much life could flip upside down with no warning?

She turned her head when a female voice echoed in the hallway. "Linzee?"

A familiar masculine voice answered.

Linzee appeared at the door, Ken towering behind her. Nobody would ever describe Linzee as petite, but Ken made her look as tiny as Quan.

"Hi, Mom."

"I'm so glad you're here."

They crossed to Richie's bedside, and Linzee gazed down at her brother, her mouth pursed. She brought her free hand to his cheek and stroked it. A pang throbbed in Meg's heart.

But Ken paid no heed to Richie. Judging by his warmed-over gaze on Linzee's face, he held her daughter in high regard. Was maybe even in the early stages of love. After only a week. You had to admire a man who knew what — who — he wanted, then confidently pursued her.

Quan finished her massage therapy and left the room. Jon brought in extra chairs, and they settled themselves around the bed. Meg couldn't help noticing how close Ken sat to Linzee. Couple-close, knee-to-knee. *This is my woman*, the stance proclaimed.

Linzee nudged Ken. "Tell them your latest news on the case."

He nodded. "We're currently trying to track down other Jarrett family members. There are still several unexplained points about the case we hope they can shed light on."

Meg leaned closer as he continued.

"We're trying to find out if Rose Jarrett used drugs while she was pregnant with Coby. But her parents refuse to talk to us. They claim they need time—"

"Which is perfectly understandable," Linzee said, eyeing Ken as if expecting him to object.

"Yes. It was their gun Coby 'borrowed.'" He made air quotes. "Rose was an only child, and there are no siblings for us to interview. So we're focusing on Robert Jarrett's parents. They live only about a mile from Robert and Rose, but unfortunately, the wife has Alzheimer's and isn't even aware of what happened."

Meg clutched the chair's arm. "Oh, how sad."

"That leaves the paternal grandfather. Tim Whitney. We interviewed him yesterday. When I asked him whether he knew if Rose had a history of drug abuse, he acted surprised and said not since he'd known her. Then he told us he's actually Robert's stepfather, and Coby was three when Tim married Robert's mother."

"Did he have any insights as to Coby's motive?"

"None. He was as baffled as everyone else."

"What about Robert's biological father?"

"He died in Desert Storm in 1991."

"Wow. You keep hitting dead ends. Rose must have had some close friends."

"Yes, we went there next. We tracked down a good friend of hers from high school, a woman named Karen, who told us she couldn't imagine Rose ever using drugs. But she admitted she'd lost touch with Rose after high school. Rose attended college at the University of Oregon, where she and Robert met, and Karen went to UC Riverside. They didn't reconnect until about seven years ago when they finally found each other on Facebook."

"So she probably has no idea, either."

Ken shook his head. "She doesn't. Rose and Robert stayed in Oregon for a few years after they were married, and Coby was a toddler when they moved back here. So any friends of hers who knew her then are most likely in Oregon."

"So, now what?"

"We're going to search her social media contacts to see if any of them hail from Eugene, Oregon. If we can find someone who can vouch for her drug use during pregnancy, we'll have one unanswered question out of the way."

"You mean, his motive?"

"Yes. We suspect he blamed prenatal drug use by his mother for his mental breakdown. It must be a pretty miserable life to be trapped with a mind that doesn't work right. And when you find it could have been prevented, well, we think he just snapped."

Jon cleared his throat. "Good work. Have you determined his reason for shooting the teacher and the mom?"

"Not yet. That's going to take a lot more digging. Coby researched both of them for months, but why, we don't know."

Linzee nodded. "So bizarro."

Ken continued, "Even more bizarre, there's no apparent connection between the two. We've interviewed their family members, checked their histories." He flipped his palms up. "They didn't attend the same schools, they had no mutual social media contacts, didn't live anywhere near each other. Bottom line, Sandy Milliken and Geoffrey Hope seemed to have had absolutely nothing in common."

Meg shook her head. "When he stalked them online, what was he looking for?"

Ken brought his palms to his knees. "He tracked their

social media activity and followed both of them on Twitter and Facebook. He conducted searches on their employment history, background checks, that sort of thing. Pretty detailed stuff."

"Did you find any clues on the parents' computers?"

"Yes, lots of emails to and from Coby's mental health professionals. And, like Coby, they did a lot of research on mental illness. But nothing to connect them to the other victims."

Jon planted his palms on his knees. "It had to be revenge." He turned his gaze to Meg. "Linzee's kidnapper had been stalking her too. We learned later it was for revenge." He shifted toward Ken. "Mr. Hope and Mrs. Milliken must have crossed paths with Coby at some point. Or one of their family members hurt him in some way, and Coby chose that way to enact his retaliation."

Ken nodded. "Those are all valid possibilities. And we hope to have some solid answers after the funeral this Saturday. It will be a triple funeral, so we're hoping all those AWOL Jarrett family members will show, and at least some of them will talk."

Four more days before she had some answers. Not that having answers would make a difference in the outcome. But it might lay to rest her constant whys.

Chapter Seventeen

Painting in the Wilderness – Megan Shaw Paulson
(1767 followers)

"But I will sing of thy power; yea, I will sing aloud of thy mercy in the morning: for thou hast been my defense and refuge in the day of my trouble." Psalm 59:16

My poor husband. It seems he's gone gray overnight. He was salt-and-pepper the day we met. But today I noticed more salt than pepper. Not only that, my face has sprouted a few new wrinkles. This must be our bodies' way of telling us, you're too old for this.

We met with Dr. Nguyen today, and the prognosis he gave for Richie is too uncertain to pin any hopes on. Unfortunately, the brain monitor shows no change. Ironic, then, that modern technology is forcing Richie's body to work almost normally. Tomorrow, Dr. Nguyen is going to try removing Richie's catheter to see if his bowels work again. His blood pressure has stabilized, and they are no longer pumping enormous quantities of pain meds into him. He no longer needs the respirator (praise the Good Lord!) The compression socks and all the physical therapy are keeping his muscles activated.

But what good is a perfectly-working body when your brain doesn't work?

I left that meeting discouraged once again … yet I don't want any of you to give up praying or feel

discouraged that God isn't hearing us. All this
proves is, we need to keep the faith-strengthening
prayers going. We don't know what God has in
mind, or His timing. So please keep knocking on
Heaven's door with us.

Love to all,

Meg

~~~~

Candy waited for Meg near First Baptist's basement entry. She clasped Meg in a desperate hug when she drew near.

Meg held her close for a moment, then pulled back. "I've been worried about you."

"I'm so sorry I didn't call. I'll be all right, honest."

Meg narrowed her eyes at her friend. Candy wasn't all right last time they talked. Guilt squeezed the breath out of her, and she sucked in a ragged current of air. "I should have called you. I owe *you* an apology." But she'd been so preoccupied with Richie, she'd given Candy barely a thought. So much for putting others' needs ahead of her own.

She and Candy followed Jon to the same row they occupied last week. Meg looked up in time to see a stiff-faced woman on the front row twisted around, peering at her as though Meg were a celebrity. As if any second now, the lady would approach her with a pad of paper, asking for her autograph.

Dream on, Meg.

The pastor called the room to attention and again opened with a prayer and Scripture, ending with, "We have some guests tonight who were greatly impacted by last week's tragedy." He gestured to the front row. "The parents of a student who lost her life last week are here tonight—Sabrina Anderson's mom and dad."

The woman who'd eyed Meg raised her hand, along with the gray-haired man beside her.

"They're here for prayer and comfort. Be sure to offer

112

both while they're here."

No wonder the mother's pinched face resembled the El Greco *pieta* of Mary cradling the body of her son, Jesus.

Meg had probably witnessed more grief this past week than in her entire lifetime. But she couldn't fathom why the woman had peered at her with such curiosity.

Unless she'd seen the video of the interview already.

Meg nearly gasped aloud. She'd been so busy with Richie today, she hadn't bothered to look for it. Or was it that, deep down, she didn't really want to see herself on camera?

Pastor Fred now eyed her as he talked, squinted, then moved his gaze to Jon. Meg had no idea what he was saying. She kicked herself for failing to look at the video today.

They broke into small groups again. Addy gave Meg a hug and said, "I saw your interview with the Mercury."

Meg drooped. "I'm almost afraid to ask you, how was it?"

"It was awesome."

Her husband, Paul, nodded, flashing a white-toothed smile.

"It got a ton of likes and comments."

"Wow. And I haven't even seen it yet."

"It brought tears to my eyes. I sometimes forget that God knows what He's doing, but you reminded me that He does."

Meg lifted her mouth in a relieved smile. *Thank you, Lord.* God was so full of surprises. He could use even a barren soul like herself to inspire others. God had heard and honored her feeble words of faith and used them to bear fruit.

~~~~

"Jon, honey, come look." The interview headlined the Marin Mercury's home page. Meg turned up the volume and shifted the laptop away from the glare of the ceiling light. Jon came up behind her chair and ruffled her hair as her face appeared on camera. "You looked nice, my love."

They watched in silence for several minutes, then she chuckled. "You looked a little ticked when he brought up the gun issue."

Jon shook his head. "I suspect he was trying to get a rise out of me. I think he was hoping I'd come off like an angry, right-wing gun owner."

"You did a good job restraining yourself."

She listened to herself declare, "God's got this."

Jon reached around and cupped her chin, then tipped it up to meet his gaze. "You sounded a lot more confident than you thought, sweetheart."

She grinned at Jon's reversed smile, the corners of his mouth slanting south instead of north. He leaned over to give her an upside-down kiss, and his whiskers tickled her nose.

As she scrolled through the comments, the word "hypocrisy" jumped out at her. Just as she feared, the bashing had already begun. Her heart plummeted, but her finger had frozen. She couldn't move on if she tried.

"I listened with interest," a commenter named FourByFour wrote, "to this couple who was so deeply affected by lax gun laws. I waited, and waited, for them to tell us what we need to do to eliminate gun violence. But all I heard were religious platitudes. No solutions except to 'pray' to some imaginary guy in the sky. From the way the dad defended gun ownership, I can only conclude they own guns themselves. I consider it the height of hypocrisy for these religious folks who are presumably against killing to refuse to give up their own guns ..."

Meg made a face at the screen. "How dare they judge us." She leaned her head back against Jon's torso. "They don't know anything about us, yet they try to convict us."

Jon leaned in, his finger on the screen. "But look, most of them are positive. Look at this one: 'I pray every day for our country, that God would bless and heal it.'"

"I like this one. 'In a time when evil seems to have taken over our nation, we need to pray against it even more fervently.'"

"And this: 'We need God more than ever. I Chronicles

says if we who belong to the Lord will humble ourselves and turn from our wicked ways, God will heal our land.'"

Meg's phone vibrated in her pocket. She took it out, glancing at the display. "Candy?"

A moment's silence, then, "Are you home?"

"Yes."

"I think I need another painting session."

"Now?" Meg blinked at the urgency in Candy's voice.

"I know it's past nine, but tonight's meeting made me feel worse, not better."

Meg stood and paced toward the kitchen, away from Jon's quizzical gaze. "How did it make you feel worse?"

"Meeting that mom whose daughter was killed. How awful for her. I just couldn't bear it."

Meg scrunched her face in thought, deciding Candy must be an empath—one of those tender souls known as angst-sucking sponges. How else could you explain the way she absorbed others' traumas as though they were her own?

"Let me check with my husband. Call you right back."

Finding Jon still sifting through comments, she hurried through an explanation.

"That lady needs professional help," was all he said.

"I know. She's in counseling. But I want to do whatever I can."

"My wife and her heart of gold." He reached for her hand. "Just one of the many things I love about you. I'm going to bed soon. So then I'll see you in the morning?"

"Okay." She bent over for a kiss. "Good night, love."

Chapter Eighteen

"Let's both paint what's on our hearts," Meg suggested as Candy followed her into the studio, then pointed Candy to two easels side-by-side. She planted herself at one, then spun to face her friend, who stood at the other easel staring at the blank canvas, her expression equally blank. "I'm so sorry the meeting upset you tonight. Are you sure you're ..." She didn't know how to voice her fears without putting unwanted suggestions into Candy's mind. "I mean, sometimes I worry that you ..." She stopped, wondering if Candy could see in her eyes her unspoken fears.

But Candy merely shrugged those frail shoulders. "Everyone says they're worried about me. My sister called me a breakdown waiting to happen."

Meg kept her voice gentle. "Maybe there's a reason people are so concerned."

Candy jerked her hand along the easel as if seeking a resting spot and finding none. She picked up a clean brush, dipped it in black paint, and swept it back and forth. "They can't go back and undo the past." Her forced monotone frightened Meg even more. "That's the only thing that will make all of this better." She shifted her gaze to Meg with a suddenness that startled her. "Don't you feel that way too? Wish you could go back and undo everything that happened to your son?"

"Well, of course ..."

"Don't you ever lie awake at night with 'if onlys' swirling through your mind, keeping you from sleep?" The black swathes were multiplying with a startling swiftness on the formerly white expanse.

"Sure." Yet there hadn't been a thing Meg could've done to prevent Richie's injury. "It sounds like you're holding yourself responsible for your son's suicide." She grasped Candy's free arm and clung there. "Please don't blame yourself."

Candy's jaw hardened. "Are you serious? It was my fault he grew up all messed up."

Meg stepped back, narrowly missing the easel leg. There was something else going on that Candy wasn't telling. Had she abused the boy? Meg's longing to know was expanding by the second, yet she couldn't bring herself to pry. "Does your counselor think it's your fault?"

Candy stopped, set the brush down. "He understands why I think so."

"Really?"

"But he says I need to work toward forgiving myself."

If Candy had confessed to abuse after the fact, the counselor was required by law to report it. Since that didn't appear to be the case, Meg checked off abuse as unlikely. But maybe someone else abused him, and Candy did nothing to stop it.

"He's right, you know. Nothing good can come of constantly heaping all this toxic blame on yourself. It's not going to undo the past. Nothing will." She peered at Candy's easel, where a heart-shaped array of angry black streaks filled half of it. "At first, I blamed myself for my son's tragedy."

"You did? But why?"

"Jon and I had turned off our phones during the time the college kept calling, trying to reach me. We didn't want to be bothered if you know what I mean. It wasn't until hours later that my daughter finally got hold of me. So I do know what you're feeling. If I'd answered the first time they called, I would've been home with him much sooner."

"But would that have made a difference?"

"Looking back on it, no. I came to realize that my actions didn't change the outcome at all."

Candy leaned against the wall, her face dark. "That's not the same thing at all. You didn't do anything to contribute to the shooting."

Meg's breath caught. "You actually believe you caused your son to take his own life?"

"Maybe not directly, but if I hadn't been so young and stupid maybe things would've turned out different."

"Young and stupid?" Meg went to her and embraced her. "Sweetie, we've all been young and stupid. That's how we learn. What could you have possibly done that was so terrible?"

Candy sniffed against Meg's knit sweater. "For one thing, I got mixed up with the wrong man, someone who wasn't ready to be a father. The minute he found out I was pregnant, he couldn't get away fast enough." Another sniff. "And then there were the drugs …"

Oh, no. That could explain the high-strung nerves, the twitchy gestures.

"But I'm clean now." She felt Candy's head move side to side as though to shake away the memories. "It's been years since I've gotten high." She lifted her head but kept her gaze downcast. "I did a lot of things I regret."

Meg lifted Candy's chin and peered closely at her eyes for telltale signs of drug abuse. Her steady gaze betrayed no unnatural brightness or dilated pupils. Apparently, grief could masquerade as substance abuse.

"You aren't ultimately responsible for your son's choices."

"As far as the world is concerned, it's always the mom's fault."

Candy's declaration made her think of poor Rose Jarrett, whose son had apparently blamed her for his mental illness. Why did mothers get so much blame heaped on them?

She glanced at Candy's easel. "Don't let the world's messages sway you." She gestured at the canvas. "This isn't you. Your heart is righteous." She moved to the other easel and picked up a red charcoal. As Candy watched, a white heart outlined in red took shape on the canvas. Meg added swirling embellishments then turned to her friend. "This is how God sees you."

Candy nodded and brushed a finger beneath her eye. "I've heard that a million times. It's just difficult to believe, at times." Her gaze strayed to her watch. "It's late. I better get going, let you get to bed."

Meg cupped her friend's face in both hands. "Promise you'll call me the minute you start feeling overwhelmed with guilt and self-blame?"

Candy nodded, and reluctantly, Meg let her go. As soon as Candy was out the door, she made her way to the laptop she'd left on the kitchen table and powered it on. There had to be something in the news about Candy's son, and it had to have been recent. Meg longed to know how long Candy had been carrying this burden. Weeks? A month? A year or more? She started with the leading local news site, wracking her brain for the name Candy called her son. His childhood nickname Mikey — that was it. On the obituary page's search box, she typed in Michael Burton and narrowed the search to the last ninety days.

Nothing.

Well, perhaps he had a different last name than his mom — a common occurrence these days. But her name would be in the obituary as the mother of the deceased, so she tried Candice Burton.

After coming up empty, she tried possible variations of Candy's name ... Candace, Candie. Still nothing.

She keyed in just the surname Burton and expanded the search to the last six months, although skeptical it had actually happened that long ago. No obituary for Candy's son appeared.

Next, she scrutinized recent local death notices for any nineteen-year-old males. A young Asian man had passed away two weeks ago — no cause of death listed. Going further back, she discovered a Michael Bailey, aged nineteen, from San Rafael, son of Keith and Jade Bailey. She remembered a news item from about a month ago—a young man had died in a head-on collision with a pickup near Mt. Diablo. Speed and alcohol had contributed to the fatality. This young man was probably one and the same.

Obviously not Candy's son.

Still, he'd been someone's dearly loved son. Her heart twisted as she stared at his photo for a moment, noting the intelligent eyes gazing into the distance as though his mind were rehashing an algebraic equation. For the Baileys, every parent's worst fear had been realized. She couldn't count the times she'd gripped the side of her bed and cried to the Lord in fear whenever Richie got into that sports car he called the Richmobile and roared away. And the times her heart throbbed in relief to hear the distinctive syncopation of the engine when he returned home safely.

Would he ever drive that snazzy green Richmobile again?

With shaking hands, she returned her attention to the screen, and after another fruitless search, concluded that Mikey's death hadn't been reported to the newspaper. Not surprising. She couldn't blame Candy for not wanting to publicize it.

She opted not to search the public records, and instead logged onto Facebook and searched for Candy's name. Surely she'd posted photos of her son, and hopefully details of his death.

She found her friend's profile after sifting through several Candices and Candaces, finally locating Candy Burton in Lagunitas, California. Eight miles west of here. Meg guessed her profile photo was posted pre-tragedy—Candy knelt next to an enormous boxer, her arm around the dog, her face not actually smiling, yet far more relaxed than Meg had ever seen it. Her fawn-colored hair matched her pet's coat. Meg scrolled to her photos. But Candy had her profile set to private; the scant few visible pictures of her revealed nothing of her personal life. Most of them were cartoons or memes, with an occasional dog photo in the mix. No son or other family members.

In order to see her posts, Meg needed to send her a friend request, so she clicked the button. Hopefully, Candy would respond soon, and Meg could satisfy her curiosity. She could come right out and ask Candy how long ago Mikey had died, but her friend kept erecting walls whenever she talked about him.

Her tired gaze sought the time. She needed to go join her husband in bed. The answers would have to wait. She turned off the laptop and made her weary way to the master bedroom, sending fervent prayers heavenward that her friend, in her grief, wouldn't do anything drastic.

Chapter Nineteen

Painting in the Wilderness – Megan Shaw Paulson (3915 followers)

"I can do all things through Christ which strengtheneth me." Philippians 4:13.

Thank you, new and old friends, for your interest in our son's recovery! I know many of you discovered my blog after my interview with the Marin Mercury. I'm so thankful word is getting out, and we've gathered six-hundred-some additional warriors for our team!

This morning we held a prayer vigil, right here in Richie's room. Friends from church, even some of the nurses, gathered round to place hands on him and cover him with prayer. Through it all, Richie's eyeballs moved around under his lids, like he could hear us. I have to ask myself if he was praying silently too. Is he still aware of God, I wonder? I know God can do anything, including reaching my son in his dark pit. But does He, and will He? The doctor says the next two weeks are crucial. If Richie doesn't awaken during that time, the chances that he ever will significantly diminish.

I know it's time to plan for the future, but I so don't want to broach the subject with Jon. What if Richie never recovers? Do I have what it takes to care for him the rest of my life? Dear God, there was a reason I never considered the medical field.

We need a miracle, my friends. Even a small one.

An opened eye, a hand squeeze. Anything to let us know our son is still in that shell, just waiting to get out.

Mega Hugs from Meg and Jon

~~~~

"I have a boyfriend," Linzee declared, then grinned when Claire gawked.

The Carlito's son Heath jumped off her lap, toddled across the patio to his plastic car, and climbed in. "Room room!" His cries drowned out Claire's astonished reply as his little legs propelled the pretend Jeep along the concrete. "Room room!"

Claire took a sip of the kombucha Linzee had poured them. "A boyfriend? You mean that humongous cop I saw you talking to at the rally?"

"The humongous, *cute* cop." Her face had better not flame and give Claire more ammunition. "The very one."

"What's his name?" Somehow Claire managed to infuse a sly tone into the simple question.

"He's got the coolest name ever. Kentucker."

"What?"

"Ken. Tucker."

"Oh. As in the famous derby?"

Linzee sipped her own kombucha. "Or the famous fried chicken."

"How tall is he, anyway?"

"Six five, plus three hundred pounds of solid muscle."

"When did you start liking men?"

Linzee shrugged. "When I met Ken." She jerked forward. "Heath! Get away from that planter!"

The little boy looked at her for a moment, then reluctantly changed course, still eying her.

But Claire kept talking. "Wonder what Nena would say if she knew."

Another shrug. "I don't see why she would care. She's

123

moved on too."

"I still see her, you know. She goes to the Starbucks at my store about once a week. With her new girlfriend." Linzee felt her friend's gaze on her as if gauging her reaction.

She stretched her mouth in a mock-yawn, tapping it twice, to remind Claire she no longer cared. "Tell her hello for me, will you?"

Out of the corner of her eye, she saw Claire turn away, and smiled to herself. If Claire was hoping to stir up drama, she had the wrong girl. With this weird feeling for Ken growing in her heart by the day, her split with Nena no longer registered on her angst-o-meter.

Claire tugged on a thick tress of her red hair. "So what's it like to, you know ... after being only with women?"

"I don't know. We're not there yet."

"Really?" Thick silence. "Have you told him?"

Linzee whirled to her friend, but Claire was watching Heath drive his car in circles. *Play dumb.* "Told him what?"

"About Nena."

Drama queen. "A little. He didn't ask for details." She watched Heath shift direction and head directly toward her legs. Like Heath, she needed to steer the subject elsewhere. "How about you? Making any progress with Ian?"

"We've had coffee a couple times."

Linzee lifted her feet just in time for the Jeep's bumper to collide with them. Heath gave a couple of half-hearted pushes against the soles of her flip-flops, then gave up and reversed course again.

"Oh no." She bounded up and darted toward the boy, who was on a collision course with the pygmy date palm's thick trunk and grabbed the plastic car just in time. "Heath! I told you not to drive your car into the tree."

The little boy burst into tears and Linzee stroked his wet, soft cheeks. She needed to leave soon to meet the two older Carlito kids at the bus and walk them home. "C'mon, little man, let's get you in the stroller. Wanta go for a walk? See

Sissy and Bro-bro?"

Heath grew alert. "Bo bo!" He climbed out of the toy car and galloped across the patio to the garage door.

Linzee grinned at Claire. "So much energy! Want to walk to the bus stop with us?"

"Sure."

She retrieved the stroller from the garage and bundled Heath into it, then strapped him in. Pulling the Giants baseball cap lower toward her oversized sunglasses, she and Claire set out for the bus stop two blocks away. Without her cap and shades, too many people recognized her whenever she ventured out.

Curiosity was practically radiating out of Claire's ears. "What did you tell Ken about Nena?"

"You're just full of questions today!"

"You brought it up."

"Okay. If you must know, I told him I've been engaged. I just didn't tell him to whom."

Claire gawked. "Have you thought about what you'll tell him?"

"Of course I have! I just ... just ... don't know yet."

"You're worried it'll be a deal-breaker."

"Wow, you must be psychic." Linzee's feet pounded into the concrete sidewalk.

A '90s-vintage Corvette roared up, then screeched to a stop between the cars parked at each curb. "Hey!" The door flung open, and a head of spiked hair emerged first. Glaring at Linzee, the young driver shouted, "Want to know what I think of your stupid video?"

He launched something toward the Carlito's living room window, where it splatted directly onto the reflected sunlight.

Streaks of egg yolk dripped yellow stripes down the glass.

"Hey!" Linzee charged toward him, but he was already racing away. She squinted at the license plate, but couldn't make out the digits.

A swear word flew out her mouth. "The Carlitos are going to be so upset."

"Clean it up now while it's still fresh."

"I have to go get the kids." She whirled and pounded her way toward the bus stop, Claire hurrying to stay with her. She never should have agreed to do that interview. "How did he know where I live? And how did he recognize me?"

"Good question."

She lurched to a halt as the bus stopped at the curb and the folding door squealed open. She tapped her foot, her mind filled with visions of flying eggs and spiky hair, as the kids poured out of the bus. Naturally, Hannah and Hogan, preferring the rear seats, came out last. She grabbed their hands. "Kids, we need to hurry home."

"How come?" Eight-year-old Hannah yanked her hand away. "You said we'd do something fun after school today."

"It will be fun. Have you ever washed windows?" She watched Hogan skip a few feet ahead, then turned to Hannah, who was shaking her head. "You'll love it. It's a lot like painting, only with water and a squeegee."

"Really?" Hannah gave an excited leap. "I love painting."

"I know you do. That's why I know you'll enjoy this."

They reached the house, and Hannah's eyes widened. "What happened to the window? How did it get an egg on it?"

The vision of the flying egg would not go away. Linzee motioned Hannah into the garage. "Someone with really bad aim. But now you can learn a new activity that your mom and dad can be proud of you for."

They gathered the soap and two buckets, and Linzee showed Hannah how to work the squeegee. She wanted to take this squeegee and wipe that guy's spikes right off his head. In the most painful possible way.

As Hannah set to work, Claire winked at her. "You did a Tom Sawyer on her, didn't you?"

"Not at all. I plan to help too. It's just that more hands

make light work. And she needs to learn how to wash windows."

"Sure wish we'd gotten that guy's license plate number."

"Ditto. Because then I could sic Ken on him." All it would take would be the sight of Ken at his door, and she felt confident he'd never, ever do that again.

Chapter Twenty

She didn't belong here, at the Jarrett family funeral. As Linzee walked beside Ken into the somber sanctuary, she regretted agreeing to go with him. St. Mark's Catholic Church overflowed with sorrow, from the mournful statues on the platform to the unsmiling faces in the stained glass windows following her every move. The perfect funeral venue. Mourners filed into the wooden benches and whispered in the aisles.

Ken gestured her to a pew close to the back. He didn't want to call attention to himself, he'd said. He was dreaming if he thought nobody would notice him. His size alone would result in double-takes. She slid to the middle, behind a squirmy, suit-clad little boy and his mother. She opened the program in her hand and read the bios of the two deceased parents while the organist played a selection in a minor key. Linzee couldn't picture that dark, massive organ ever producing any happy music. The frowning faces in the stained glass would probably shoot lightning at the stage in outrage.

Whoever had written the bios had taken the sensitive route, not mentioning the murder or suicide, plus they'd also omitted the son's bio. Linzee eyed the stage where two large, shiny coffins covered in flowers sat, lids open. She nudged Ken. "Weren't there supposed to be three coffins?"

Ken, his eyes dark with grief, shook his head. "They're not including the son in this funeral. The Catholic Church's doctrine on suicide means he doesn't get a Christian burial."

"That really sucks," she whispered. "Then what did they do with his body?"

"I imagine someone in the family arranged for a private

burial," he whispered back.

"You seem to know a lot about Catholicism."

The little boy swiveled in his pew and eyed them, his gaze swinging from her to Ken, and back again, as though their conversation were of great importance to his little three-year-old mind.

"I've picked up a few things about Catholics over the years. My line of work has taught me a lot about the different faiths."

"But you're not Catholic?"

"No, I was raised Presbyterian."

The little boy's grin seemed out of place among all these tortured faces, but she appreciated the comic relief. She smiled back. He let out a protest when his scowling mother grasped his arm and spun him back into place.

Linzee spoke into Ken's ear. "I was raised non-denominational Christian."

"Would the church you were raised in give a Christian burial to someone who committed suicide?"

She nodded, then hesitated. "To be honest, I'm not sure. My mom would know." The only people she knew who'd killed themselves had been high school or college acquaintances. Her chest felt heavy inside her; considering the destruction Coby Jarrett had wrought, his family must be suffering as much her own.

The organ stopped, and a priest moved to the front of the stage. Linzee tuned out the droning monologue and the Latin prayers, then fidgeted while most of the congregants filed to the front, bowed to the Virgin Mary, and partook of the Eucharist.

If all went according to plan, Ken would get the answers today they so desperately wanted. She wasn't sure how he'd know who was who, but she'd leave that up to his keen cop judgment.

There must be a least a hundred people here. All of them strangers to her, gawking at the plastic-looking corpses in the caskets. When the pallbearers picked up the caskets and made their way down the aisle, Ken went on alert—straightened shoulders, narrowed eyes, scanning the departing crowd. "Let's wait at the back."

They eased out of the pew and followed the grim-faced pallbearers to the foyer and watched folks file out, waiting for Tim Whitney, who could if he were willing, steer Ken to Rose Jarrett's parents, who still had not returned any of Ken's calls.

Ken shifted and craned his head back and forth. His astonishing height sure made his job a lot easier.

"Do you see him?"

"Yeah. Here he comes."

She'd guess Mr. Whitney, a grandpa, must be in his sixties, so she wasn't expecting the youngish-looking man with a full head of American Crew hair and Johnny Depp glasses who snuck a glance at Ken then looked quickly away. But Ken wouldn't let him off the hook that easily. He waved. "Mr. Whitney."

Hard to believe this youthful-looking man had a wife with Alzheimer's. "Hey." A smile, obviously forced, creased the taut skin around the man's mouth as Ken closed the distance between them. "Nice to see you again."

"And you. It was a nice service." Ken placed a hand on Linzee's back and made introductions. Tim Whitney shook her hand with his firm grip and met her eyes with no flash of recognition. Up close, the wrinkles on his face deepened in the afternoon sunshine and highlighted the gray streaks in his artificially black hair.

So, an older man trying to look young, as if he were back in the dating scene.

"Nice to meet you," she said. "Your son and his wife seemed like wonderful people."

The man's eyes darkened, and his mouth flattened. "Thank you. They were."

Ken cleared his throat. "Mr. Whitney, if you don't mind pointing me to Mrs. Jarrett's parents, I'd like to express my condolences to them."

"Sure." The man's eyes flashed with something suspiciously like relief as he gestured behind him. "They're coming out right now."

A sixty-something man and woman, who did look their age, exited the sanctuary, their hands entwined together in weary bewilderment. Ken beelined in their direction. "Mr. and Mrs. O'Callahan," he said. "My deepest condolences."

They raised watery eyes to him, and Linzee caught her breath at the grief and trauma in them. Ken introduced himself, and they visibly shrunk back.

He held out a hand. "No pressure. I was just hoping to set up a time to meet with you," he hastened to assure them. "We'd like to conclude this investigation and ..." he appealed with an upraised palm.

And get the chief off his back, Linzee heard in his unspoken plea. And give the non-stop callers the answers to their whys.

Mr. O'Callahan wrapped a shielding arm around his wife's shoulder as he aimed his feet toward the exit. "We need to get to the cemetery."

Mrs. O'Callahan stepped out of her husband's shield. "Dear, they're not going to stop calling until we give them what they want. Let's just get this over with." She looked at Ken, her lips firmed. "You seem like a nice young man. No more than five minutes, okay?"

"Yes, ma'am. Can we sit down?" He pointed to a bench, and they sat, the two couples facing each other.

"Thank you for this," Ken began. "We know how rough this has been for you. So you must have some insight into Coby's motive."

Mrs. O'Callahan huffed. "Motive? He was a mentally ill young man. He didn't need a motive."

Linzee heard Ken take in a slow breath, giving Mrs. O'Callahan time to compose herself. "We're trying to understand why he would want to harm his parents."

"We're trying to understand it, too. Both of them were excellent parents."

"Yet according to his internet search history, he seemed to be curious about how drug use by pregnant mothers impacts the future mental health of their unborn children."

Rose's mother cocked her head, her hands clenching and unclenching her black linen blazer. "I don't understand."

"Did he blame Rose for his mental illness?"

"That doesn't make any sense." Her husband sat like a stoic statue beside her.

"Why do you say it doesn't make sense?"

"Well, Rose was never pregnant."

Ken just stared at her as if she were the one not making any sense.

"Coby was *adopted*." She stressed each syllable, and the air around Linzee froze. "So if he was curious about whether his mother's prenatal drug use caused his mental problems, it would've been his biological mother."

Ken sat very still, as if afraid to spook her into silence. His voice came out low, smooth. "And who was his biological mother?"

Mrs. O'Callahan widened her eyes at Ken. "Don't tell me you don't know."

Ken lifted his hands, palm up, his eye twitching. A little sliver of shame crawled up Linzee's spine on his behalf. Ken was anything but stupid. How dare this woman imply it.

She had to say something. "Why? Is it common knowledge?"

"Well, he's a cop." Mrs. O'Callahan's teary gaze pinned Linzee. "Don't they specialize in finding dirty laundry from people's pasts?"

Ken shifted. "Only if it can be found. If you would please tell me the name of Coby's biological mother, it will save me and my cohorts a lot of effort."

"Okay, but I can't believe you aren't making the connection. The other woman who was shot? Mrs. Milliken?

132

She's the one who brought Coby into the world, not my daughter."

Chapter Twenty-One

"Quite the revelation." Linzee blinked in the sudden brightness of mid-day. The air, sunny and alive, seemed to mock the somber spectacle they'd just witnessed. Cars roared by happily, children laughed in the park across the street. She grasped Ken's arm. "You really didn't find anything about him being adopted?"

"We hadn't gone back that far." Ken's voice held an edge, and she knew he was annoyed at being made to look incompetent. "I'm sure we would eventually have found it. But Mrs. O'Callahan's statement saved us a lot of time."

"I wonder if Mrs. Milliken's family knows."

"The husband never said anything about an adopted baby in his wife's past, so I would presume he doesn't know. Or didn't make the connection."

A block from the church, Ken opened the passenger door of his Toyota, and Linzee climbed in. "Are you going to tell him?"

Ken cranked the ignition, then thrummed his fingers on the steering wheel. "No need. But we need to talk to Mrs. Milliken's parents. They're taking this really hard, too. They may not realize Coby is the son their daughter gave up for adoption nineteen years ago. I think it's only fair to let them know."

"I don't know, Ken. If it were me, I think that might just add fuel to the fire."

"They can always decline. But as the detective in charge of this case, I have to perform due diligence."

"So. Who's the biological father? I wonder ..." She dug out her phone and searched the internet for Coby's photo, which popped up within seconds. "Can I borrow your phone?"

"Uh, sure. What for?"

"Just checking something." He handed her the phone, and she repeated the action, this time searching for Geoffrey Hope.

"Aha." She held the phones up, side-by-side. "I knew it. Ken, look."

He pulled his attention from the cars whizzing by to the phones in her hands. She heard a sudden intake of breath. "Holy cow," he breathed.

"I know, right?"

"Can't believe we didn't see it."

"If you're like me, you're not likely to see something you're not looking for."

"But it's my job to see things like that. I'll have to ask Mary if she noticed the resemblance between the two."

"Especially the nose and chin."

"And the shape of the face."

She handed the phone back. Ken pulled out onto the street, then stared straight ahead, a frown slashing across his face. "So ... twenty years ago, Sandy Martin and Geoffrey Hope had an affair, and she got pregnant. I wonder if she gave up the baby willingly, or if he was taken from her by the state. If so, there will be a record of it in the state archives."

"Coby wouldn't have any way to know if she used drugs."

"Maybe he was stalking her because he wanted to find out. Mary and I need to search further back in both their histories. We couldn't find a single connection between the two."

"Well, obviously they knew each other twenty years ago. She must've still been in high school."

"He may have been a teacher where she attended school." He gave the steering wheel a celebratory slap. "Awesome. We've got some more threads to explore. I knew Jarrett had a motive. And now I'm pretty sure I know what it was."

"But why Mr. Hope? What could Coby have against him?"

"It could be a lot of things. Maybe he felt Hope had abandoned his mother. Maybe he thought his mother used drugs because of it. We'll just have to dig deeper."

~~~~

"Okay." Ken met Linzee's eyes as they gazed at their reflections in his black laptop screen, perched on his outstretched legs. "Are you sure this won't bore you?"

She gave him a quick head shake. "Not at all. Your work fascinates me. I watch CSI, you know."

He grinned at her, pulled her close and kissed her hair. "One of the many things I like about you."

This was her first time in his duplex, where he lived with his trained German Shepherd, Fletcher. It exuded "man cave." The sofa where they sat was long and deep for stretching out on. Ken's size-fifteen feet rested on a simple wood coffee table, next to a neatly-stacked set of beer logo coasters. Over there in the corner, the requisite big-screen TV, seeming out of character in its silent, dark-gray beauty instead of broadcasting football or baseball.

An all-male habitat reflecting the man who lived here.

"Found it."

She leaned against his shoulder when the public records site booted up. He wrapped one long arm around her and the other around the computer.

"Twenty years ago, Geoffrey Hope was in graduate school, student-teaching at Emerson Middle School in San Rafael."

"Really? According to the magazine, he coaches—coached—basketball there." Linzee tipped her head to get a better look at the screen, and her hair brushed Ken's cheek. "He would've been twenty-three. By the way, where'd he get his degree?"

"Sonoma State."

"Was Sandy Milliken connected to Sonoma State somehow? Maybe had a sibling who attended?"

"She lived in San Rafael all her life until her marriage, according to her husband. But I like your idea. We'll have to find out if she ever visited Sonoma State for any reason."

"Yes."

"By the way, your hair smells good." He had apparently lost interest in the laptop, because he set it on the coffee table, turned, and drew her in to his massive chest. His eyes were so close, she could make out the tiny blue starbursts around the iris. Then the starbursts disappeared, and he lowered his lips to hers.

As he gathered her tighter against him, Linzee was only vaguely aware of her arms snaking around his thick neck, her senses overpowered by the determined pair of lips exploring hers. Her whole body went lax as the sensation went on and on.

"Mmm."

Startled, she opened her eyes to see Ken's a millimeter away and grinned. "That was nice."

"Linzee." He breathed her name in a voice she'd never heard him use before, a half-husky, half-crooning caress. His gaze bored into her, then he eased her back against the sofa. "You're quite the distraction, you know."

"I don't mean to be."

"I know, you can't help yourself. But I'm finding it difficult to focus on my job." He didn't look upset at all. In fact, he looked pleased, the sides of his eyes all crinkled.

Her grin matched his. "You want me to go home?"

The crinkles deepened. "No, no, not at all. Just the opposite. The problem is, I don't want you to leave."

She cocked her head at him to squelch the adrenaline jolting her heart. Was he implying what it sounded like? "Well, I ... um ..."

He released her with a sudden movement. "Sorry. I didn't mean to scare you." He kept his hand on her waist. "It's just that I think about you a lot."

"I think about you a lot, too."

His hand made circles on her back. "I don't want to rush you. I'm just happy you're letting me spend time with you."

"And you didn't even have to arrest me."

He laughed. "That's another thing I like about you. You're always so upbeat. I don't know how you do it with all you've been through."

She squinted at the intensity in his eyes. "My friends accuse me of being naïve because I tend to see the good in people before the bad."

"That's an admirable trait, actually."

"But it would make me a lousy cop."

He chuckled again, his hands still circling her back. She searched his face for a clue as to what he was thinking as his sharp gaze studied her. He gathered her into his embrace, and she rested her cheek against the rough fabric of his blue polo shirt.

"I should warn you," his voice rang through her head, "in case we have a future together, a cop's life isn't easy. Every day we risk our lives."

She was having a hard time wrapping her brain around the fact that Ken wanted a future with her. A year ago, if someone had produced a crystal ball and shown her this scene, she would say the crystal ball was insane.

A month ago, she'd never heard of Ken Tucker. And here she was, falling in *like*?

Um, no. She couldn't fall in *like* with him. Then she'd have to tell him about Nena.

But she didn't know how she could stop herself.

~~~~

"Dear Linzee and Meg," read the email from KNK-TV. "We would like to invite the two of you to be our guests next Friday on our Morning by The Bay show. We believe you have a compelling story to tell and would be honored if you accept our invitation. Please reply to this email at your earliest convenience, and I will be happy to send you the details. Sincerely, Kate Steiner, Executive Producer, KNK-TV."

Chapter Twenty-Two

Painting in the Wilderness – Megan Shaw Paulson
(4523 followers)

"Therefore, my beloved brethren, be ye steadfast, unmoveable, always abounding in the work of the Lord, forasmuch as ye know that your labour is not in vain in the Lord." I Corinthians 15:58

My dear friend Camille texted me this verse today. At first, my heart resisted. I'm so tired, God, I thought. Steadfast? Unmovable? More like exhausted. Wasted. Jon and I fall into bed each night, with romance the furthest thing on our minds much of the time. Neither of us dreamed marriage would be like this. But I am so thankful for him. He's the steadfast one. The unmoveable one. He's my rock of Gibralter in a fierce storm. Nothing ruffles his feathers. As I pondered this today, I realized God had sent Jon to me at just the right time. He knew my weakness and knew I needed someone beside me to help me live out this verse.

My darling Jon, you are a precious gift, and my love for you has only grown during this trial we've faced together. I'm SO grateful for your commitment to me and my family, your concern and care for Richie, who isn't even your biological son. What a gem you are. I am the luckiest, richest woman in the world.

And I'm also lucky to have so many new friends ... over 500 new followers at last count! Those of you who've taken the time to message me ... words can't express how you've buoyed my spirits. I pray bushels of blessings over each of you, each and every day.

Lifting up prayers for you,

Meg

~~~~

Linzee snuck a look at Ken when the words to Awesome God flashed on the screen behind the worship team. According to him, this was his first church service in forever, but all through the songs and sermon, his expression had betrayed nothing—neither interest nor boredom. Oh, if only he weren't so hard to read. Mom and Jon raised their clasped hands. A tremulous smile curved Mom's lips. How could she be so happy with all the awful stuff happening to them?

People had been giving Ken curious looks all service long. Across the aisle, Darrell, a young single guy who seemed to meet her eye more than she thought was normal, took his turn looking Ken up and down, then gave her a quick glance before sliding his eyes back to the front.

When the last note echoed, Ken took her hand. "How about lunch at Grandma's Diner?"

"Sure. Here's hoping the line isn't a mile long like the last time I was there." Despite the name, the place was popular with Millennials, perhaps because of the fat sandwiches served with oversized bowls of hot soup, like those found in grandmas' kitchens everywhere.

In Ken's passenger seat, she adjusted her denim skirt. "What did you think of the service?"

He took a right on Red Hill. "It was great. Good music, interesting sermon."

"I'm glad you liked it."

"I miss church. I used to go all the time."

"Why did you stop?"

"The job. I was always on call on Sundays. So I'd stay

home rather than disrupt my church experience by being called away. I always intended to find some other way to do church, but it didn't happen."

"But you're off most Sundays now, right?"

"I'm always on call, but I've come to realize I can't let that stop me from the important things. Like church." He slowed, signaling a right turn into Grandma's parking lot. "And you."

His quick smile arrowed straight to her heart. As if Cupid hadn't already shot a dozen of them into her aorta.

Only two people waited on the plush benches inside the door, and ten minutes later they ordered BLTs and clam chowder. She sat with her back to the restaurant. As long as she couldn't see anyone's stares, she could pretend her life was still normal.

She pulled her baseball cap lower.

Ken set his menu aside. "I've been wondering something."

"Is that good?"

He smiled. "I hope so. Remember when I saw you at the gun control rally?"

How could she forget the place where he'd first asked her out? She smiled and nodded.

"So, uh …" With jerky fingers, he wiped the corners of his mouth with a napkin. "Where do you stand on the Second Amendment?"

Not what she'd expected. "I can't believe you'd ask me that."

He tilted his head, gave her his best earnest look. "By now, I should be able to ask you anything. And I hope you'll do the same to me."

She took a sip of water. "I'd think my presence at that rally spoke louder than words."

"I gathered you're for gun control. But how far would you go? Would you abolish the Second Amendment?"

"In a perfect world, nobody would need guns."

"But we don't live in a perfect world."

"True." She looked up as the waitress plunked their food in front of them, and then picked up her soup spoon to tackle the chowder first. "I'm not sure I'd go so far as to totally abolish it. But I think there are plenty of people who've forfeited their right to gun ownership." Steam snaked from the creamy chowder; clams dotted its pristine surface. She dug into the creamy concoction. "I think *their* Second Amendment rights should be taken away and there should be a whole lot more restrictions. How about you?"

She blew on the steamy spoonful as Ken replied. "I'm pro-Second Amendment." When she opened her mouth to argue, he held up a hand. "Please, hear me out. As a cop, I see the need for self-defense. If we take away guns or make further restrictions, we keep guns out of the hands of good guys, the ones who can help protect our world from bad guys. There are only so many of us law enforcers. We can't stop all the bad guys. Which is why I appreciate the help."

His words rolled around in her mind, gathering momentum like stones rolling down a hill. "But most gun violence is due to bad guys shooting good guys, not vice-versa."

"In reality, eighty percent of gun homicides are gang-related. The Second Amendment isn't the problem. Gangs are."

"But if we make guns scarce, gangsters won't be able to obtain them."

"If we make guns scarce, the law-abiding citizens won't be able to defend themselves. Which reminds me. I've been meaning to ask you, have you ever considered a concealed carry permit?"

"Serious?" Linzee shuddered at the image of herself pointing a loaded gun. "What do I need to carry a gun for?"

"Say you come home and find an intruder. What are you going to do, say, 'Wait just a second while I open my locked cabinet and retrieve my gun and ammo'? No, you'll want to have it close enough to stop him. A gun in his face is an excellent deterrent."

"Unless he has a gun, too."

"I can take you target shooting."

"No way."

"Then what? Let him steal your belongings?" He plunked the spoon in the bowl and scooted forward. "Let him attack you?"

"I know karate and tae kwon do. Besides, I pray for protection every morning."

"Hmm." Ken finally shoved in a bite of chowder, chewed and swallowed. "Maybe God's protection comes with a barrel and bullets."

"Ha ha."

"Don't you ever wish you'd had a gun on you when you were kidnapped last year?"

Linzee blew on another steaming spoonful of chowder to give herself a moment to formulate a response. "It wouldn't have made a difference. First of all, I didn't realize I was being kidnapped. Secondly, I was drugged and completely helpless." She thrust the spoon into her mouth and bit into a potato cube. "Anyway, speaking of guns, now I have a loaded question for *you*."

His face relaxed in a grin. "What, funny girl?"

Reassured by his grin, she plunged in. "Where do you stand on gay rights? Specifically, same-sex marriage?"

He shook his head before she'd even finished. "Not in favor. Never have been, never will." He chomped a large bite from his BLT, determination in every plane of his face, then set the sandwich down and looked at her. "You?"

His eyes almost dared her to contradict. "I go back and forth," she said. "I used to be totally on board with it, but anymore, I'm not so sure."

Ken narrowed his eyes at her. "So you're ambivalent."

"Yes."

"It seems pretty clear-cut to me. Marriage is between a man and a woman. Right?"

"Traditionally, yes." She had to know now if he'd be receptive to her history before she fell too far. "But don't you think it's possible for people of the same sex to fall in love?"

"I suppose you could call it that. But it doesn't mean they should marry."

A sudden urge to play devil's advocate seized her.

"What would you do if someone you cared about was in a same-sex relationship?"

The blue in his eyes intensified, and he scrunched his face at her. "I can tell this is an important issue to you. Where is this coming from?"

She lifted her shoulders in a half-shrug, desperately floundering for a diversion. "Just seeing if my suspicions are correct."

"What suspicions?"

"That you're a Republican."

To her surprise, he laughed. "Guilty. And you're a Democrat, I'm pretty sure."

She nodded, the pressure of her secret evaporating like the steam from her coffee cup, bringing a relieved smile. "But I still like you." She forced a teasing note. "As long as you still like me."

Chapter Twenty-Three

Painting in the Wilderness – Megan Shaw Paulson
(5888 followers)

"But they that wait upon the Lord shall renew their strength; they shall mount up with wings as eagles; they shall run, and not be weary; and they shall walk, and not faint." Isaiah 40:31

Tomorrow my daughter and I will be guests on Morning by The Bay. Of course, we are beyond excited. We're going to be on television! I know many of you live in other states, even faraway countries like Australia, India, and The Philippines, and can't watch it locally. So I hope you'll watch it online, some way or another. I'd love to hear what you, my readers, thought about it.

Eternally grateful for the internet,

Meg

~~~~

Linzee had no idea TV studio lights were so bright. If she hadn't known she was on the set of Morning by The Bay, she'd never have recognized it from this side of the TV screen. Apparently, cameras must distort dimensions. Everything was set further apart than it looked from the outside. The potted palms, rather than sitting adjacent to her, sat about ten feet from where she sunk into the familiar leather sofa. The coffee table appeared three feet wider than the camera made it look, only accentuating the impression that a shrunken version of herself had been dumped into a blown-up story world.

Starting with the chauffeured studio car picking them up at seven a.m. at Mom's house, to the hair and makeup artists who transformed them, and here under the brightest lights she'd ever seen—it all felt like it was happening to someone else, and she was merely watching herself from afar. She watched herself jostle her knees, chew on her thumb. Then notice she was doing it and thrust her fists in her lap.

She shook away the surreal sensation and eyed the glossy-haired hostess, Antonia Whats-her-name, through squinted lids. On the adjacent leather sofa sat Sabrina Anderson's parents, Lester and Catherine. Beside her, Mom's thin hands clenched her kneecaps; her shoulders jutted forward, and her eyes were fastened tightly shut like a locked door as if she were desperately tossing silent prayers into the sky. Apparently, she'd forgotten Jon's pep talk over breakfast this morning—"You'll have all kinds of prayer cover. You're going to be just fine."

She tucked Mom's white-knuckled hand in hers. Mom cast her a smile as stiff and forced as her own. Thirty seconds till show time. The tip of Linzee's nose itched under the greasy foundation the makeup artist had slathered on her, and she longed to scratch at it. But Antonia had instructed them to keep their hands away from their faces. Instead, she fingered the tiny, already-perfectly-placed mike in front of her mouth. The itch persisted, and she feared it might pester her when they went live. No way could she last for fifteen minutes with an itchy nose. She poked at it with her fingernail, no doubt leaving a crescent-shaped dent. Not that anyone would notice.

Antonia squared her shoulders as the curtain opened, showing off an expanse of shiny white teeth in that TV-hostess smile of hers as the audience applauded. Linzee gaped at all the faces staring back at her. Well, maybe not at her, but certainly in her general direction. On the front row, a red-haired, model-like woman caught Linzee's eye and smiled before turning to the suited gentleman next to her.

"Good *morning*, San! Fran! *Cisco*!" Antonia's trademark greeting never varied from day to day, and Linzee had wondered more than once if the hostess lip-synced it. But apparently not. She'd practiced it so much, every inflection, every pause was now second nature. "Our guests today, as promised, were affected, up close and personal, by the recent shooting at Ignacio College." She made quick introductions, then told the audience, "Help me welcome them."

The applause jarred her already frayed nerves, sounding almost canned, unreal.

Antonia stepped to Linzee's side and gave the audience a brief rundown on their relationship to Richie. "Now what's so interesting about this mother-daughter duo is that they stand on opposite sides of the gun control issue, even as the national debate heats up. We're going to hear their thoughts on how the shooting has affected their daily lives, and let them each share their feelings on the Second Amendment." In one practiced movement, she sat in her leather hostess armchair and tucked her legs to the side. "Meg, let's start with you. All of a sudden, in the blink of an eye, your life was turned upside down. Tell us what your new normal looks like."

Linzee couldn't decide if Mom was nervous, or just picking her words carefully. Her halting delivery and frequent "ums" might suggest either. Linzee listened to the heartfelt narrative with calm detachment, but soon her mind wandered to Ken, wondering if he was watching. He'd promised he would. She was tempted to wink at the camera just for him but thought better of it.

Antonia skooched forward on the black leather. "Now recently you and your husband were interviewed by the Marin Mercury. You two did great, by the way. Anyway, in that interview, you both expressed sentiments that suggest you are in favor of gun ownership. Here's a small clip of that interview."

Linzee and Mom turned as one to the monitor on their left to watch the minute-long segment.

Davis was asking, "Has this tragedy caused you to give thought to current gun control laws?"

"We prefer not to discuss that," Jon replied. Beside him, Mom nodded.

"But surely you can see how stricter laws might have prevented this tragedy?"

"Not at all. The perp used a gun that belonged to another family member. Tell me, Mr. Davis. How would stricter laws have kept him from borrowing someone's gun?"

"The state house introduced new legislation to solve that very issue."

"You mean, the gun turn-in thing? It's a terrible idea."

"Even though it might prevent more tragedies like yours?"

"I don't believe it would. Has outlawing hard drugs prevented overdose deaths?"

A pause, then the film jumped forward to Meg saying, "I know God's got this."

In the ensuing silence, someone in the audience coughed. Antonia rustled on the chair.

"Now let's take a look at Linzee's interview with Ted Corban of the Chronicle, when she expressed the opposite sentiment as her mother, an interview that went viral on YouTube." She jabbed the remote, and Linzee's earnest face filled the screen.

"Someone's letting the crazies slip through the cracks," she heard herself say. "That guy shouldn't have had a gun."

"From what we understand, the shooter had access to an unregistered shotgun that belonged to his grandfather."

"Then the grandpa should've reported it stolen. Maybe we should prosecute him, huh?"

"Do you feel that holding gun owners responsible for reporting lost or stolen weapons is the answer?"

"I do. Believe it or not, gun owners are not required to.

But with all of us working together, we can turn this tragedy into a positive force for change."

The picture disappeared, the cameras seeming to scrutinize her and Mom, and suddenly she couldn't breathe. The audience held their breath as if each mind were thinking, Now what?

"Linzee," said Antonia, "wise words well stated."

"Thank you."

"Ever since the shooting, the gun control issue is once again the topic of the day. Tell us what else you're doing to spread your message."

"Probably not as much as I could," she admitted. "I've written to my state and federal representatives. I post my opinion on social media. I donate to groups that are working hard to get more restrictions in place." She shrugged. "I wish there were more I could do. But if everybody does their part, and doesn't just ignore it, gun violence can be a thing of the past. So write those letters. Get familiar with the laws in your state, and encourage your leaders to plug those loopholes."

"Thank you, Linzee. I admire your passion. Maybe you'll inspire someone watching today to take those steps."

Antonia turned to the Andersons. The dad glared back at his hostess, while the mom hadn't stopped dabbing her eyes since they arrived. "Mr. and Mrs. Anderson." A poignant pause later, Mrs. Anderson put down her tissue and grabbed her husband's hand. "I can't express how sorry I am." Sympathy shone from Antonia's eyes and puckered her mouth. "What a horrible thing, to lose your only daughter."

A low growl erupted from Mr. Anderson's throat. "Folks need to stop raising killers."

Antonia's brows rose. "What's that you say?"

"You heard me." His stare could shear those perfectly-shaped eyebrows right off her face. "Why're all these shooters suddenly showing up? Killers aren't born. They're made."

"I know you're hurting and grieving, but—"

"You think? You ever hear the expression, garbage in

garbage out? If you let kids fill their minds with violent video games and watch filth on their computer, what can you expect?"

"There's no evidence that—"

"Oh, bullcrap." The man bent far forward, closing the distance between him and Antonia. She shifted back a few inches, her eyes suddenly wary. "There's plenty of evidence, you just don't want to admit it. The porn industry and the video game companies have made sure the public stays blinded to the damage they're doing to young minds." He turned to the audience and raised his voice. "If you're a parent of boys, stop letting the internet raise your sons!"

A low murmur rippled through the blurred faces; the red-haired woman shook her head, her eyes wide with disbelief.

"Hey, wait a minute." Linzee couldn't stop herself. "I think most parents are like my mom. They do their best, but sometimes the kids make choices the parents don't agree with. It's hardly the parents' fault." She gestured at Mom. "My mom raised us by herself for several years while working outside the home. It wasn't possible for her to keep me from pulling crazy stunts. And I did my share. So did my brother. With all due respect, Mr. Anderson, I think you're way off base."

Mr. Anderson clamped his crossed arms tighter. "If you don't believe me, research it for yourself. It's no secret that video games and internet porn have exploded among young men. And nobody is there to stop them."

"The young man who shot your daughter," said Antonia, "was mentally ill. Video games had nothing to do with it."

"That's the other thing." Mr. Anderson uncrossed his arms long enough to point an aggressive finger at Antonia. "What's with the sudden increase in mental illness among teens? Why is depression and suicide so rampant? That's what I'm trying to say. Something is broken in our world. Gun violence is a symptom, not the cause."

"Where are you getting your statistics?"

He rattled off some website names unfamiliar to Linzee, but Mom was nodding along as though she recognized them. Movement in the back of the darkened auditorium shoved all else from Linzee's mind. Three indistinct figures sidled along the rear wall. One silhouette rose a few inches higher than the other two. The girth on another could hide two small adults. The third fell somewhere between the other two.

On the surface, there didn't appear to be anything sinister in their actions. She couldn't even tell their genders. So why did the hair rise on her suddenly cold arms?

She continued to watch them from the corner of her eye while tilting her head toward the interactions around her. How odd. The trio didn't seem to be looking for an exit. Or seats. Their heads were turned toward the set as they moved—no, snuck—along. There was something furtive about them.

"That's all for today, friends." Linzee jerked her head in time to see Antonia air-hugging and blowing kisses to the audience, which was disappearing chunk by chunk behind the closing curtain, and suddenly their escort—Frank?—stood before her, telling her they were free to leave now.

She leaned her weary head on Mom's arm as they traversed the busy hallway. People hurried here and there, some frowning at or talking into phones, others moving with purpose to unknown destinations. As she and Mom passed a recessed doorway, three bodies abruptly appeared in front of them, forming an impregnable wall.

"Excuse us." Mom steered herself and Linzee to the left. The tallest one synced with her. Linzee jerked back and took a closer look. From their physiques, this was the trio from earlier. The tall guy, younger than Linzee, had ringleader coming out every pore. A heavy-set African-American woman about Linzee's height hardened her expression when Linzee met her eyes. The third one, a solidly-built blond man, crossed his brawny, tattooed arms and planted his Nike-clad feet when she tried to go around him.

"Excuse us," she repeated. Why were these weirdos just standing there?

Every time she moved, so did they. "What do you want?" she exploded.

"Stop trying to take away our rights."

The tall dude looked at her with creepy pale eyes; a shiver shuddered through her. "You are bullying the wrong person. I don't have the clout to take away anyone's rights."

The woman made a lunge at her, hands extended toward Linzee's face. Those were some dangerous-looking metallic rings on those fingers.

Before she could even think of a scathing comeback, Linzee spun and ran.

Chapter Twenty-Four

Painting in the Wilderness – Megan Shaw Paulson (8301 followers)

"Fear not: for they that be with us are more than they that be with them." 2 Kings 6:16

A disturbing thing happened after the show today. Three thugs accosted my daughter and me. They accused us of trying to take away their rights. I gathered they were pro-gun advocates, who were apparently willing to do anything to push their agenda, including threatening us. Their threats seemed more aimed at Linzee than at me. She started to run, then at the last second, she grabbed my hand. My heart was pounding so hard, I was glued to the spot, and nearly stumbled when she yanked me away. We practically ran back toward the studio and found a security guard standing there, who then escorted us safely to the exit. We saw no sign of the three troublemakers, thank the Lord, but we gave the man their descriptions.

My daughter and I talked about it on the way home. Even though she and I see gun control and gun rights differently, we both agreed that people using violence or aggression to make their point only make their side look despicable. Most people believe their own viewpoint reflects the moral high ground. After all, why believe it if you don't consider it superior to all other views? So to use immoral means to push your own moral high ground seems an oxymoron to me.

Linzee thinks those three prove what is wrong with the Second Amendment movement. She asked me why I would side with people like that. So I explained that it has nothing to do with the adherents, but the issue itself. It's about freedom and self-defense. She, however, claims we've forfeited our freedom to bear arms because so many criminally-minded Americans have abused that freedom. Then I countered with the fact that the vast majority of guns are NOT used for criminal purposes. We went back and forth all the way home.

As you can imagine, it was quite the spirited discourse in the back seat of that chauffeured car. The driver kept glancing back at us through the glass panel as though he saw the smoke rising and was considering if he would need to stop and intervene. I love my daughter dearly. She is one of the kindest, most thoughtful daughters a mom could ever wish for. However, she sees the world through hot pink glasses, and I see it through a muted shade of aquamarine. We do our best to keep our disagreements civil, yet whenever we try to switch glasses, suddenly we can no longer see.

I console myself with the knowledge that this is very common in families. Am I right? It was true in my family of origin, and it's true again for this one too.

Keeping it civil,

Meg

~~~~

Still no answer from Candy. Meg let the phone call go to voicemail. "Hi Candy," she said to the recording. "Camille and I are leaving in a few to come pick you up."

After stuffing the phone in her bag, Meg placed three wrapped sandwiches in a wicker basket and closed the lid, tucked the basket under her arm, then picked up a shiny tin plate containing a dozen muffins. "Honey, I'm leaving now."

Jon intercepted her at the front door. "Here, hand me one of those before you spill something." He took the basket from under her arm and accompanied her out the door.

"You're a gem."

On the driveway, he bent down for a kiss. "Have fun with your girlfriends and forget your troubles for a few hours. Richie will be in good hands."

He stowed the basket in the back seat of Camille's idling Toyota, and Meg climbed in front, clutching the plate on her lap.

Camille's mouth curved into a welcoming smile. "Hey, Superstar! You look great on TV."

"Did I look as nervous as I felt?"

"Pfft. Nervous, my foot." She pointed at the tray Meg held. "Whatcha got there?"

"I made extra muffins for Candy."

"Oh, right, your famous cinnamon coffee cake muffins. They look delicious. What kind of glaze is that?"

"Streusel with lemon."

"Yum yum." She chuckled. "My tummy's growling already. Found the route to Candy's place?"

"I did." Meg showed her the map app, and Camille backed to the street. "She lives off Francis Drake Blvd. in Lagunitas. She said she knows the perfect picnic spot in the state park."

As Camille drove, she sang along to Mercy Me in her rich, Carly Simon contralto. "I can only imagine ..." After two songs, Meg shook her head. "I'd sing with you, but you don't want to hear me croak."

The wooded Marin Hills, as dense with firs and laurels as they were sparse with people, loomed larger and higher as they proceeded west on Sir Francis Drake. They were entering the rural outreaches of the county, where houses hid in forested shadows and perched on larkspur-dotted hillsides and stayed at arms' length from their neighbors.

A sudden shiver surprised Meg. "I can totally see Candy living out here."

"How so? From what you've told me about her, she doesn't sound like your typical carefree liberal. She sounds like a basket case."

"Carefree, no. Liberal? I have no idea. Actually, I see God's hand in my crossing paths with her. It's like He's reminding me I'm not the only one with agonizing circumstances. We're both grieving for a son, and somehow we help ease each other's sorrow."

Camille nodded. "God's timing is right on."

"I seem to be less inclined to brood on Richie's situation, which is healthy."

"But you're brooding more on hers, which isn't."

Meg gaped at the huge hot tub on someone's deck. Much larger than her own. "I need to keep those arrow prayers going whenever God brings her to my mind."

"A good faith-strengthening exercise."

"Indeed."

The phone chirped. "Turn left—fifty feet."

Camille steered left from the boulevard onto a narrow wood bridge spanning San Geronimo Creek, then a sharp right. Swaying tree branches cast dappled shadows over the skinny street and obscured the sun, forcing another shiver out of Meg. She clutched the tin plate tighter. What would they do if they encountered an oncoming car? Camille's little compact nearly spanned the breadth of the crooked lane.

The road made a gentle curve beside a steep rise where a house perched, its wraparound deck almost directly above them. Camille glanced over. "How much further?"

Meg peered at the map. "Stay right at the Y, then another eighth of a mile."

The road cut through the woods for as far as Meg could see. To the right, the land descended at a sharp forty-five-degree angle. Twenty feet below them, another house appeared, this one sadder and shabbier than the showpiece they'd passed, piles of debris scattered about its yard.

At the Y, more of the same. Meg rolled her window down. No birds chirped, no humans appeared. The slowly-waving tree branches seemed to beckon them forward.

"Not much further." Meg's voice creaked, and she cleared her throat. The sound echoed off the car roof. "It's to the left."

What would they find at Candy's house? Since Candy lived alone now in this isolated place, Meg couldn't help wondering if she had much human companionship during the day. No wonder she battled depression.

"Here it is." Around one more bend, a cottage that must have once been as green as the swaying firs sprang into view. Set fifty feet up a grassy slope, its hue had softened to a ghost of its original self, like an aging garment washed too frequently. Shamrock-green moss formed such a thick blanket on its roof, it seemed to become one with the high cliff behind it. A sorry-looking shed tilted among some graceful laurel trees, a sliver of sun burnishing the rusty tin roof to a nearly fluorescent orange.

A few patches of California poppies bloomed cheerfully on the front lawn, oblivious to the scraggy grass surrounding them. Camille pulled into the gravel drive behind Candy's ancient Ford Explorer, and they got out.

Meg, balancing the muffin plate on one forearm, winced at the sharp pebbles poking into the thin soles of her shoes as they strode slowly up the cracked, potholed walkway. At the front door, Meg, seeing no doorbell, gave two sharp raps.

She heard nothing but their breathing for ten seconds. She knocked again.

Expecting the scratched wooden door to spring open any second, she stood very still.

Again, nothing but trees whispering to the sky in the waiting quiet.

"Candy?"

Camille stepped around an empty terra-cotta planter to

the front window and ventured a peek. "Sure we've got the right house?"

Meg checked the number above the door. "Yes, 440. And that's her van in the drive."

Camille moved to a smaller window, cupping her hands on the glass to peer inside.

"Do you see her?"

Camille shook her head, her hands still propped on the pane.

"Do you hear her dog?"

"Nope. Maybe you need to text or call her."

Meg lowered herself and the muffins to a cracked vinyl chair and took out her phone. "I'll call her." Two rings became four. Then eight. Somewhere overhead, bird wings rustled through the laurel branches superimposed over the pale blue sky.

Camille's face tightened with each ring. "I'm too worried to stand out here. Something's wrong."

Meg dropped her phone into her bag, stood, and cocked one ear toward the door. "No answer."

"I'm going in." Camille elbowed Meg aside and jostled the doorknob. "It's unlocked. Come on."

Meg shoved away her hesitance. Holey socks, they'd been knocking for several minutes. She forced her legs over the threshold and into the shabby living room.

Smells of fresh coffee, old mildew, and sorrow hung heavy in the air. A seventies-style plaid sofa took up one wall, contrasting with the big-screen TV opposite broadcasting a basketball game.

"Candy?" Camille's voice boomed over the TV clamor.

To the right, Meg spied the kitchen, its round Formica table scattered with cheap plastic dishes. But no Candy. Stepping through a pink archway, she peered deeper into the kitchen, finally depositing the muffins on the only cleared spot she could find, next to the oven.

Back in the living room, Meg opened her mouth to speak,

but Camille had disappeared. Meg stood, uncertain what to do next, already feeling like an intruder. An open book on the scratched coffee table caught her eye, its pages plastered with mug shots. A yearbook. She bent to take a closer look. Terra Vista High School, 1995-1996, said the heading.

A scream startled her, and she rushed toward the sound coming from the rear of the house. Through an open door, she saw Camille's panicked face.

"Meg, call 911."

Heart racing, she followed her friend's pointing finger and doubled over.

Candy lay in a heap on the worn carpet, face toward the ceiling, mouth open in a silent scream.

Chapter Twenty-Five

Meg grabbed the door handle as Camille, following the speeding ambulance to Kaiser Hospital, cursed at the slow Nissan from Nevada blocking her progress to San Rafael. She clapped one hand over her mouth as she glanced at Meg. "Oops, sorry."

Meg waved away her apology, too worried about Candy to care about expletives. She felt like hurling a few herself. "She'd better be okay. We did everything the 911 operator told us to do."

"Just wish the paramedics had gotten there a little sooner." Camille braked again with a jerk as the Nissan slowed. "The whole time I was so scared she'd be gone by the time they got there."

"The timing is just so odd. Why would she OD on pills when she knew we'd be there any minute?"

Camille pinched her lips together. "I have a hunch it was deliberate."

"But why?"

Her friend shrugged. "Beats me." She cast another loaded glance at Meg. "It's like she wanted us to find her. A bid for attention, maybe?"

Meg shook her head, then called Jon to update him. He promised to pray.

After fifteen white-knuckled minutes, Camille swerved into the Kaiser lot. They rushed through the emergency entrance and asked the young brunette behind the reception window about Candy.

The receptionist gave a hurried nod. "She just arrived in the ambulance. Are either of you next of kin?"

Meg shook her head. "Close friends."

"You'll have to wait in the lobby, then." She gestured to the seats behind Meg. "Only authorized family members are allowed back there." She thrust a thumb over her shoulder. Meg and Camille turned to the chairs.

"Oh wait a minute." Ms. Brunette, whose name badge identified her as Kaycee, waved them back. "Since you're close friends with the patient, do you happen to know a family member we could talk to?"

"I know she has a sister," Meg said. "But I don't know her name, or where she lives."

Camille shrugged, and the receptionist gave a skeptical lift of the eyebrows as if to say, what kind of close friend doesn't even know their friends' families? Meg wilted, berating herself for not thinking to question Candy about her immediate family. Knowing her friend's instability, Meg should have been prepared for this.

They found chairs in the far corner of the crowded lobby. A few magazines lay around, and Meg thumbed through them. Most of them dated from last year. A shiny new issue of USA Today caught her eye, and she picked it up. No headlines about the shootings stared her in the face. New crises — bombings and accidents and people gone missing — had crowded out her family's tragedy, and the world had moved on, which both relieved and saddened her. Sure, she didn't miss the media scrutiny. Yet it seemed the nation had forgotten about poor Richie lying alone in his netherworld.

Every fifteen or so minutes, she checked with Kaycee on Candy's condition, with no results. After the third time, she finally got some news. "The patient is stabilized." Kaycee, digging through a file cabinet, tossed the words over her shoulder.

"She's going to be okay?"

"Apparently so. We found her sister in Sacramento, and she should be here within the hour."

Almost an hour had elapsed by the time the sliding doors whooshed open, and a tall woman in a navy blue sweater dress strode through, straight to the front desk. "Hi, I'm Bonnie, Candy Burton's sister. How is she?" she asked, her words as brisk as her stride.

Meg went to the woman's side while Kaycee updated her. Both sisters possessed the same fine gold-brown hair; otherwise, the resemblance to Candy diminished as Meg drew closer. Bonnie's healthy plumpness contrasted with Candy's gaunt physique. Whereas Candy skittered like a spooked cat through life, her sister sauntered like a lioness, regal head held high.

Meg laid a hand on Bonnie's arm. "Hi, I'm Meg. My friend and I found her."

Bonnie whirled. "You ... you found her?"

"Yes." Meg dropped her voice. "We'd just gotten to her house to take her picnicking with us, but she didn't answer the door. So we went in, and ... and ..." She paused and swiped at her eyes. "She had collapsed on the floor."

Creases etched across Bonnie's forehead, around her eyes. She clutched Meg's forearm with both hands. "Thank you, thank you for doing that. You might have saved her life."

Meg shook her head. "I've been worried about her for a while."

"You and me both."

Meg squeezed her fingers until they hurt. "I attempted art therapy with her, but it didn't really seem to do any good. But then, I'd be grieving too if I lost my son that way. In fact—"

"Bonnie McDougall?"

A nurse beckoned at the door, and Meg quickly thrust her business card at Bonnie. "Call me with an update, will you please?"

Bonnie nodded, took the card, and disappeared behind the swinging double door.

~~~~

"Hi, Bonnie. Thanks for getting back to me." Meg paced her yellow-checked kitchen floor and glanced out the window at the palm tree swaying in the morning breeze. "How's Candy doing?"

"Her doctor admitted her to the psych ward, and they're going to adjust her meds. I'm at her house now, tidying things up and packing a bag for her."

"Sounds like she'll get the care she needs. What a relief. By the way, I left a tin of muffins there. I'll need the plate back. It was a wedding gift."

"Do you want to come pick it up? Then we can chat in more detail."

"Sure. Give me twenty to thirty minutes."

She made it to Candy's place in twenty-five. The sun gleamed into Candy's yard, transforming it into a shining emerald. She found Bonnie in the bedroom, near the spot on the frayed carpet where she'd found Candy. Had it really been twenty-four hours ago? The hours since had both dragged and whizzed by, as though a malfunctioning clock was dictating the pace.

"Hi, I'm here. Can I help?"

Bonnie looked up from where she knelt next to an ancient chest of drawers. "No, I'm just about done here. I stored the muffins in the freezer, and your tin is waiting for you in the kitchen."

"Thanks. You can have a muffin if you'd like. They're kind of my specialty."

Bonnie's face lit. "Okay, if you're sure. They did look scrumptious."

Luckily the muffins hadn't frozen yet. Bonnie found two clean plates and warmed two muffins in the microwave. They settled themselves on the living room sofa and dug into the warm, butter-slathered treats.

Meg picked up a plush tie-dyed pillow. "How cute."

"Isn't it? Candy made that. She loves to sew."

"I didn't know that." She tucked the pillow behind her back. Another tie-dyed pillow graced a cracked vinyl armchair. Paisley sleeves covered the chair's wooden arms.

"Does she buy the fabric already tie-dyed?"

"No, she designs the pattern herself. She also sews peasant skirts and dresses and sells them at outdoor markets."

"Very cool. I'd like to see more of her handiwork sometime." The tall laurels outside Candy's living room window blocked the sun, but the few artsy splashes of whimsy scattered about drew her eye — tiny beams of cheer in the otherwise barren room. Apparently, Candy had tried hard to bring her home to life on a slim budget.

Meg glanced around at the bare walls, the nonexistent shelves, for any family photos. Surely Candy had photos of her son somewhere. Then her attention was caught by the open yearbook on the coffee table.

Meg bit into a spicy morsel, savoring the hint of cinnamon and nutmeg. "When I was here yesterday, this yearbook was open, just like this. As though she'd been looking at it just before she … she …"

"Took the pills? It's okay, you can say it."

"Yes. But why did she? And it also seems odd that she did it when she knew we were on our way to pick her up. Don't you think?"

Bonnie cocked her head to the side, eyeing the yearbook as though it held answers. "Yes, I agree. But I've never understood why my sister makes the choices she does."

Meg picked up the yearbook. What had Candy seen to send her over the edge? She scanned the air-brushed color photos of smiling kids, poker-faced kids, and kids making faces at the camera.

"This would have been her senior year." She scanned the column of names — Miller, Mitchell, Mohammed, Monteith, Moran. "Where is Candy's photo?"

She didn't hear Bonnie's reply. A photo of Sandy Martin, almost unnoticeable in the top right corner, froze her in place. "Sandy Martin. That's who she was looking at." Meg set the yearbook on her lap and shifted to Bonnie, whose head tilted closer. "When I first met Candy, it was just after the shooting. She told me she and Sandy had been close in high school, and she was very distraught over her friend's murder. So maybe after the trauma of losing her son, the news of her friend finally broke her, and the grief became unbearable." Meg thumbed through pages and pages of faces in various stages of smiling. "I remember thinking she seemed way more upset than I would be in the same circumstance."

"I vaguely remember Sandy."

"Does it seem in character for Candy to take a friend's death so hard? Especially one she hadn't seen for a long time?"

Bonnie placed a piece of muffin carefully on her tongue, her forehead scrunched in thought. "She's gotten worse over the years. Once I left for college, I didn't see much of her." She finished the muffin and set the plate down. "In the last few years, she's become more and more unstable."

Meg flipped more pages, skipping through the sports and school clubs, then slowed when she got to the teachers. "I bet a lot of my teachers were still there in '96." She scooted closer to show Bonnie. "There's Ms. Vecchio. I had her for sophomore PE. And Mr. Thomas for history senior year. When did you graduate?"

"In '94. I was two years ahead of Candy. And you?"

"1990. So we just missed each other." The more she flipped pages, the more familiar faces she saw. "They even have a section for student teachers ... Holey socks."

Her breath hitched at the photo staring up at her.

"What?" Bonnie's hair brushed Meg's arm as she leaned closer.

"Geoffrey Hope." Meg jabbed the page. "The college instructor who was shot. He was a student teacher at Terra Vista in 1996. So that's the connection."

"What connection?"

"Between him and Sandy Milliken. According to the cop in charge of the investigation, Coby Jarrett was adopted, and

Sandy Martin was his biological mother." The story Linzee had told her poured out. "The shooting was not random, as everyone thought at first. He deliberately set out to kill both sets of parents." She stifled a shudder. "The ones who conceived him, and the ones who raised him."

Chapter Twenty-Six

Linzee rested her head on Ken's chest, which must be as broad as a grizzly bear's. The words he spoke vibrated through his rib cage into her ear. "Fine, I'll notify them by phone." Ken let out an exasperated sigh, but Linzee didn't care. Even though she couldn't tell him how to do his job, she most certainly could offer her opinion.

The morning sun reflected off Lagoon Park's pond, warming her chilled hands and the fuzzy blanket underneath her. The sprinklers shot geysers over the lake's surface. She propped herself up just enough to take a swig of Vitamin Water. "Just put yourself in Mr. and Mrs. Martin's shoes, Ken. Your daughter's been murdered, then some cop you don't even know tells you the shooter is your biological grandson. This is going to take mega-sensitivity on your part."

"I know, I know. It's one of the worst parts of the job—bearing bad news." He drummed his fingers on her back and gave her a penetrating look. "This calls for a woman's touch, don't you think? Maybe Mary would be better for the job."

"Yeah, her bedside manner beats yours by a mile." She chuckled to show him she was only kidding. Ken didn't let his soft side show often, but every now and then it leaked out. Like now.

"Or ..." She scrunched her face at him.

"Or what?"

"You could not tell them. What would it hurt?"

"It would hurt the department's credibility. As long as everyone thinks it was a random shooting, they'll stay fearful. But if we can prove target and motivation, the incident loses its power to frighten the public."

"Right, right, I get it."

"Chief wants us to wrap this up and make a public statement by next week. The good folks of San Rafael have been waiting three weeks for answers. That's why we need to inform Mrs. Milliken's parents ASAP who Coby Jarrett really was."

"And her husband, too, I take it?"

"Of course. But I feel bad for him. It will probably blindside him."

~~~~

Meg set the yearbook back on the table and shot to her feet. Words tumbled from her mouth as quickly as her pacing feet gobbled up the space between sofa and TV. "So Sandy had an affair with student teacher Geoffrey Hope, apparently while still in high school. She put her baby up for adoption and went her merry way, later marrying and having a couple more kids." Her flip-flops slapped the floor with each step. Bonnie listened, her eyes agleam with interest. "The baby also grew up and developed serious mental problems. Knowing he'd been adopted, he somehow discovered his mother's name and set out to locate her—"

"How do you know all this?"

"Detective Tucker has been keeping us apprised. But there's one thing about this I don't get."

"What's that?"

"Sandy obviously graduated. All the seniors are wearing their graduation caps, including her. So she didn't drop out like a lot of pregnant girls do. How did she go for nine months without anyone knowing who the father was?"

"Someone had to have known."

"If word ever got out, he'd have a statutory rape conviction in his background." She stopped and dug out her phone. "I'm going to text my daughter about this, and have her ask Ken if he can check on that."

Her fingers flew over the tiny keyboard. *Mr. Hope was a student teacher at Sandy Martin's high school her senior year. Can Ken check his background for statutory rape?*

She finished the text and returned the phone to her bag. "But I'm almost sure he won't find anything. If Mr. Hope had such an incident in his history, he'd never teach again."

She flopped to the sofa and leaned back, crossing her arms at the same moment her phone beeped. *Oh Mom, you rock!* said Linzee's text. *How did you find that out?*

Will explain it all later.

She shifted back to Bonnie. "Now, I want to know about Candy's son. She wouldn't tell me any details. How long ago did it happen?"

"When she lost him?"

Meg nodded.

"Only a couple months ago, from what I understand. She and Jared's father had been battling for months. He claimed she was an unfit parent, which was total rubbish. She loved that boy. Losing him was the final blow."

Something in Bonnie's statement struck her as odd, but she couldn't think what. Grasping for a reply, she scanned the room. "I didn't see any photos of him on her Facebook page. Or here. Where are her photos?"

Bonnie stood. "I know exactly where they are. Excuse me a minute." She left the room, returning in minutes with an old brown photo album. She sat next to Meg and opened it. A cute brown-haired boy grinned up at her, and Meg tracked his progress from exuberant toddlerhood through middle school and beyond, his expression growing increasingly hard with each passing year.

Suddenly she knew what she'd wanted to ask. "What did you say her son's name was?"

"Jared Michael Burton."

"Oh. That's why she called him Mikey."

"Really? I've never heard her refer to him that way."

"She said it was his childhood nickname."

"Hmm." Bonnie closed the album and set it atop the yearbook. "But like I said, I haven't seen her or Jared much over the years. I've been in Sacramento for almost twenty years."

"It must have hit you and the rest of the family hard."

Bonnie tilted her head, an odd expression that Meg couldn't identify darkening her eyes. But she merely nodded and got to her feet. "I need to get to the hospital now. My sister is waiting for her stuff."

"Sure, we should go now." Meg also stood, pulling her purse's strap over her shoulder. "Give Candy a hug for me, and tell her I said don't ever scare us like that again."

Chapter Twenty-Seven

Painting in the Wilderness – Megan Shaw Paulson
(8787 followers)

"Let no corrupt communication proceed out of your mouth, but that which is good to the use of edifying, that it may minister grace unto the hearers."
Ephesians 4:29

Dear Friends – This is going to be a hard post to write. I was dismayed – no, outraged – by how the comments deteriorated into a free-for-all after my last post. It seems there's no middle ground when it comes to gun control vs. Second Amendment. Many of you feel strongly, passionately, about your position. But a few of you resorted to insults and name-calling on my blog, and that was not okay. I finally had to close the comments, delete the most combative of them, and block the perpetrators. I don't mind disagreements and civil discussions. But I have to draw the line at belligerence on my page.

The offenders are using the same M.O. as the three assailants at the TV studio. I wish I could ask them the following questions: When was the last time you changed your position just because someone insulted you for it? Can you name anyone you've verbally abused whose mind you have changed? Do you know why you can't think of anyone? Because it doesn't work that way.

People, please be kind and respectful when you comment.

Ministering grace,

Meg

~~~~

A rare afternoon rainstorm pounded its fury on Richie's hospital room window, but even the noisy torrent didn't wake him. Rain pitter-pattered on the roof, dripped from the eaves, and gushed through the drainpipe. Meg reached for the light switch, and artificial brightness awakened the room. Yet his eyes stayed closed.

On the other side of his bed, Kassidy sobbed as she crooned to him. "Please, baby, wake up. Please, please ..."

Would Kassidy's voice awaken something deep inside his frozen brain, like before? Meg didn't dare move or breathe as Kassidy kept pleading, begging, his brain to revive.

For countless long minutes, nothing happened. His chest rose and fell with his steady breathing, eyelids flickering occasionally as they did on and off throughout the day, but never fully opening.

When Meg's phone beeped, she jumped as though it had sent an electrical bolt through her. A text from Linzee lit up the screen. *No rape conviction in Mr. Hope's background check. All squeaky clean. Got some news ... can we come over?*

She stared at Richie's motionless eyes as she pondered what Linzee's news could possibly be. Good news, or bad? She peered again at the text as though clues hid there. Probably not an engagement—far too soon. So they must have an update on the case. Hopefully good news. Something to make them forget the gloomy rain streaking the windows. Maybe today they'd all finally reach closure, and they could move on with life.

Yes, I'm at the hospital.

Kassidy broke into a jagged rendition of "My Boo," her voice wavering on the pitches as tears rolled down her face. She stopped for a brief moment, meeting Meg's eyes. "He used to call me his Boo. This was our song."

Kassidy resumed her wobbly serenade which brought tears to Meg's eyes too. But wait, what was that?

Groans emitted from Richie's mouth. Meg gripped the edge of the mattress, every nerve standing at attention.

"Hunnnn." His head jerked back and forth, furrows erupting on his forehead, eyeballs moving rapidly under his shut-tight lids. "Hmmnnn."

She and Kassidy gasped almost in unison. Richie flailed his head harder, and Meg grasped it between her hands. "Richie. Can you hear me?"

His eyes flew open. Blue orbs looked directly at Meg. "Mmum?" he croaked out.

"Richie!"

Kassidy leaped nearly on top of him and wrapped her tiny arms around his neck. "Richie! You're awake!"

"He's finally awake?" They whirled to Linzee, who leaned on the door frame, her arched brows almost hidden beneath a shock of hair.

In seconds, his bed was surrounded. Richie glanced at Linzee on his right, squinted at Ken next to her, then focused on Kassidy for several seconds. "Bay ... bay?"

Kassidy's face lit with ethereal joy, and she bounced on her heels like an excited five-year-old. "Baby! I knew you'd wake up! I knew it." She lowered her lips to his forehead and smacked a kiss on the furrows. Meg's smile stretched so far, her facial muscles protested. With each shift of his gaze on their faces, she thought she saw recognition flash in his eyes. She rested in the thought that if he knew them, then the old Richie was not far behind.

"Mom? Mom!" Linzee's voice shook her back to reality. "Maybe you should call his nurse? And Dad?"

"Oh! Yes. And Jon. He's at work."

Meg punched the call button, then stepped away to call Jon, the joyful background voices blending with the whisper of gentle rain, curling into her head, flooding her heart. Returning to her son, she smiled down at him and patted his cheek as he struggled to speak. All he could manage were stammers and groans, making Meg wonder how extensive his brain damage was. He was probably facing months of therapy.

As she texted the news to her husband and her ex, Richie kept trying to lift his head, with Kassidy playing the squealing cheerleader role. After he made several unsuccessful attempts, he flung off the blankets, exposing his bare chest half-covered by a striped hospital gown. The tubes in his arms and chest stretched as he shouted, punctuating each wail with a flailing arm.

"No, young man." A stocky nurse rushed in and grabbed his arms. "You'll disconnect something! Don't try to remove anything."

The minutes rushed by—everyone was talking at once. Meg and the nurse struggled to keep Richie from yanking out his IV. His wild, staring eyes flipped from face to face as though seeking an anchor, or a place to rest.

Phillippe rushed in, followed closely by an intern, all brisk business, who reached Richie's side in seconds.

"Okay, young man. You can wake up now."

Chuckles followed in a sudden release of tension. Meg gladly turned the reins over to the pros. Expecting Jon any second, she avoided Phillippe's intent look and turned her focus back to Richie. This corpse-like figure thrashing beneath Cecily's capable hands didn't look or sound like her Richie. Except for his height. His six-foot-three frame hadn't shrunk a centimeter. He still sprawled the entire length of the bed. Or he would if he would only lay still.

"Cecily, why is he so freaked out?" Linzee whispered.

Her son's mangled words and agitated shouts drowned out the nurse's reply and tore at her heart. She blinked back tears. Kassidy's tears joined hers, and Meg watched her eyes, so full of hope for a happy ending, and shook her head. Kassidy might as well have soaked in all the hope in the universe. Because there wasn't any left for Meg.

Jon rushed in, and it was as though someone had thrown her a lifeline. In seconds, he had her in his embrace. "How's he doing?" he asked as she sobbed on his shoulder.

"Oh Jon," she sniffed. "Looks like Cecily's calmed him down now, but just before you got here, he was so disoriented. Yelling, trying to get out of bed, yanking on his tubes." They walked hand-in-hand to the bedside, where Cecily was taking his vitals and squeezed in next to Phillippe and Linzee. "Richie? Can you speak?"

"Nnnn," he croaked out, bewildered creases between his eyebrows. His eyes latched onto hers, and the turbulence in his eyes subsided, leaving them as clear and untroubled as a summer sky. "Mmmum?"

She clasped his hand tight. "I'm so glad you've come back to us. You're gonna be okay, hon. You wouldn't believe how many people have been praying for this day." She turned to Cecily, whose expression filled Meg with another bout of throbbing fear. "Cecily? What is it?"

The nurse looked up briefly, then back to the patient, her reply so low Meg barely heard her over Ken and Linzee's conversation. "Some residual brain damage," she muttered. "He'll need lots of therapy over the next year, and likely longer."

~~~~

Linzee clasped Ken's hand as they left the hospital. "We didn't get a chance to tell her our bizarre news."

"Yeah, too much drama going on."

Linzee swung their joined hands. "The good kind of drama."

"Indeed. I'm really happy for your family. When things have calmed down, we'll give them the update." He stopped next to his car and turned her to face him. "I have an hour before I have to be at the station. How about we run and get some tacos at El Ranchito and eat them in the park?"

"Sounds epic."

They got in and reached the crowded Mexican restaurant

in five minutes. In the drive-thru, it seemed that each of the three cars in front of them spent precisely five excruciating minutes placing their order and getting their food. Ken was mumbling something about missing out on their picnic when Linzee caught a glimpse of a nondescript red car at the gas station next door.

It sure looked a lot like Nena's 2005 Honda Civic. Faded paint job. UCLA decal in the rear window. The familiar swirly A on the bumper—Nena proclaiming her love for the Oakland As, naturally.

Linzee craned her neck to catch a glimpse of the driver. The gas nozzle was attached to the car, but no driver. Nena must be inside paying.

A sudden urge to see her ex again nearly sent her reeling. How fun if they could reminisce about the happy times they'd had. Did Nena even look the same after all this time? And what was she doing here in San Rafael? As far as Linzee knew, Nena still lived and worked in Mill Valley.

"Earth to Linzee."

She whirled to see Ken watching her, his mouth twisted in amusement.

"I asked you, what do you want?" He peered around her as if to see what had caught her attention.

She flipped her hair back with shaky hands. "Uh, how about a Mongo Taco? With. And a diet Sprite."

"You got it."

As Ken replied to the disembodied voice coming through the speaker, she returned her scrutiny to the gas station, expecting any second now to see Nena's boyish stride. The front door swung open, and here she came. Linzee squinted. Nena had cropped her black, angular hair even shorter, all spikes and severe edges. She wore one of her black tees with a rainbow stenciled across the front.

Nena glanced over. And met Linzee's eyes. A shocked expression flashed across her face, then disappeared just as quickly, as though she'd slipped on her poker-face mask.

And then Nena was heading her way, her eyes riveted on Linzee, and Linzee wished she could duck and hide. Instead, she lurched from the car and faced Nena on trembling legs. She couldn't let Ken hear their conversation.

"Nena! What are you doing here?"

Nena stopped and tilted her head at Linzee, studying her for a brief moment. "Heard you're into guys now." Still the same raspy, abrupt speech.

"I heard you're happy in your new relationship."

Nena nodded slowly and leaned in for a better look at Ken. "You didn't go for just any guy, did ya? You chose a macho cop."

"I sure did." Despite her best effort to keep the irritation out of her tone, it leaked out anyway. "A kind, good-looking macho cop." Who was probably watching them right now, his kind eyes narrowed in curiosity, his handsome face scrunched with inquiry.

Nena shot her a look. "Did you tell 'im about you and me?"

"No."

"Why? You ashamed of us?"

"Nena. We are not having this conversation."

"Yes, we are. Why can't you just tell 'im?"

"I have my reasons, and they're none of your business."

"Then maybe I should." She made a move toward the car, and Linzee stepped in front of her, blocking Nena's way.

"Back off. You don't get to decide what I should or should not tell him." She pulled in a ragged, steadying breath. "I think you'd better go now."

"Ha."

She remembered the way Nena's eyes snapped black sparks whenever she was ticked. She remembered a lot of things. Sudden memories flooded her mind and left her breathless. This was the person she'd loved, had promised to spend her life with. Something that big couldn't be forgotten so easily.

"Look, he's summoning you. Better go, before he drags you back into the car by your hair."

"Oh, shut up." Linzee clenched her fists to keep from slapping her ex, and the lovey-dovey feelings vanished. She spun, grabbed the door handle, and hopped back inside, trying to still her breathing. She didn't look at Ken but felt his eyes boring into Nena's retreating figure.

"Who was that?"

"An old friend."

"Really? I got the feeling she was no friend of yours."

She stared at the vanity license plate on the rear bumper ahead. B A LERT. "What made you think so?"

"You both seemed angry. I heard a little yelling."

B A LERT moved ahead one spot. Ken let off the brake, and the car rolled forward.

Her heart slowed its racing. "Okay, then. My former roommate. We didn't part on positive terms."

"I could tell." From the corner of her eye, she saw him glance over. "Is she the same roommate that figured out who kidnapped you?"

"Yes."

"And you two are mad at each other? Rather surprising. Did she shaft you?"

"No."

"Need to talk about it?"

"No."

He shrugged, then moved into the vacated spot at the pickup window and grabbed the two bags the server held out, then handed Linzee two dew-covered drinks.

"Thanks."

His Toyota hummed out of the lot as Linzee's heart hummed with relief.

Close one.

Maybe Ken didn't have to ever know that sordid bit of her history. To paraphrase an old adage, what he didn't know wouldn't hurt him.

Chapter Twenty-Eight

Meg scarcely left Richie's side. Two days became three, then four, until the days blended together in her mind, pouring in a continuous stream like syrup. Each day, she tracked his progress on Facebook.

Today he sat up.

Today he was able to eat solid food.

Today he walked if you could call it that. Hobbled, more like. Hey, I'll take any small victory. PTL.

She'd done the same thing when he was a baby, carefully recording each precious milestone; when he sat up, ate his first solid food, took his first toddling step. If only her emotions could march in sync with each victory as they did eighteen years ago. But eighteen years ago, each victory came with joy. Here, each small victory only underlined struggle, and no one yet knew when it would reach his limits.

Meanwhile, Jon went to work each morning as before; dropped by to check on Richie, sometimes carried on a one-sided conversation with him. Then he and Meg would down a quick dinner and resume their vigil. They'd watch TV in Richie's room, or at least have it on for his favorite shows. And Meg would watch him, not the screen; watch his mouth form a laugh, listen to his broken ha-has at the funny parts.

Tonight we watched Big Bang Theory, and Sheldon made him laugh. Just like before. Maybe his brain isn't as damaged as we feared.

Four days after Richie awoke from his coma, Meg sat on his bed and worked the remote while she waited for the physical therapist to arrive. When her cell rang, she punched the button. But the name on her screen made her jaw drop. "Candy?"

"Hi, Meg." The voice held a world of weary resignation.

"Girlfriend, you gave us all a big scare."

"I'm sorry." Was that a sniffle, or a crackling connection?

"You're doing better, I take it?"

"For now." Meg could visualize Candy's bowed shoulders, her pacing feet. "I hear you met my sister."

"Yes, I did. She was very nice. And very concerned."

"What did she tell you about my son?"

"Well, um …" Meg cast her mind back, thrown by the unexpected question. "She told me his name was Jared, and she showed me some photos of him."

"Anything else?"

Meg blinked at Candy's intensity. "No, not really."

But whatever her motive for asking, Candy left it unspoken. "How's your son?"

"I'm so glad you asked. He finally came out of his coma."

Meg wasn't sure if the strangled sound she heard was a gasp or a sob.

"But it comes with its own set of challenges." Like getting Richie interested in something besides TV, she thought as she glanced over at his tall frame sprawled on the elevated bed, his blank eyes glued to the Mad Men rerun.

Candy's voice grew even softer. "May I come by?"

"You sure may. It will be good to see you again."

Candy made it in twenty minutes. Meg hugged her tight, then stepped back to assess. Candy's eyes had lost the dull sheen they'd had last week, her hands hanging straight to her side, no longer fidgety. She tilted her head, eying Richie. He didn't even glance over. "How wonderful to see him awake." She placed light fingers on Meg's arm. "What a relief."

Meg picked up the remote and lowered the volume. "I'm relieved that you seem so much better. I … um …"

"I know. You want to know why I did it."

"Well …"

"I hit bottom, that's why."

Meg grasped her friend's clammy hands. "Come sit."

They found a couple of empty chairs in the hallway and settled there, and Meg shifted so that Candy had to meet her eyes. "When I was at your house helping your sister, I saw you'd been looking at your high school yearbook. Did something you saw there trigger you?"

Candy's eyes widened, and just like that, the spooked colt was back.

Meg gripped Candy's bony arm just in time and sat her back on the chair. "No, don't leave." She folded her arms. "Talk to me."

Candy gazed at the floor, rubbing the fabric of her Star Wars T-shirt between her fingers.

"Maybe it's none of my business, but I'm concerned for you."

Candy's voice whispered across the twelve inches separating them. "I was sitting there, thinking about my son, wishing I could go back and undo everything. Then I saw Sandy, all smiling, looking just like I remember her." She clamped her lips together and shut her eyes tight, yet tears still leaked out.

Meg pulled her friend's head to her shoulder, and let her use it as a crying post. Poor Candy. Too many tragedies piled on at once could make even the strongest person snap.

When Candy's sniffles had fizzled to steady breathing, Meg patted Candy's soft hair. "You must have cared deeply for your friend."

She felt the nod of Candy's head against her shoulder. "Of course I did."

"Then you must have known about her and Geoffrey Hope."

Candy's spine stiffened even more—more than Meg had known was possible.

"That man deserved what he got," she spat into Meg's neck. "Sandy didn't."

Meg scooted back, the air suddenly chilly. "And he was never found out, apparently."

Candy lifted her head. "I should've said something. But I figured nobody would believe me."

"Why wouldn't they believe you?"

"Everybody liked him. He spoke and came across all respectable, like Denzel Washington. And it would've been his word against mine." Her eyes shone with emotion. "But I keep picturing him standing before God, being held accountable for his sins. Then I always feel just a little bit better."

Chapter Twenty-Nine

Painting in the Wilderness – Megan Shaw Paulson (10017 followers)

"Glory in his holy name: let the heart of them rejoice that seek the Lord." I Chronicles 16:10

As my daughter would say, it's been a strange, yet epic day. Even though Richie is technically out of his coma (thank you Lord!), he's seemed confused and dazed ever since, as though he's not sure who he is and how he got here. But today, he looked straight at me and uttered what I'm sure was meant to be "Morning, Mum." British accent and all! (I've heard of people awakening from comas who suddenly are able to speak other languages, or who speak in a distinctly foreign accent. But I suspect Richie wasn't really speaking with an accent. It was just the effort of his mouth to form coherent words.)

For the first time in weeks, I feel hopeful we're going to get our old Richie back!

Words can't express how much your prayers and thoughtful comments mean to us.

Praising Yahweh,

Meg

~~~~

The Ignacio College football stadium was packed by the time Linzee arrived. She spied Ken on the stage a hundred yards away, his twiddling thumbs betraying his nervousness as he waited for the noontime press conference to begin. Mary

Lethbridge, to his left, leaned her head around Ken, apparently carrying on a last-minute conversation with her boss, Chief Gale Grieve, also known as Chief Grief. On the chief's other side sat somber, bespectacled Mayor Christine Hall.

Something electric shook the air around Linzee; the din of a thousand voices roared in her ears. She looked around for Section B, Row 8, where Claire had promised to meet her. Two minutes later, she found her seat overlooking the twenty-yard line and plopped down beside her friend.

She'd barely said hello to Claire when Chief Grieve stepped to the podium. He twisted the mike upward, closer to his face, and opened his mouth.

"Good morning—er, afternoon, ladies and gentlemen." He gave a brief nod to the rows of journalists directly in front of him. "Members of the press. We've called you here today to present an update on the tragic shooting that took place on this campus roughly three weeks ago."

Linzee only half-listened to his five minutes of condolences to the victims' families, and then a review of everything already covered in the media. She stifled a yawn, wishing she'd ordered an extra shot of espresso in her morning latte. But she perked up when Grieve announced, "We want to reassure and inform all of you that this was no random school shooting. We now know Coby Jarrett's motive, thanks to the two detectives who've worked so hard on this case." He turned and gestured toward Ken and Mary. "Please give a hand to Kenneth Tucker and Mary Lethbridge."

Applause and cheers exploded as Ken and Mary stood.

Linzee lifted her phone and zoomed in, capturing Ken's bashful smile and reddened ears before the blush disappeared. She showed the photo to Claire, who grinned. "Perfect shot."

The chief continued. "After much footwork, these two discovered not only Coby's motive but also some previously

185

unknown details about the victims." Grieve looked down and shuffled the papers in his hands, then lifted his head and slowly panned the crowd. "Many of you already know Coby targeted Mrs. Milliken and Mr. Hope. What you may not have known was that he was adopted by Robert and Rose Jarrett when he was a few days old. And the names of his biological parents, the names on his birth certificate, were Geoffrey Hope and Cassandra Martin whom we know as Mrs. Sandy Milliken."

A commotion on the end of row three, on the side nearest Linzee, drew her attention as the chief's words faded to background noise. A man steering a Channel 7 camera and a newswoman rushed to a woman draped in scarves who'd stood and now yelled something indiscernible at the chief.

The newswoman listened for a moment, nodding along as the woman's gesturing hands punctuated each syllable. Linzee recognized the newswoman as Karla Anthony, the young blonde anchor on the six o'clock news.

Chief Grieve, eyeing the commotion, called for questions from the media. Karla spun and waved jazz hands in his direction. The cameraman shifted the equipment her way when Grieve nodded at her.

Karla placed a hand on the scarved woman's shoulder. "Chief, I have Sandy Milliken's mother here, and she has something she wants to say." She shifted to Mrs. Martin and brought the mike closer. "Mrs. Martin, tell the chief, and our TV audience, what you just told me."

The woman tugged one end of the multi-colored scarf, straightened her spine, and spoke into the mike. "Sandy was not Coby Jarrett's mother." Her tear-filled voice wobbled. "My Sandy was not pregnant nineteen years ago. And she never used drugs." She glared at the chief. "I told those two cops so, but they obviously didn't believe—"

"Ma'am." Grieve's tone commanded compliance. "We're not saying she *was* his mother. We're saying Coby believed she was."

The conversation reminded Linzee of the children's storybook, "Are You My Mother?"

"Well, he shot the wrong woman. Please set the record straight." Mrs. Martin plopped to her seat, mouth tight and hard, her folded arms shielding her from news she didn't want to hear.

Linzee watched the tight-lipped woman swing one leg over the other and clamp herself against the back of the chair as though she were turning herself into a fierce, immovable statue. It occurred to her she'd meant to tell Mom about Ken's interview with Mrs. Martin, but then Richie had awakened, everything exploded, and … well, it must have slipped her mind. She could only sympathize with Mrs. Martin's attempt to deny the terrible news. What parent or grandparent would want to receive news like that?

Sometimes fiction couldn't hold a candle to real life. Mom would've loved to hear this. But Mom, unwilling to leave Richie, had declined Linzee's invite, reminding her to tell her all about it later.

A male reporter jumped up next. A city employee hovering nearby brought him a wireless mike, and the reporter held it beneath his chin. "Since the shooting, the police are everywhere. In malls, in office buildings, driving the streets. Why did you feel the need to increase police presence if you don't believe we're in danger?"

Grieve unfurrowed his brow as he replied. "This is just a temporary measure to prevent any copycat crimes. We expect to gradually reduce our presence over the next few months."

A female reporter called out, "Do you have reason to believe there might be a copycat out there?"

The man with the mike held it out, and Grieve asked her to repeat her question.

This time her question boomed through the stadium, and Grieve replied, "There's always a slight risk after a highly publicized shooting like this one. We want to assure all of you that the risk is quite small." The chief leaned forward, his earnest gaze inspiring trust. "However, we felt that during the aftermath of this tragedy, more forces on the street would help ensure public safety."

"Speaking of highly publicized," shouted a teenage boy on the fourth row, "isn't it time we stop giving so much power and publicity to these shooters?"

Grieve gestured at the boy. "And you are?"

Microphone Man rushed over.

"Joe Bloom," said the boy into the mike, "student body president at Terra Vista High School." Confident, college-level maturity permeated every gesture, every word. "These shooter dudes are seeking attention, and we keep giving it to them."

Linzee found herself nodding along. The kid had a point.

Grieve nodded also. "You might be right. But that's not under our control. Restricting the press from reporting certain news would violate the constitution. If you're serious about this, contact your congressman."

The reporter who'd interviewed Linzee that day at the college—Ted Corban—turned around and glared at Joe. Although Linzee couldn't hear what he said, his lips seemed to form the question, "You're trying to restrict my first amendment rights?"

Linzee couldn't see Joe's expression, but he seemed to shrink under the journalist's stare.

"He's right, you know," Claire whispered beside her. "If some unstable young dude has been ignored all his life, can you imagine how tempting it must be to go on a shooting rampage?" Her volume amped up a couple notches. "He knows his name will be all over the country afterward. Might be the only time he's ever gotten so much attention."

"I know, right? Everyone remembers Dylan Klebold—"

"Hey, look." Claire's elbow nudge nearly knocked her into the man beside her. "Your boyfriend is checking you out."

"Sshh," demanded the lady directly in front of Linzee.

"I'd like to hear if you don't mind."

Claire made a face at the woman's back, but Linzee rolled her eyes and hoped she didn't look as embarrassed as she felt. Loud-mouthed Claire still hadn't learned to control her tongue after years of Linzee's protests. She peeked at the stage. Sure enough, Ken was peering in her direction. When he met her eyes, he winked.

She grinned and winked back, feeling her cheeks warm, marveling at the thrill in her chest. Ken had just set a record — the first, and only, man to ever make her blush.

Chapter Thirty

Painting in the Wilderness – Megan Shaw Paulson
(11045 followers)

"Praise ye the Lord. Praise the Lord, O my soul. While I live will I praise the Lord: I will sing praises unto my God while I have any being." Psalm 146:1-2

Today marks the four-week anniversary of the day that changed our lives forever. In these twenty-eight days filled with hope, discouragement, fear, and faith, all of you prayed and trusted the Lord's mysterious plan. Because of your faithful intercessions, Richie has shown all of us, the doctors and nurses, this whole hospital, that God can and will do miracles.

Especially this past week, since Richie has been out of his coma. My son has undergone intense occupational therapy. Endured endless poking and prodding by the medical staff, albeit with much resistance on his part. Been unable to communicate his discomfort except through groans and yells. How frustrated he must be. This same young man, who was once so vibrant and talkative, can now barely form words. Once so active, he now can't perform the most basic of functions without assistance.

Please keep praying for his complete healing. We miss our Richie and love him more than words can express. The good news is, so does God.

Clinging to Love,

Meg

~~~~

"**W**ant to do lunch?" Claire said as they filed out of the stadium. "Me and Emma and you and Ken?"

Linzee glanced behind her at the stage. Ken stood conversing with Grieve, his tense posture suggesting an intensity level she wasn't sure how to interpret. He didn't look as though he'd welcome an interruption.

On the other hand, maybe he needed a break. She swiveled, replying as she went, "I'll ask him and text you, okay?"

When she reached the stage, Ken was smiling again, and Grieve had slapped him on the back. A gust of wind sent a whiff of fresh-cut grass into her face and carried the tension away.

Ken smiled, gave her a shoulder hug, and an enthusiastic yes to lunch. In moments, they were on their way to Ken's car to meet Claire and Emma at Ortega's. Ken headed out to the boulevard then to the southbound 101.

"That poor woman. Mrs. Martin." Linzee shook her head in Ken's direction. "I can understand why she's in denial about Coby being her grandson."

"Which reminds me." Ken glanced over. "I meant to tell you, she could be right, you know. She made the same claim in our interview with her. Which is why the chief clarified that Coby believed it was so, not that it was."

"What are you talking about?"

"After we interviewed her, she denied everything so vehemently, we decided to search for others of the same name as her daughter on the off chance she was right. Guess what? We found a total of three Cassandra Martins in the area."

Her jaw sagged. "Really? I would think Coby would want to be totally sure he had the right person if he was out for revenge. Don't you think?"

"You'd think." He slowed at the off-ramp. "But he didn't have access to the same records we do. He used a public site on which people can remove or hide their information. On that site, we only found two Cassandra Martins nearby. One was Sandy, and the other was too young. So he made the reasonable assumption that Cassandra Martin Milliken was the woman he sought." After braking to a complete stop, he flipped his right turn signal. "Her age and location seemed to fit."

"Well, what do *you* think?"

He tugged his ear. "I think we need to keep an open mind, do more digging. We're going to look more closely at Cassandra number three. If she turns out to actually be Coby's mother, we can give Mrs. Martin the reassurance she needs. Of course, it won't bring her daughter back." He threw Linzee a quick look. "Remember, until further notice, this is just between you and me." His grin softened the no-nonsense words.

"You mean we could be dealing with a case of mistaken identity? Wow. Mind-blowing."

"Yes. It's entirely possible Coby shot the wrong woman."

~~~~

At Ortega's, the lunch crowd had dwindled to a handful, and they had no trouble finding Claire and Emma, especially considering Emma's newly-dyed rainbow hair. They exchanged hellos and introductions and spent the next several minutes picking apart the press conference. A dark-haired, dark-eyed waitress named Ximena, who couldn't be any older than fifteen, brought a basket of chips and salsa to their table. The owners' daughter, perhaps?

Linzee took a bite of burrito smothered in cheese, and Ken dug into his tamale.

"Oh hey." Emma tapped Linzee on the hand. "Isn't this the restaurant that Nena's uncle owns?"

With a jolt, Linzee shook her head. "No, you're thinking of Ortiz's." She glared at Emma in hopes she'd get the message to shut up. She thought she saw Claire nudge Emma.

She could feel Ken scoping her. "Isn't Nena the roommate you ran into the other day?"

Linzee popped a chip into her mouth and nodded. The crunch rippled through her mouth and into her head. She pulled her chin in and fixed her eyes on the chips.

Claire was still elbowing Emma, who whirled on Claire. "What?"

"Shut up."

"Why?" She turned to Linzee again. "Aren't you over her now?"

Linzee went hot from head to toe. She felt, more than saw, Ken's scrutiny.

She dared a peek at his scrunched face. "What?"

"'Over her?'" Ken echoed. "What does that mean?"

The other side of the table went silent. Was this just a horrible dream? From the clacking silverware and cheery Mexican music over the speaker, this was for real.

Her mouth opened, and words croaked out. "It … it means, we had a tiff, and I'm over it now."

A distinct snort carried from across the table. Linzee glared at Emma's smirking face, her own flaming hot, then sought Claire's empathetic gaze. But there was no empathy there. Claire was carefully placing a piece of fish on her tongue, looking everywhere except at Linzee.

Ken put his fork down. Linzee tensed.

"What are you not telling me?"

Chills ran down her arms at his quiet voice, laced with a tone she'd never heard before.

"Um …" She fingered a corn chip, rubbed her thumb along its surface, as rough as her emotions. "This isn't the time or place."

Without a word, Ken picked up his fork and finished his tamale. Linzee choked down one more bite. "I need to go home."

Ken nodded, his eyes laser beams, then picked up the

check.

"Bye." Emma's guilt-ridden voice swept over Linzee, who tossed a wave in that general direction as she followed Ken out. If they weren't in a public place, she'd use a different gesture.

Linzee gripped the seat and stared at gray pavement all the way home. Ken's clench-lipped silence overpowered her racing thoughts and Coldplay's Adventure of a Lifetime piping from the radio.

Some adventure. More adventure than she bargained for. She took another peek at Ken's rock-hard expression. She needed to disarm him. Act casual. Normal.

"Thank you for the yummy lunch."

He merely nodded.

"What are your plans for the rest of the day?" she tried again.

"To try and figure out what was going on back there." He jutted a crooked thumb behind him.

"Going on?"

"Yeah. Why did you clam up as soon as your old roommate's name came up?"

She clutched her knees.

"Your reaction was telling, you know. I'm around enough criminals to know a guilty conscience when I see one."

She swallowed hard.

"I know you had a falling out with the lady. But getting over her? That's something you say about a romantic relationship."

"Emma is full of …"

"But it can't have been romantic. You've been engaged."

They'd reached an intersection, and he slowly braked, then turned his head. She could almost see the wheels in his mind grind to a halt as they arrived at the correct conclusion.

To her horror, a tear rolled down her cheek. She dropped her wet face into her hands.

"I get it. You were engaged to her." Thick pause. "That would explain why you're so close-mouthed about it."

She sniffed. "I'm straight now," she said through her fingers. "My history doesn't need to come between us."

He accelerated with an uncharacteristic jerk. "You should've told me."

"I'm sorry." Her hands sent wet streaks across her cheeks. "But you made it clear what you thought of same-sex marriage."

He swung a right onto her street. His silence was freaking her out. She watched his face, his eyes, for any softening.

"Is this a deal-breaker for you?"

When he braked in her driveway, instead of reaching for her as he usually did, he stared at the Carlito's garage door and thrummed his fingers on the wheel. "Dishonesty is a deal-breaker for me."

"When was I dishonest?"

"When you didn't tell me who Nena really was to you."

"After you expressed your views on same-sex marriage, you really think I'm going to confess something like that?"

The drumming halted. He looked at her, his eyes blank, unreadable. "What a mess."

"I know, right?"

"I really like you, but this is a lot to take in." He gestured. "Come on, I'll walk you to the door."

Her legs went numb at his flat tone. Then the shaking began. "You'll call me, right?"

"Yeah."

But from his tone, and the way he avoided her eyes, she feared he would not.

Chapter Thirty-One

Richie's homecoming should have generated a celebration. Instead of smiles, there were somber faces. Instead of cheers, hushed voices. Meg tailed Jon who wheeled Richie into his old bedroom, but Richie stared straight ahead, seemingly oblivious to the posters of rock bands and classic cars all over his walls. Before they left this morning, she'd pulled back the Star Wars curtains on both windows, flooding the room with life-giving sunlight.

She sighed as she recalled the instructions from the physical therapist on how to help Richie with his PT homework. "He may fight you," the pretty redhead had warned. "But you have to keep on him. Remember the three types of patients?"

"Yes– 'I'm only here because the doctor told me to.' They are depressed and won't do their homework."

"Correct. The second type only do their homework half the time, because they forget. The third types overdo it because they think they will improve faster."

Jon clasped Richie under his arms and lifted, grunting with exertion as Meg watched, frozen.

"Your son will go through stages of grief." The physical therapist's warning echoed in her mind. "He'll have times of anger and depression. As his mom, you'll want to help. But sometimes the temptation is to help too much. You can help him with his Therabands exercises, but they will hurt, and he may struggle. Just be sure to get him to the massage therapist as soon as you can. It will hurt, but it's 'good pain.'"

"Will it help him sleep?"

"He might still have trouble sleeping during recovery. He may take naps off and on all day, and be awake at night.

The length of recovery time depends on the person. But I'm optimistic about your son's chances. He's young and seems robust. But you need to be prepared for the worst."

"Like what?"

"He'll likely have anxiety in public. Seeing a group of young people might frighten him. Or even seeing someone wearing all black. When Halloween comes, I suggest you keep him away from anything or anyone with masks or costumes, especially gory ones."

Hard to believe her big, strapping son could ever be afraid of pseudo-scary Halloween revelers. Especially since he'd been one himself. In earlier days, Halloween had been his favorite holiday after Christmas. The scarier the character, the more likely he was to be one. One year he'd been a zombie, with dripping red paint all over his face. Another year, he ignored her vehement protests and dressed up as Death.

Her throat tightened as she realized Richie, former football player and fearless extrovert, had reverted back to scared little boy.

~~~~

Linzee lay curled in the fetal position on Heath's bed, his soft snores tickling her arm where his head nestled. Her blank phone sat beside her, agitating her with sinister silence.

Ken hadn't called or texted for two days.

"Emma ruined everything," she'd told Claire yesterday. "And yes, you can tell her she's on my dirt list now."

"She's really sorry."

"Too late for sorry."

"Why don't you just text him?"

"Because." The innocuous word spit into in the air and hung there, breathless with dread. "I couldn't bear it if he didn't reply."

Linzee eyed the phone now, and her fingers crept toward it, picked it up.

No new messages.

Her head dropped to the pillow, and the phone chose that moment to chime. She snatched it up. Ken, finally?

No. Claire.

Claire could wait.

The phone beeped again, and her heart surged. It had to be Ken.

But no. Claire again.

She nearly threw the phone at the wall but pulled her hand back at the last minute. Then punched in a frequently-used number.

"Thank God you answered," she said when Mom's quiet hello dispersed the emotion gathered in her chest. She swung herself off the bed and snuck into the hall, after ensuring that Heath was still fast asleep. "Can you talk?"

"Sure. What's going on?"

A sob erupted. "My worst fear came true." The story spilled from her aching throat.

Mom made little sympathetic noises throughout, ending with, "I'm so sorry, baby girl." Long, heavy pause. "You know that saying—'If you love somebody, let them go, for if they return, they were always yours. If they don't, they never were.'"

Linzee sniffed. "That's beautiful. Who said it?"

"Kahlil Gibran."

"Does it apply if you're only in like, not love?"

Mom chuckled. "Yes, I think you could substitute the word like for love, and it would still count. In fact, something similar happened to me when Jon and I were dating. And look at us now, happily married."

"What happened?"

"Well, we'd been dating for about six months. He'd hinted around about marriage a couple of times, but the conversations didn't really go anywhere. One weekend he went camping with some men from church. I expected him back on Sunday. He'd promised to call me as soon as he got back."

A rustling from the bedroom reached her. She peeked through the slightly-open door while Mom kept talking. Heath had shifted, his mouth wide open as though watching a riveting cartoon. *Must be an interesting dream.*

"Well, Sunday came, and he hadn't called. So I texted him just to check he'd made it home safely. He had, and then he said he'd talk to me in a couple of days. No explanation. So I began to imagine all sorts of scenarios. He was planning to end the relationship. He'd met someone else."

Linzee stepped away from the opened door, her heart resonating with Mom's words. "Oh Mom, you always come across as so secure and together. I can't believe you have those kinds of thoughts too."

"Surprise, your mom is human."

"So why did he do the disappearing act?"

"Well, while I was fretting and anxious, Jon was seeking God. About our relationship. And I had no idea. Finally, on Wednesday night, he asked to come over. By this time, I was convinced he was planning to break up. Remember Barry, the one who made me drive half an hour out of my way so he could dump me?"

"That schmuck? How could I forget?"

"If you recall, he didn't contact me at all for a few days prior. That's why I jumped to the wrong conclusion about Jon's silence. Anyway, Jon came over, and when I saw the bouquet of red roses in his hands, I knew."

"Ah, the night he proposed. How cool."

"He simply wanted to get God's stamp of approval before he asked me to marry him. That's when I knew he was the man for me."

Linzee swiveled and paced along the hallway runner. "Cool story, Mom. But I don't think you can make a parallel with Ken. I doubt he's making plans to propose."

"Maybe not, but I'm saying he might just need some space to figure things out."

"I don't know. He was pretty grim that night. Accused

me of dishonesty." Her voice broke, and she swallowed. "With you and Jon, it wasn't anything like that."

"Just remember that if things don't work out with Ken, it was still a good learning experience for you."

"Yeah, I learned certain friends can't be trusted." She gave a bitter chuckle. "Actually, I know I need to be upfront about my past from the get-go. And to remind myself that if someone has a problem with it, he's not the man for me." She sniffed again. "But I was starting to believe Ken *was* the man for me."

"I'll pray real hard, Baby Girl. I'll pray that God will bring Ken back to you if it's His will."

A small wail echoed from the bedroom. "Mom, I need to go. The baby is awake. Thanks for praying."

She clicked off and hurried to Heath, then picked him up. She drew him to her shoulder, where he burrowed, sobbing. "Sca-wy."

"Shh, the scary dream went bye-bye." If only her own real-life scary dream would go bye-bye. Linzee stroked his soft head, lowered her hand to his tiny back. "Poor baby. I know exactly how you feel."

Chapter Thirty-Two

Painting in the Wilderness – Megan Shaw Paulson (15517 followers)

"Being confident of this very thing, that he which hath begun a good work in you will perform it until the day of Jesus Christ." Philippians 1:6

Dear friends, my days have become a whirlwind of transporting Richie to his physical therapy appointments every day, followed by occupational therapy, followed by speech therapy, followed by doctor checkups. No, they're not really one right after the other. It only seems that way because my days are so repetitive now that they all blur together. Jon helps me lift Richie and get him into the wheelchair. It's not motorized; he's not ready for one of those. No telling where he'd race off to if it were.

Isn't that a lot like life? Right now, my life is like a non-motorized wheelchair. Nothing is easy. Lots of work resulting in very little progress. Yet I know, someday my son's body and mind will be well enough to use a motorized chair. And eventually, he won't need a chair at all.

And this – this shall pass, I tell myself every day. Someday I'll be out of this wheelchair of a trial. Someday, a long, long time from now … life will be normal again.

Until then, I cling to my Savior.

Coveting your ongoing prayers,

Meg

~~~~

Meg's eyes snapped open to a dim room, sounds of gunfire and screaming still ringing in her head. Shuddering, she flung her hair away from her face, unable to shake the intimidating image of Coby Jarrett's hard, determined face, the face of a madman. Eyes of a killer. And still so lifelike in her mind, more so than a dream ought to be. He'd held a smoking gun, and she'd seen inside his outer shell to the empty center where his soul should be.

A headache throbbed at her temples. The numerals on her bedside clock read 3:30 pm. She'd napped for more than two hours!

Blinking away the dream, she hoisted herself up, swung her feet to the floor, then regretted it when her head pounded. Why was the room so dim? She didn't remember closing the curtains.

Trying to ignore the headache, she slithered along the hall in her red anklets, only to find Linzee in Richie's room holding a spoonful of chocolate pudding in front of his mouth.

"Linzee!"

Glancing up, Linzee's mouth opened in sync with Richie's, as though she were refreshing him on how to eat. "Mom."

Richie ignored the spoon and turned his head. "Mmmmum?"

She went to his side and planted a happy kiss on his cheek, then rested her arms around his neck and drank in the sight of her daughter being the big sister he needed. "You must be the mysterious angel who closed my drapes."

Linzee stuck the spoon into Richie's opened mouth. "Mmm hmm, I did. Your door was cracked, and I saw you were sleeping. I was worried because it's not like you to crash in the middle of the day."

"How were you able to get away from the kids?"

"It's Mrs. Carlito's early day. It couldn't have worked out better."

"I hope you can stay awhile. I could use a break." Despite her best efforts to mask it, she wondered if Linzee could hear the desperation in her voice, the utter weariness, the I'm-at-the-end-of-my-tether.

"You got it, Mom."

After Linzee shooed her away, promising to tend to Richie, she wandered to her studio, her fingers suddenly itching to pick up a brush. Closing her eyes, she tried to conjure up a visual of her current emotional state. What did soul-sucking weariness look like? What color was exhaustion? Maybe it was the heavy gray of menacing storm clouds rolling in from the Pacific. Or endless dull beige, perhaps, like sand in a desert that hasn't seen rain for years.

Out on Reno Drive, a motorcycle rumbled by, making her jump. She opened her eyes, examined the palette, then dipped the brush into the deepest brown she had—burnt umber—and smeared it across the canvas. She should add some pale grays, the color of birch tree trunks. Washed-out browns and barren greens of an oak quaking in the wind. All twisting together and spiraling off into nothingness.

She shook her head, unsatisfied, and kept swabbing. She was wasting her time. This was frankly a mess.

But then, so were her emotions.

Twenty minutes later, she stepped back and gave it her customary once-over. *Sheesh!* It looked like a kindergartener's finger painting. In the meantime, inside her head, Coby Jarrett floated back into view, glaring at her with his crazed, vacant eyes.

Aha. She ripped off the mess in front of her and replaced it with a fresh blank sheet. As she dabbed more paint, a face emerged. The face from the newspapers, TV, and the internet, which now lived in her head and refused to leave. Almond skin. Empty, hopeless green eyes. The colors of a broken soul.

Coby Jarrett.

"Why?" she whispered to him. "Did you want your parents to suffer the way you did? Did you even care about the destruction you'd wreak?" She dipped the brush in goldenrod, dabbed flecks in the eyes. "You destroyed several families, including mine. Your bio mom and dad weren't perfect, but they certainly didn't deserve what you did." She added more olive green to the eyes. From the photos she'd seen, he'd had arresting eyes, an odd mix of yellows and greens that would have been attractive if not for the hard stare.

Hard to believe he'd ever been an innocent little boy. Had he enjoyed the same things Richie had? A vision rose of Coby at the Little League field, clad in a striped uniform, a diminutive, hopeful Babe Ruth. She wondered if he'd played Sim City at the neighborhood Boys and Girls Club, as Richie had. What terrible event had made the childlike hope in his heart morph into deadly intent?

She stepped back and assessed. She'd captured the ironclad set of his jaw, the unique eye coloring, the grim planes of his face, the mouth a thin slash. But she'd unwittingly captured something else as well.

Depths of misery swam in his eyes, along with another expression she'd seen recently. She shook her head, trying to think. Then it came to her. The same haunted expression had twisted Candy's face just before she attempted suicide.

She dropped her brush. Candy! She hadn't thought about her friend in days. Guilt clenched her heart as she pulled her phone out of her pocket and texted.

How are you doing, my friend?

As she continued her muttered diatribe at Coby's image, she waited for Candy's reply, casting anxious glances at her phone. Five minutes became ten, then fifteen. But her phone remained blank.

Candy almost always returned texts right away. Except for the day that ... Her shaky fingers fumbled over the tiny keys as she dialed Candy's number. Straight to voicemail.

204

Heart surging, she left a voicemail, hoping the tremor in her voice didn't betray her. "Candy, hope all is well." She forced an upbeat lilt. "We haven't talked for a while, and I was hoping to catch up. Call me!"

She paced to the window. The side yard's yellowed lawn heralded the end of a long, hot summer. Clumps of ice cactus splashed pools of green next to the fence. She told herself Candy was okay, just busy, but couldn't convince the quaking in her gut.

Returning to the easel, she pondered on the phenomenon of the pre-suicidal expression right there on the canvas, plain for all to see. She wondered if this was common knowledge among counseling professionals if they could see the telltale signs on people's faces.

She couldn't wait any longer. Something could be wrong with Candy. She sent a text to Bonnie.

Have you heard from Candy? I'm worried about her because she hasn't answered her phone.

Bonnie texted back.

Not since yesterday. She seemed fine then. But just to ease our minds, can you go check on her?

Meg promised she would, then went to tell Linzee she needed to leave. Linzee, perched beside Richie as they watched CNN, threw her the okay sign.

Meg hopped in her car and sped five miles over the limit toward Lagunitas. When she turned off Francis Drake Blvd onto the narrow, dim street, the dappled tree shadows again sent a quiver up her arms. They sheltered her all the way to Candy's ramshackle home.

It should be right around the next bend. She crept on until she reached a gleaming emerald of a yard. Candy's yard. But this time, an off-white sedan was parked behind Candy's van. Meg pulled in behind it, noting the license plate. An official government plate. She scrutinized the car more closely. If she recalled, this car was very similar to the car Ken drove when he first came to interview her and Jon.

She sucked in a breath. What in the world were cops doing here? Did someone break into her house? Or worse?

She reminded herself when cops responded to a crime reported, they didn't use unmarked cars. It was probably nothing serious. So why the quavery breaths, the unsteady heartbeat?

She couldn't very well interrupt whatever was going on in there. Yet if she waited until the cops left, no telling how long that would take. She'd best go on home and tell Bonnie what she saw.

Backing out, she jerked the accelerator a little too hard, then slammed her brakes when a car passed in her rear-view mirror. Whew, close one. *Meg, calm down.*

She prayed for Candy all the way home.

Chapter Thirty-Three

The football stadium at Peninsula Christian Academy echoed with noise and purposeful activity. Squeals from the band warming up mingled with cheerleader yells and the din of adult and children's voices. Meg, determined to enjoy herself, pushed her worries about Candy out of her mind. This afternoon she'd wasted no time calling Bonnie with an update. "Have you heard from her? I'm afraid she's in some sort of trouble."

She could almost see Bonnie shaking her head on the other end.

"Best case scenario? She witnessed a crime. Worst case? I don't even want to think about it."

But so far she'd heard from neither Candy nor her sister. No news was good news, she reminded herself. But the questions still nagged: crime witness or crime victim? Or worse?

From the first row, she and Jon watched the stadium bustle with excited anticipation. She patted Richie's back, who was seated in front of her in his wheelchair. His smile had flashed when she told him that the school wanted to honor him at halftime at the homecoming game. That Richie could understand what she said warmed Meg's heart. So many old friends were greeting him and wishing him well. The crowd seemed to animate him, and she was thankful most of them, except for a small child or two, weren't rude enough to stare at his drooping head, or the way he kept rocking back and forth, over and over again. She heard the effort behind his guttural replies, yet the improvement from last week gave her hope that he'd eventually recover his old self.

She glanced back to a row halfway up the stadium, where Linzee sat with Phillippe. She and Meg's eyes met, and they exchanged a smile and a wave.

Chad and Brandon, the quarterback and tight end from last year's team, came up to Richie. One grabbed him around the neck, the other pumped his hand. "Hey, buddy, how ya doin'!"

"H-h-aaaay." Richie twisted his head and looked up at his old friends.

A voice from somewhere nearby said, "Is this Richard St. John?"

Meg turned to see the woman next to her peering at Richie with kind eyes. "It is. I'm Meg, his mom."

The woman extended her hand, and Meg shook it. "He sure has come a long way since that day." *That day.* Her meaning was unmistakable. "I've been keeping up on his progress on your blog. I remember him from last year's football team. He was such an athlete." Her voice trailed off, as though she knew she was treading dangerously close to pity zone.

"I'm just so grateful he came out of his coma. Every day of improvement feels like an undeserved blessing."

The woman paused for five seconds, as if unsure how to reply. "I'm Danielle Schwartz." She gestured at the man on her other side. "My husband, Dave."

He gave Meg a quick nod, and Danielle flipped her sunglasses to the top of her head. "Our son Trenton played JV football last year, and he remembers Richard. You'll see him on the field tonight. Number 73, defensive tackle. Following in his dad's footsteps."

"I'll watch for him. I'm glad you guys have good memories of Richie." She glanced at him, noticing his rocking had spcd up, and his smile broadened as his two friends chatted with him.

Danielle pointed to the green turf below. "And my daughter is down there on the field with the homecoming court."

Meg looked to where Danielle indicated. A group of gowned girls and tuxedoed boys shifted back and forth, whispering and giggling. "She's one of the homecoming princesses?"

Danielle beamed a proud smile. "Freshman Princess. Her name is Molly."

"Do you have any other kids?"

"No, just the two."

"Did you say your husband played football too?"

Danielle ran her hand along Dave's back. "He did. Right here on this field, all four years of high school, back in the 90s when they won district."

"I remember that. Did you attend here too?"

"No, I graduated from Terra Vista in 1997."

"That's my alma mater too. Class of 1990. Did you know Sandy Milliken? Class of 1996?"

"I did know her. And I remember Mr. Hope too. What a tragedy. They were both such nice people."

"I have a friend who was a classmate and good friend of Sandy's. Candy is her name."

"I remember Candy. They were both a year ahead of me, so I didn't know them super well. They were known as the Andys."

A sudden yell from the field startled Meg. The team had streamed out to the fifty-yard line and now stood in two evenly-spaced queues. The loudspeaker drowned out all else as the introductions began.

Not until the crowd finished applauding after a talented senior girl sang the national anthem did the stadium quiet enough to resume the conversation.

Meg wanted to ask Danielle what Candy was like back then. Was she as messed up as she was now? But she clamped her lips lest Danielle construe it as gossip.

Instead, she said, "Candy took her friend's death so hard. They must've been very close."

Danielle thrust her palms up. "I know they were together a lot. Now that I think about it, Candy wasn't there the second half of her senior year."

"You mean Sandy?"

"No, I'm pretty sure I remember Sandy being there all year."

So Sandy hadn't dropped out during pregnancy. Meg wondered if she'd endured shaming or shunning during that difficult time. She couldn't think of anything harder than knowing the whole school saw the results of your indiscretions. Like the adulterous woman in The Scarlet Letter, Hester Prynne. Good thing for Sandy they no longer lived in Puritan times.

Danielle tapped Meg's knee. "Speaking of Sandy Martin, did you go to the press conference?"

"No, I missed it. Except for work, I've been out of touch with the outside world lately. I try to avoid the news. What happened at the press conference?"

"We were finally told why the shooter targeted Sandy and the teacher."

"I heard about that. The two of them were his biological parents."

Danielle nodded. "Well, at least the shooter thought so, according to the police chief. But Sandy's mother was there, and she claimed her daughter was not his biological mom."

"Then what was his motive?"

Danielle lifted her palms. "I don't think anyone really knows for sure. The birth mother's name was Cassandra Martin, but Sandy's mom claimed it was not her daughter."

Linzee had been there, at the press conference. Why hadn't she told Meg about this? But then she remembered. Since that day, Ken's vanishing act had dominated Linzee's thoughts.

"And I don't recall ever seeing Sandy and Mr. Hope together," Danielle went on, "or hearing any rumors about an affair. You know how it is in high school. If anyone is carrying on, somehow word gets out."

A shout from the crowd prevented Meg from replying. The Peninsula Crusaders had kicked a field goal, and they led 3-0. The band broke into the school song, and the cheerleaders bounced out a yell. Soon the noisy chaos overpowered any conversation Meg could have had with her new friend. But the revelation rang in her head. If Sandy Martin was not Coby's bio mother after all, then her murder made absolutely no sense. Bad enough that his injuring Richie made no sense. A fist squeezed her heart. A loved woman, a cherished son, gunned down for no reason. The hardened face of the madman who'd altered Richie's life forever floated into her mind, and the clamor around her faded. She shuddered and clutched the back of Richie's wheelchair. He shouted along with the crowd, but she had no idea why. Until she noticed the home team players celebrating in the end zone. She checked the scoreboard. 10-0.

She wouldn't be able to enjoy the game if her thoughts kept wandering. But a vibration from her pocket once again pulled her attention away. She slipped out her cell phone and then collapsed like a rag doll when she saw Candy's long-awaited reply.

Hi Meg, Bonnie said she asked you to come check on me. Everything's fine. I had company and didn't see your texts until now.

Meg responded.

Glad all is well.

"Company?" she wanted to say. "Funny way to describe a cop." She longed to ask why a cop car had been there, but she wasn't sure if Bonnie had divulged that detail.

Bonnie, she wrote amid the roar of the crowd cheering for another touchdown. *Candy texted me, and she's fine. Did she say why the cop car was there?*

No, she wouldn't tell me a thing. Just that everything was fine.

Meg shook her head and put her phone away. Candy must be the most secretive person she knew.

The buzzer marking the end of the half jerked her out of

her head and back to her surroundings as Jon stood. It was time to wheel Richie out onto the field.

Chapter Thirty-Four

Later, Meg would wonder why she hadn't seen it before. But on the way home, warmth from tonight's memories hugged her mind like a stocking cap. Memories of Richie's big grin when Phillippe wheeled him out to midfield at halftime, the plaque that the coach had bestowed on him. The principal's speech extolling Richie's amazing recovery and the flashbulbs going off all over the stadium like fireworks. Phillippe and Linzee's proud faces as they posed with her and Richie.

Richie still glowed in the passenger seat, squinting at the plaque inches from his eyes.

"See how much people care about you?"

Turning his head to her, he grunted and nodded. "F-f-f-fun."

"Yes, it was fun, and your dad and I are so proud of you."

And Jon had been proud, too, as proud as if Richie were his own son.

"Do you remember Trenton Schwartz? I met his mom and dad tonight." She didn't expect a reply, but she needed to keep talking to keep herself from dwelling on Danielle's bombshell news. For if she did, the prickling in her eyes might overflow with real tears. She'd have to give in to the horror of knowing some poor woman out there, Coby's real mom, had escaped a tragic death, while innocent Sandy took the fall for her.

She wondered about the unknown woman if she indeed existed or had any idea what she'd been spared.

On the other hand, she argued with herself, maybe Sandy had actually borne Coby, and her mom just couldn't accept reality. Assuming the media had gotten his birth date correct, Sandy would have been pregnant her senior year. Yet there seemed to be no evidence to support that theory.

But suppose Coby's birth year had been reported wrong, and Sandy had borne him sometime after graduation—say, the following year. There had to be occasions when determining birth dates of adopted children proved murky.

She half-listened to Richie's staccato delivery on his impressions of tonight's experience and nodded in all the right places while her mental arguments fought with themselves all the way home. If Sandy and Mr. Hope had an affair her senior year, maybe there'd be photos of them together somewhere.

Like in a yearbook.

By the time she pulled into the driveway, she knew what she had to do.

~~~~

Inside, Meg opened her high school alumni page on her laptop, where she could download digital copies of all the yearbooks for the past thirty years. For a fee, of course. Starting with the class of 1996, she opened it to the senior class page and entered Sandy's name into the search box. Within seconds, five entries popped up—the senior class photo that Meg had seen at Candy's house. Two photos of Sandy blocking a forward pass on the soccer field, another of a bored-looking Sandy singing in Varsity Choir, and finally eating lunch with friends. Meg studied each photo to see if she could spot Mr. Hope hovering nearby. But she saw no fresh-out-of-college student teacher anywhere.

No photographic hint of an illicit affair.

Nor did she see Candy anywhere near Sandy. Had she even attended her senior year long enough to make the yearbook?

Since she didn't know Candy's maiden name, she inserted only her first name in the search box.

Nothing came up under Candy.

Next she tried all the variations of Candice she could think of. Still nothing. Sighing, she decided to download the class of 1995's yearbook, when the two girls would have been juniors.

After she entered Candy's name, a page of classroom photos came up. Candy Martin said the caption. This girl had the same wispy hair and serious expression as the present-day Candy. Meg focused on the name—something seemed odd. Until the name to the right caught her eye—Sandy Martin.

Candy Martin and Sandy Martin? Funny. Maybe they were cousins or something.

But Candy had referred to Sandy as a dear friend, not a relative.

After searching under the name Martin, she found one more photo of Candy—her face still distinctly Candy, but without the pools of desperation in those luminous hazel eyes. She was seated in a classroom, her chin propped on her fist, gazing at some unknown spot in the distance. The planes of her face lay soft and youthful over rounded cheeks. Anticipation and focus swam in her teenage eyes.

Meg checked the page heading. *Fine Arts Department.* The caption read, "Candy Martin listens intently as Ms. Moore talks fashion design. 'This was my favorite class of all,' said Candy. 'I think I've found my niche in life.'"

And so she had. But in the years hence, life had snuffed the light from those expressive eyes.

She found her attention sliding to Candy's eyes. Unique, yes. In fact, her best feature. But also reminiscent of another pair of eyes she'd seen recently.

Picking up her laptop, she stayed riveted on the photo as she tottered toward her studio, where the painting of Coby Jarrett still glowered at her from the easel. Slowly, she lifted the laptop. Dread twisted her gut as she held the yearbook photo next to the painting, and she felt the color drain from her face.

His eyes—nearly identical to hers. The same unusual color, both sets of eyes shaped like a cat's.

An unthinkable possibility tickled the edges of her mind.

What if Candy were short for Cassandra, not Candice? How crazy was that?

"No," she whispered. "No way."

She tilted her head to the side, pondering the odds. In a school of six-thousand-plus students, it wouldn't be at all outside the realm of possibility for two of them to have the same name.

Her blood ran cold when she saw where this was leading.

Two Cassandra Martins. One nicknamed Sandy, the other, Candy.

Which, if it were true, would mean ...

The bullet that killed Sandy had been meant for Candy.

~~~~

Meg pounded on Candy's tattered front door. The morning sun reflected off the worn siding and stoked the heat already filling her chest, like a poker stirring up embers. Sounds of a happy crowd and ringing bells filtered to her ears from inside. Some TV game show, apparently.

The door flung open. Candy stood there in a flowered sundress, her fearful expression breaking into a relieved smile when she saw Meg.

Her smile faltered as she searched Meg's face. "Meg. What are you doing here?" She opened the door wider, as if going through the motions of inviting Meg in, but stayed rooted in place. "Is something wrong?"

"I need to talk to you."

Candy raised questioning brows at her, but dropped her hand from the doorknob and led her to the sofa, where she sat. Meg, joining her, glanced at Family Feud on TV, wishing she could hop inside and guess the top five most popular foods at a Southern wedding, rather than do what she came here for. The homey aromas of brewing coffee and fresh-baked pastries settled Meg's emotions like they did as a child when she visited Grandma.

She took a deep breath. "Mmm. Something smells good."

Candy darted up. "Can I get you some coffee and a cinnamon roll?"

"Of course! I'm sure it tastes as wonderful as it smells."

Candy left the room, then came back with a plate and two cups, setting them on a portable tray.

Meg thanked her when Candy placed the tray in front of her. "Aren't you having any?"

Candy shook her head and lifted the cup in her hand. "Just coffee. I already had a cinnamon roll." She gestured at the tray. "I hope you like it."

"It's my favorite pastry, as a matter of fact." Meg took a thoughtful bite, all the words she'd planned to say suddenly gone. "This is delicious."

Candy merely nodded, apparently sensing something wrong as she eyed Meg and slowly lowered herself to the sofa. She clutched the coffee cup as though her hands were as chilled as Meg's.

Meg lifted her own cup and let the warmth seep into her icy hands. She needed to just blurt it out. "I have a question for you, and I hope you'll give me an honest answer."

Candy blew on the steaming cup, and Meg watched the tendril curl and dissipate into the air, as frail and insubstantial as Candy herself. Candy took a slow sip and gave a reluctant nod, her mouth in an O as if sensing she wasn't going to like what Meg was about to say.

"I know who you are." Meg knew she had to tread carefully here. She knew she trod a path covered with brittle twigs, where the wrong step could release a sudden, startling crack. Each word must be infused with gentle compassion, lest Candy hear the crack of condemnation. She reached over to place her cold palm on Candy's knee.

"I'm sure you've heard by now that Coby Jarrett's biological mother was named Cassandra Martin. But she wasn't your friend Sandy."

The shock wave transforming Candy's face startled Meg, but she went on before she changed her mind. "It was you,

217

wasn't it? You're the missing birth mother."

Candy's mouth worked, her jaw moved side to side as if her reply were sticking to her throat like syrup and wouldn't flow. With a soft gasp, she nearly dropped the coffee cup as she plunked it to the table. Tucking her legs closer to the sofa, she bent from her narrow waist and anchored her elbows on her knees. Her head dropped so that Meg could no longer see her face.

"I want to help you in any way I can."

She waited, kneading Candy's back as if the sheer force of her fingers could penetrate her friend's brittle wall. "Won't you talk to me?"

Candy's wails came in such a sudden rush, Meg jerked back. Reassembling herself, she reached for her friend, hoping to soothe Candy with an embrace.

"I'm so sorry." Candy's sobs blurred into her words. "No words can ever express how sorry I am for what he did to your son." She lifted her head, at last, fisting away wet strands of hair from her eyes. "He was supposed to shoot *me,* not Sandy. I wish he had."

"No, no, sweetie. He wasn't supposed to shoot anybody."

"It was my fault. He blamed me for his mental problems." She sniffed and wiped her eyes on the puffy sleeve of her dress, leaving a dark smear of mascara, still not looking at Meg.

"It was wrong of him to blame you."

"Maybe if I hadn't abandoned him, maybe he would've turned out normal."

"I doubt it would have made any difference."

Candy's sobs made an eerie contrast to the cheerful noises from the TV. "I should have told someone what Mr. Hope did. I'll always regret that I was too scared to say anything."

"You didn't tell anyone? Even a girlfriend?"

"No." By now, her hands were clasped so tightly

together, the sharp protrusion of her knuckles resembled boulders with skin on. "I almost told Sandy, but chickened out. By Christmas, I was starting to show, and I told Mr. Hope. He told me I'd better have an abortion, or we were through. But I couldn't go through with it."

"He wasn't married at the time?"

"No, he was only twenty-three. Not that much older than me. I threatened to report him, but he said he'd make me sorry if I did. So I just quit school."

No wonder she'd said Mr. Hope deserved what he got.

Meg ran her finger along the seam of her jeans, back and forth, warming her fingertips. But it didn't ward away the chill in her veins. "Didn't your family know?"

Candy shook her head, sending strands of fawn-colored hair rippling like fall leaves. "No, I just left home one day and headed to the city. I remember I spent a while on the streets. Not sure how long. It's all a blur now." She sat straighter and rested her chin on her palm, much as she had in the yearbook photo, her gaze in the direction of the TV. "One day, while I was crashing in a house in Haight Ashbury, I found a shelter for unwed mothers where they can stay until they have their baby. I'll never forget the lady's name. Peggy. She was my angel. And she referred me to an adoption agency."

"Candy, do you plan to tell the cops all this?"

She finally turned her attention to Meg. Her eyes were dark with fear and grief. "They already know. They came to my house last night and asked me point-blank if my maiden name was Cassandra Martin, and if I'd had a baby in 1997."

Aha. The cop cars in Candy's driveway. Had one of them been Ken?

"I was so scared when they confronted me with the truth. I'm so worried this will end up in the media, and turn me into Public Enemy Number One. You know how vicious people can be on social media. So I begged the cops not to reveal anything to the press. They said there was no need to. They were going to close the case, and that would be that."

Candy dropped her head into her hands again. "Oh, if only I could've stopped him. I'll never forget that day. The minute I saw him on TV, I knew who he was. He looked exactly like Geoffrey looked at age 23. And his last name matched the couple who adopted him. I wanted to shrivel up and die. Then when I met you at the grief group, I thought maybe God was giving me an opportunity to make it up to you. I felt so terrible for you. And responsible." She kept her face lowered. "But you were so kind to me, so compassionate. I hope you're not mad at me."

Meg decided Candy didn't need to know about her oscillating emotions on the way over here. Anger that Candy had kept her identity a secret, mingled with compassion for her predicament, all twisted together in a confusing tangled knot.

"I'm not mad at you, Candy."

She sniffed again, then grabbed a tissue and honked into it. "I just don't think there's any way to make it up to you."

"You can't. Please don't feel obligated. You shouldn't have been afraid to tell me who you were."

"How could I?" Her tone had turned strident, harsh. "Would you want the world to know you'd given birth to a son who grew up to be a killer? That you ruined him?"

"Why do you keep saying you ruined him?"

Five-second pause. At last, words wisped from her mouth. "I'm embarrassed to admit this. I used crack off and on when I was pregnant. When Michael — I mean Coby — was born, he went through withdrawals. It was the most terrible thing I'd ever seen. He screamed non-stop for hours, and the whole time the nurses were looking at me as if I were the world's worst criminal. I know all about his internet searches about drug babies, so I know he blamed me for his schizophrenia."

She burst forth with an audible sob, like a child lost at Disneyland. Meg couldn't see her face, but surely it was scrunched in agony.

"I'll never forgive Geoffrey for what he did to me. He seduced me, and then couldn't get away fast enough when I told him we were expecting. He said, 'Not we. You. I thought you were on the pill.' When I told him I was going to report him, he countered by saying he was going to report *me*."

"For what?"

"Sexual harassment. Can you believe I was so naïve that I thought that was a valid threat?"

"You were seventeen. It's amazing the things we believe at that age."

"I never told my parents. Or Bonnie. The years went by. I married, but I always wondered what happened to my little Michael. I always hoped he was happy. I married Bob Burton, we had a son, but the marriage didn't last."

"But your son. Jared. I thought he was the one who committed suicide."

"No, I lost custody of him last year."

Ah. The pieces were starting to clink into place. The inconsistencies. The timeline that didn't make sense. She had no more words of comfort for her friend. All she could do was gather Candy's broken self to her bosom and let her cry her heart out.

Chapter Thirty-Five

Painting in the Wilderness – Megan Shaw Paulson (15877 followers)

"Yea, though I walk through the valley of the shadow of death, I will fear no evil: for thou art with me; thy rod and thy staff they comfort me." Psalm 23:4

Another school shooting this morning! Friends, what is happening to our world? Why are there so many broken young men? From what I've heard, this particular broken young man came from an equally broken home. I'm hearing some discussion about the effects of broken homes. Broken homes producing broken kids, who turn into destructive adults, etc. More discussion about the danger of guns, and on and on.

Instead of debating about guns, how about we get to the root of the problem?

We know that many broken homes do not produce broken kids. And many intact homes do produce broken kids. We also know that most gun owners are responsible citizens. So we need to find the one missing thread these boys all had in common. We need to set aside the political agendas and get this thing fixed.

I've compiled a list of the more notorious shooters from the last twenty years, along with disturbing facts that may or may not have had a bearing on their crime.

Coby Jarrett – Lived with his adoptive parents. Diagnosed with schizophrenia and other mental illnesses. Behaved aggressively as a child.

Dylan Klebold and Eric Harris – gifted as children, bullied incessantly, ostracized by other students.

Chris Harper-Mercer – Parents divorced, lived with his mother. Had Asperger's Syndrome. No social life. Spent a lot of time on the internet.

Adam Lanza – Parents divorced, lived with his mother. Diagnosed with Asperger's. No social life. Isolated himself in his room where he spent almost all his time playing video games.

Charles Roberts – a suicidal family man angry at God.

James Holmes – raised by biological parents, obsessed with killing people, took multiple medications for mental health, displayed clear mental deterioration in the months before the shooting, expert at the online game Warcraft.

Jared Loughner – raised by biological parents, heavy drug use, showed obvious mental deterioration in the months prior to the shooting.

Kip Kinkel – raised by biological parents in a healthy, loving home. Struggled in school as a youngster, but overall was an average kid.

Not all these men were raised in broken homes. Not all were bullied in school. Not all were isolated loners. Many obtained their guns illegally, ergo, more laws would not have stopped them. But most of these men suffered from some form of mental illness, and they were all bent on their destructive plans. Many of them had friends and family who worried they were about to do something tragic.

I graduated from high school in 1990, years before Columbine. I remember my school years and the various misfits that you find in all schools. I remember the Dylan Klebolds and Eric Harrises, the Adam Lanzas and the Jared Loughners. But none of them ever brought guns to school, or went to the mall, or theater, with intent to shoot people.

Why not?

Gun ownership hasn't really changed to any large degree. People owned guns then, too. So what has changed in two and a half decades?

From where I sit, looking back over the last twenty-five years, here's what I've observed.

• More kid-centric homes. We parents sometimes forget that we're in charge, and it's okay to assert our authority. Because when kids grow bigger than us, they can become intimidating if we haven't taught them limits.

• The internet. Kids can access anything they want in cyberspace. When I was a teen, theaters wouldn't let me and my friends into R-rated movies. And even if they did, it wasn't possible to fill our minds with them for hours per day.

• Misandry — lack of respect for men. Fathers are demeaned on TV, in movies, in books. I see young girls sporting tees that say things like Girl Power, or Girls Rule. I have yet to see a boy wearing a tee saying Boy Power or Boys Rule. Girls are encouraged to "be the best they can be." Are we giving our boys equal encouragement? I'm afraid the answer might be no, in light of the fact that the vast majority of the prison population is male, and more women than men are college graduates. Girls are surpassing boys in several areas. Could it be we've neglected to nurture our boys, and now these

angry boys are lashing out in the most destructive way they can?

• Very little religious influence. Only 37% of Americans attend church regularly. Church attendance in America has been on the decline for decades. Yet it's in church and homes where children learn right from wrong. Schools can help, but a strong religious foundation from an early age solidifies those values.

The sad thing is, this isn't something that can be fixed with more laws. It can only be fixed one boy at a time.

I welcome your opinions, but please, please refrain from verbal attacks or name-calling. The Comment Monitor is watching, and he loves his job! He takes delight in snuffing out comments, especially the mean ones. Okay, you've been warned.

Kindly yours,

Meg

~~~~

"No," Linzee muttered. *Click* went her mouse. Bye-bye to that prospective date. She fingered a couple of Skittles out of their crinkly bag and popped them in her mouth, sucking furiously on all the chewy goodness.

"At least try smiling," she said to the next image on the dating site. "Maybe if you smiled a little you wouldn't look so anal."

She glanced at the clock on her phone, resting beside her on her bedroom desk. 8:30 pm, the perfect time to browse the dating sites. Not only was the Carlito house at its quietest with the kids in bed, everyone knew Sunday evening was the busiest chunk of time for internet dating.

Next!

Click. So far she'd found most of the guys on

MeetAChristian-dot-com had something deal-breaking about each of them. Either too far away— no, she wasn't going to drive all the way to San Diego for a date, Mr. PadresFan— too old—men older than thirty-five need not apply—or still lived with mom and dad. Granted, she might be okay with someone still in college, as long as he had some source of income. As long as he turned out to be the one man who could make her forget about Ken.

If only the thought of Ken didn't cross her mind five-hundred-seventy-five times a day. The only cure for non-stop reminiscences? Replace him. And pop some more Skittles. She chewed the wad of candy like a desperate sugar addict until it dissipated, wishing she could spit those images of Ken out of her head as easily.

Since she hadn't heard from him in over a week, she guessed he'd replaced her by now. Already. With no hesitation, no looking back.

If only it were that easy for her. Life could be *so* unfair.

"Next." She found herself staring at someone calling himself Romantic@Heart. Finally, someone promising. Surfer-dude-blond hair. Eyes that promised her a good time. Mischievous grin that said, "If you're looking for non-stop laughs, pick me, Babe." From his profile, she learned he'd been a Christian most of his life, and recently graduated from a Bible college in Southern California. Check. And he lived right here in San Rafael—check, check—and served as a youth pastor at an unnamed local church—check, check, check. A fun-loving, young-at-heart youth pastor.

She didn't hesitate to click *like*.

"Next!" She clicked ahead to someone named GoodCop, then lurched backward. "Oh, good Lord!" None other than Kentucker eyed her from under drawn brows. The better to channel the scary-cop look. "Hi, don't let the cop face fool you. I'm really a softie inside. Don't believe me? Just message me. What am I looking for? An honest, kind Christian girl who rocks it whether she's in sweats or an evening gown.

Hey, we all have baggage from our past, but it's what we do with it that matters. I'll be upfront with mine, and I'll expect the same from you."

Linzee gasped her palms on her burning-hot cheeks. He might as well have spit in her face. Her insides blazed like the desert sun, her breath sputtered like a dying animal. A light breeze from her screened window fluttered the floral curtains but failed to cool her head.

How dare he make insinuations about her on the internet for all to see.

With shaking fingers, she blasted off a reply. "You sound like a very judgmental person. How can you expect your date to be upfront about her baggage if she knows you're just going to judge her?"

Since she hadn't made a profile yet, he'd only see a blank avatar.

Instead of clicking *Send*, she rested her back against the chair and stared at the words she'd written. Ken's image seemed to sneer at her, in all its baby-faced, mock-fierce charm. To her horror, tears stung her eyes and made tracks down her cheeks. Oh, if only she had been honest with him. If only she hadn't gotten so attached to him. If only …

She sniffed and erased the message, but immediately punched in another one. "How soon should you and your date talk about your relationship history? Don't you think one month is too soon?" His expectations needed adjusting, that was it. No doubt she would've eventually told him about Nena. But they were still getting to know each other when everything caved in.

"His loss," she muttered. But her loss too, if she were honest with herself. She erased the second message, pondering what to say. And how. She needed something creative, something to catch his attention. Chewing a handful of Skittles ought to stimulate those mental juices.

Frustrated, she tugged her hair, then, lowering her fingers slowly and thoughtfully, she placed them on the keyboard.

"Hi, GoodCop. I've been a very bad girl." She stopped, heaved in a cooling breath to stop the quivering in her chest. "I ought to be arrested for what I did. I was seeing a really great guy, but I blew it. I neglected to tell him something really important about my past, and now he's mad at me. If he were to forgive me, I would never lie to him again. Seeing as honesty is important to you, tell me what you think. Do I deserve to be on his naughty list? ~ Cocoa Nut."

Send.

Wow. She'd really done it. But now came the doubts, the second-guessing. He'd undoubtedly guess her identity. Would it make him laugh, or would he roll his eyes and sneer?

Too late now to retract her words. All she could do was wait.

Lord, it's in your hands now.

~~~~

A new day, full of hope, broke into Linzee's room and yanked her from sleep. Stretching and yawning, she slowly opened her eyes and took in her lit up phone on the nightstand, piercing the dimness with its electronic glow.

She snatched it up, checked the messages awaiting her.

Romantic@Heart sent you a gift!

PadresFan wants to chat with you!

Three more guys sent gifts or messages, none of them called GoodCop.

She plopped to the mattress, wishing she could sink all the way through its bulk, through the cotton layers, dodging the metal springs, to the dusty hardwood floor below. She'd curl into a fetal position and hide from the outside world, from her shame, inhaling dust that would make her sneeze.

Instead, she stared at the ceiling, at the small stain shaped vaguely like a hand marring the otherwise flawless white expanse.

Ken must have thought her feeble attempt to contact him

ridiculous.

Romantic@Heart could wait. So could PadresFan and the other three hopefuls. She opened the dating app.

GoodCop read your message at 10:15pm yesterday.

Eight hours ago, leaving plenty of time to reply. The knife in her heart twisted harder.

On the other hand, maybe he wasn't ignoring her. Maybe he was planning the perfect reply.

She forced a shrug. If she never saw Ken again, it wasn't meant to be.

Chapter Thirty-Six

Meg, clutching a fresh copy of the Marin Mercury, carried it closer to the kitchen window where the early morning light struggled its way into the breakfast nook, and Jon sat nursing a shot of espresso. The shooting seemed to have fallen off of everyone's radar, so today's update had been stashed on page twelve. Apparently, the good citizens of San Rafael, reassured by the police chief that the shooting had not been random and that the force was stepping up their efforts to prevent any more such deeds, had gone about their lives. The shooting was no longer the topic of the day.

She held up the paper to the light and began to read aloud. "San Rafael Police Chief Gale Grieve told the Marin Mercury that the case of the Ignacio College shooting on September 29, which devastated the city and left six people dead and three injured, has been closed. Evidence proved the shooter, Coby Jarrett, sought out the two people he believed were his biological parents, Cassandra Martin Milliken and Geoffrey Hope. However, further evidence revealed that Mrs. Milliken was not Coby's biological mother. The real birth mother has been found, and her identity will remain confidential."

Whew. Meg dropped the paper to the table, where it landed on a wet spot. Moisture soaked through the newsprint and blurred the words as if she were viewing it through tears. As she folded herself into Jon's arms, she realized — they were real tears.

~~~~

"No, Heath!" The baby toddled toward Linzee's phone on the sofa arm. "It's nap-nap time, sweet baby." Linzee snatched her phone out of his reach. "And you can't have my phone."

"Pone, 'Zee!" He emphasized each word with at least two bounces. "Cah Wash!"

"You can play Car Wash after your nap, okay?"

His little face crumpled, but a movement out on the street diverted her attention. Red Hill Florist said the letters on the side of the white van pulling up to the curb.

For her?

After Heath whined and pulled on her leg three times, she picked him up and let him watch the young delivery man get out of the van with a bouquet of flowers, then saunter up the front walk.

"Look, Heath. He's bringing flowers! Now who do you think they're for?" She poked his tummy till he giggled. "Are the pretty flowers for you?"

"Pwetty!"

They could be for Mrs. Carlito, she supposed. But practical, no-nonsense Mr. Carlito didn't seem the type to send his wife flowers on any day except special occasions. They must be for her. Her mind clicked through possible names. Darrell from church, the one who kept eyeing her and Ken that one Sunday? The one who turned quickly away every time she caught his eye? Or could it be Marcus, her old high school pal who monopolized her attention at their five-year reunion last month?

Or was it Ken?

She flung the door open before the doorbell rang. "Hi! Wow." The fabulous bouquet covered most of the young man's pimpled face. Crimson roses splashed amid yellow lilies and golden California poppies, interspersed with baby's breath, all of them artfully assembled in a shiny chrome vase. A blooming mishmash bursting with sunny-day warmth.

"Fows!" Heath's plump little hand tried but failed to grab at a lily. "Mine!"

"Shh." She brought her mouth close to his ear and put a

rasp in her voice. "I think they're for me."

Another grab. "Mine!"

The young man cleared his throat. "Are you Linzee?"

"I am."

"Want me to bring it inside?"

"Oh, yes." She stepped back onto the area rug which slid precariously a few inches before her foot found its grip. "Yes, please. Right this way."

She directed him to the mantel, but it was too narrow to accommodate the bouquet's breadth. It needed to be out of Heath's reach. "Here, put it on this table here." She was dying to check the card, but with her arms filled with Heath, her curiosity had to wait.

After the guy set the vase on the coffee table, he hesitated. She could see his full face now. Late teens, early twenties, maybe. Too young for her. Plus, the acne detracted from his cuteness. Without it, he'd be hot, she decided. Someday, some lucky girl ...

"Your baby's cute."

"Yeah, he's a sweetie."

A wobbly grin. "Your husband must have sent the flowers."

"Oh, I'm not married. And this baby isn't mine. I'm the nanny."

She noted the brightened expression, the hopeful eyes. "Really? I thought the baby looked a lot like you."

She had to laugh. Heath looked nothing like her. But whatever.

"Speaking of the baby, I need to put him down for his nap now. I thank you kindly for the flowers."

He backed to the door, nodding and smiling. "Sure. No problem. Have a great day."

Finally he was gone, and she covered the route to the flowers in two strides. Shifting the baby to her hip, she grabbed the tiny card and opened it under Heath's curious stare and groping fingers.

From an admirer, said the caption.

For a brief moment, her heart drooped. It couldn't be Ken. He'd be forthright and sign his name, and probably even include a little note. It had to be Darrell or Marcus. Both of them knew where she lived.

She turned the card over and looked at the printed note on the back. "This bouquet was designed with care especially for you. Along with red roses, the universal symbol for love, we included the luscious orange Eschscholzia Californica, AKA Golden Poppies, California's state flower. Next, we threw in some Solidago Gigantean, otherwise known as goldenrod, the state flower for Kentucky, to make a unique and personalized bouquet just for you. Gypsophila, or baby's breath, adds a lovely artistic touch to your arrangement. We hope you enjoy your personalized bouquet. Sincerely, Marie – Red Hill Flowers."

Her mind spun like a washer's spin cycle until dizziness forced her to the sofa. Heath straddled her knee. She was only half-aware of his whines as she bounced him over and over, hoping to keep him quiet.

The flowers she'd mistaken for lilies were actually goldenrod. She'd thought goldenrod was an ugly spiky weed, but these showy blooms had the texture and appearance of exquisite yellow silk. Only one person would think to include the Kentucky state flower in a bouquet. Ken must have figured she'd get the significance. Or was he unaware that the florist would go into such detail, enough to give his identity away?

Heath flailed and tipped to the right, and she suddenly realized she'd loosened her grip. She grabbed him just in time. *Get hold of yourself, girl.*

This little boy needed a nap. Somehow, she managed to hold him steady as she got to her feet.

Then the doorbell rang.

Just as it had done moments before, the chime pealed its announcement through the house like a strident intruder. But an unexpected quality invaded the sound this time. A sense that the someone on the other side of that door was significant, a game-changer.

Still holding Heath, and her breath, she shuffled to the door, her red fuzzy socks noiseless on the hardwood floor, and flew it open.

Ken stood there, his eyes alight like blue flames. A pair of handcuffs dangled from his index finger.

She sagged against the door frame as her chin dropped. "Ken," she managed.

He took a hesitant step forward. "You're under arrest."

"For what?"

His brow firmed, but a twinkle in his eye betrayed him. "Internet stalking." He swung the handcuffs hypnotically back and forth, like an Old West sheriff trying to intimidate the town drunk.

"I swear I wasn't stalking you."

He stepped closer, a grin hinting at the corners of his mouth.

"Are you here to play Put-the-handcuffs-on-the-girl?"

Startled pause, followed by loud laughter. Her giggles united with his, and Heath chortled in her ear, his grin saying this was all about him.

She stepped back, clamping down on the chuckles long enough to say, "Hey, come on in."

He obliged, and she said over her shoulder as he followed her to the sofa, "Thanks for the bouquet, by the way. It's gorgeous. See?"

"You're welcome." She heard the feeling behind the nonchalant tone. "Seemed the best way to get your attention."

She pulled Heath's greedy little hand away from the mesmerizing flowers and spun to face Ken. "You know you gave yourself away, don't you?"

The handcuffs were now spinning around his finger. "I figured you'd guess."

"And I figured you'd guess who your mystery contact

was."

"It was obvious it was you."

Heath squirmed and emitted guttural noises at her. Her hip bone was getting sore after all this time propping him on it. She shifted him to the other side, tilting like a marionette whose operator dropped his string. "When I didn't hear from you, I figured you'd written me off. Why'd you make me wait three whole days?"

He stood with legs apart, still channeling Wyatt Earp. Or maybe Dirty Harry. "The florist had to special-order the goldenrod. It's not a very common component for a bouquet, she told me."

"I assume this means you've forgiven me."

He folded himself onto the sofa and patted the cushion. "We need to talk."

She nodded. "Let me put Mini-Dude down for his nap first."

"Mini Doo! Mini Doo!" Heath continued his enthusiastic chant all the way to the bedroom.

"Heath, my man, you'll make a worthy cheer squad member someday."

"Mini Doo!"

She set him lightly on his baby-sized mattress. "Nap time, Mini Doo."

"Sto-wy?"

She groaned. If she didn't read him a story, he'd fuss for half an hour and refuse to sleep.

"Be right back." Back to the living room she went, then beckoned when Ken looked up, eagerness plain in his face.

"Want to sit with me while I read Heath a story? Otherwise, you might be waiting awhile."

To her surprise, he stood. "Sure. We could even take turns."

She gave him a wide-eyed smile to show him how much he'd pleased her. As they sat and read Goodnight Moon, Linzee pondered on the scene. Ken's campy delivery, her playful one. And an adorable child to listen to them, rapt with fascination. It proved a surreal combination for her to wrap her brain around. Perhaps she was experiencing a foretaste of a life to come.

Chapter Thirty-Seven

Jon popped the cork on the bottle of Moet & Chandon champagne, while Meg and Linzee counted noses and gathered wineglasses respectively. "I counted fifteen," Meg tossed over her shoulder at Linzee, "not including us."

The disposable goblets made hollow clinking sounds on the countertop, the telltale sound of cheap plastic, as Linzee set them out in rows. From the living room, the guests' voices drifted in a babbling stream. Meg caught joyful laughter and well-wishes and Happy Birthdays to Richie mingled with multiple conversations clashing pleasantly.

After Jon poured an inch of champagne into each goblet, Meg carried them on a tray into the living room. The guest of honor sat, sans wheelchair, in his favorite Lay-Z-Boy recliner, all proud grins for having walked to it with no aid.

"Here you go, birthday boy." She held the tray in front of him and held her breath as he reached for a goblet. Would he succeed in his efforts to keep from spilling it? His fingers slowly closed around the closest one. Even more slowly he lowered his hand and cradled the cup in his lap.

She felt her face beaming. "Good job, son. You have a lot to celebrate today."

"Yeah." The word pushed from his throat, but praise God, it was clear. "I do."

Beside him, Kassidy's smile widened to a breadth Meg hadn't thought her capable of. Bless her sweet heart for sticking by Richie for six whole months, through frightening coma, through grueling recovery, and finally cheering him on through long hard days of physical therapy. If Richie didn't marry this girl as soon as he was fully whole, she'd wring his tree-trunk of a neck.

Ken grinned and nodded at her as he took a goblet but just as quickly his warmed-over gaze caressed the space behind her where his lady love tailed and didn't let go until Linzee nestled next to him in a folding chair. Twice as wide as her, Ken spanned nearly two chair's worth of space. Meg recalled the early days when he'd betrayed his smitten state with a junior-high blush. And here they were, six months later, having survived a major rift, and seemed to be heading to the marriage altar. Grandchildren couldn't be too far away.

Camille and Bill, on Ken's right, exerted their usual good humor when they helped themselves to a goblet. She didn't want to think of how much worse things might have gone if Camille hadn't kept the church prayer chain going, hadn't pestered them to keep lifting Richie up to the Lord, and held the members accountable when they didn't.

Camille deserved an enormous attagirl. "I get it now why I thought Candy looked familiar that day at the café," she'd told Meg after Meg confided in her. "I saw Coby Jarrett in her face. Just like you did."

Speaking of Candy, she sat in the most inconspicuous spot in the room, tucked in the corner between the stereo and the window that framed the small fenced-in side yard. Still skittish, but no longer from anguish. Meg understood now that Candy would always emit a delicate air, like a fragile flower, that could easily fool an observer into thinking she was a pushover. Her eyes, once as wary as a wild deer, no longer mirrored her traumatized state of mind. She nodded serenely at Meg's mom next to her, who seemed to be carrying on a one-sided conversation with Candy. How fortunate that Bonnie had taken firm control of Candy's situation and gotten her the help she so desperately needed.

"I know in my head I'm not to blame for Coby's actions," she'd told Meg last month. "But sometimes my heart still tries to lie to me."

"Just kick those enemy lies to the curb," Meg had said.

The new Candy caught her eye and smiled, a loose, easy

smile that channeled contentment.

A dull clanging pulled her attention back to her husband. Jon tapped a spoon against a goblet, then flashed a rueful grin when the plastic emitted only muted thuds. But somehow, his take-charge demeanor managed to capture everyone's attention anyway.

"Okay folks, it's time for a toast!" He gestured to Meg and gave her the sideways grin that always made her heart do a little cartwheel. "My beautiful wife and I invited you all here to help us celebrate a special day." He stepped to the side of Richie's recliner and laid a hand on his shoulder. "Not only is it Richard's nineteenth birthday, but also the six-month anniversary of the shooting that nearly killed him." He glanced down at Richie's motionless form, broken only by a grin stretching across his face. "Now look at him. Walking and talking again, just like he used to."

The applause bursting around them was the final high point for Meg. Happy tears coursed down her cheeks, and she longed to wipe her tickling nose, if only she had a tissue handy.

"Here's to Richard Eric St. John, birthday boy, and hero of the day!"

"Yahoo!" Camille's yelp pierced the airwaves, and everyone lifted their goblets.

Jon gave the downbeat, and eighteen voices celebrated. "Happy birthday, Richard!"

Dear Readers

On October 1, 2015, two weeks after I wrote the opening scene to this story, a 26-year-old armed gunman named Christopher Harper-Mercer walked into Umpqua Community College in Roseburg, Oregon, and started shooting. I was driving home from work that day when I heard the news on the radio. It was so eerily similar to Chapter 1 of this book, it completely threw me. I had a meltdown right then and there in my car, crying out to God, "Why?" I may never get an answer to that question, but I do know it strengthened my conviction that this story needed to be written.

Since that day, school and public shootings have increased to the point where we have almost become jaded to it. Every time it happens, we become a little more desensitized. And I find that the most tragic result of all.

Like Meg, most of us grew up in a safer world, a world in which mass public shootings were unthinkable. I don't pretend to have solutions. My goal in writing this book was simply to tell the story of a family impacted by this new normal, and the polarization that has ensued. There was no agenda other than to portray a family who trusted in God and the power of prayer.

No matter where you stand on gun rights issues, I hope and pray you take something valuable from this story. This is the second story in my Golden State Trilogy, a series that takes place in beautiful Marin County, California, where Meg and her family live. Check out my website at dawnvcahill.com for updates on Book III, Paint the Sunrise, and my other series, Seattle Trilogy.

Many Blessings,

~DVC~

Hot Topic Fiction

About the author

Dawn V. Cahill, an indie author from the land of microbrews and coffee snobs, published her first book, When Lyric Met Limerick, in 2015. She published her first full-length novel, Sapphire Secrets, in January of 2016. "The characters in my stories face situations that would have been unthinkable even 20 years ago. We live in a vastly different world than our parents did, and that's the world I write about."

Seeing an unfilled niche in the Christian market for edgier fiction, Ms Cahill came up with the concept of Hot Topic Fiction (HTF) at an intensive four-day writers conference. HTF isn't afraid to explore the question, how does God want us Christians to live out our faith in this not-so-brave new world? Without insulting the reader by offering pat or easy answers—because there aren't any—HTF tells stories of ordinary Christians following hard after Christ in a world of terror and violence, of upside-down morality, of hostility to Judeo-Christian values.

She has written several newspaper articles and more limericks than she can count. Email her at dawn@dawnvcahill.com, or find her on Facebook, Twitter, and her website. She is a member of American Christian Fiction Writers (ACFW).

(If you enjoyed this novel, would you be so kind as to hop over to Goodreads and let the world know what you thought of it?)

Other books by Dawn V. Cahill

SEATTLE TRILOGY

When Lyric Met Limerick – Prequel

Sapphire Secrets – Book I

Moonstone Secrets – Book II

GOLDEN STATE TRILOGY

Paint the Storm – Book I